COPPER & GOLD

JESSICA D. COPLEN

Copper
and
Gold

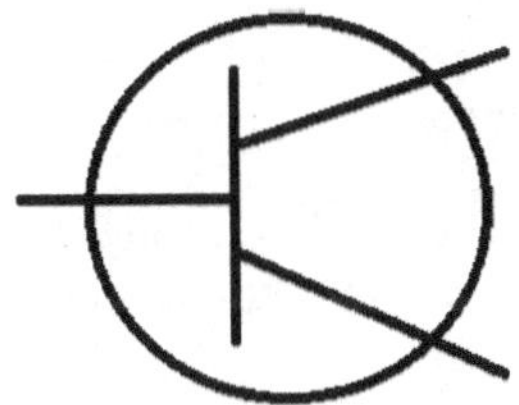

IPHI Books
Tulsa, OK

The Periodic Tales of Minni the Witch

Copper and Gold

Copper and Cobalt

Copper and Mercury

For

The TechnoMage

&

The Spark

ONE[1]

Okay, the wanton destruction of public property—that's on me—but momentarily displacing Delaware? Yeah, that… that was totally the dragon's fault.

Right, so, on Friday, I may have cut the power to New York City. It was an accident. I'd drawn enough electrical energy from the local power grid to crash it. Some kind of cascade failure occurred and, *boom*, there went Times Square. And I completely slept through the whole thing.

When I woke up Saturday morning, I could feel this excess of energy in my aura. Not magical energy, we're talking straight up AC/DC. Now, it's not unheard of for me to trip the breakers of my apartment, so I didn't think anything of it. But if I had stopped commiserating for five seconds, I might have put together that this was not a minor power drain.

Instead, I was more focused on the fact that I really didn't want to talk to anyone *at all*, ever again, or at least until Monday when I had to. So I grabbed an old iPod, completely ignored my phone, and headed to Central Park for a Saturday morning jog. I'm pretty much a regular in the park. I could probably run it with my eyes closed. No, that would actually be a horrible idea.

I was a few laps in when I decided to stop and catch a breather. As I shuffled through the iPod for something more mood specific—man I really need to update that thing—I saw the battery was getting a little low. I lightly rubbed my index finger across a sigil scratched over the Apple logo and started transferring energy to the battery. It was going to take a few minutes for it to charge because, you know, physics. I ended up walking off the path to lean against a nearby tree.

I really need to work on my situational awareness skills.

"Hey, girlie," a man said as he came from around the tree. He was a tall fellow, very cliché with a baseball hat down low and hands tucked forward in his wind-breaker. I'm pretty sure the words 'Captain Obvious' blazed over his head. "Nice iPod you got there," he said entirely too casually. "What is this, 2010?"

I stared blankly at him. "This a robbery?"

"You're a quick one." He flashed me a toothy smile, which was not at all comforting, mind you. "Hand it over and your phone."

"No phone," I replied as I pulled out the ear buds and slung the cord around my neck.

"You don't have a phone?" I'm not entirely sure if that was supposed to be a question.

I shrugged as I disconnected the cord. "Left it at home."

He scrunched his brow, genuinely confused. Considering he was one of those brick walls of a man, it was kind of comical. I would've laughed, but I'm pretty sure that's not polite etiquette in these situations.

"Who even does that?" he asked.

"Someone who doesn't want to check their messages," I answered flatly, holding the device towards him.

"I'll take that, too." He gestured to the copper, cuff bracelet I always wear on my left wrist. Then as he reached for the iPod, his fat fingers brushed against mine. It took no effort to send enough volts into him to make him face plant in the dirt. I did hold back on the amps so as not to kill him outright.

Voltage to amperage is a very important ratio.

What? I'm a witch. You really   think I was going to let him get away with robbing me? Hell no. Giving him the iPod was just a way to hide my spell. The magical community has been able to hide their existence for centuries and we would like to keep it that way. We're just a bit paranoid, you know? Too many instances of our kind being lit on fire, drowned in ponds, hung from trees, smashed under really big rocks...

So, yeah, he went down like a sack of potatoes. A convulsing sack of Idaho russet potatoes… I kicked his foot and he let out a groan. It was kind of pathetic.

Seeing as he was alive and breathing, I went back to the path and jogged the hell away from there. Mounted cops were heading in his general direction, so I'm sure he's fine. Probably.

Anyway, by now it was hedging close to noon. I was starving and in dire need of a shower. I headed out of the park and made my way to my apartment in Yorkville. That's on the Upper East Side of Manhattan Island. You already knew that, sorry. I'm used to having to explain it.

How do I afford an apartment in Yorkville as a low-level electrical engineer? Supplemental income and very careful financial wrangling. I also moonlight as a tour guide, which I find hilarious because I'm basically a tourist myself, seeing as I'm originally from Nebraska. But I like to think I do a fairly good job. I also speak fluent redneck, so that helps.

Oh, wait, sorry, I've been totally rude. I just invaded your space here and started talking your ear off without properly introducing myself. The name's Dominque Masterson. You can call me Minni. My oldest brother started calling me Minni since before I could walk and it stuck. As nicknames go, I kind of like it.

Minni the Witch.

Anyway, where was I? Oh yes, I stopped at my local Dunkin' Donuts because I may or may not be addicted to them. Waiting in line, these two ladies were talking about the blackout and how it was nothing compared to the outage of '03. Or at least I think that's what they were saying. They were speaking Spanish which I am barely conversationally fluent in. I thought about taking a class because people keep speaking it at me. They tend to assume I'm latina and some days I'm tempted to wear a nametag that reads, 'Soy Cheyenne.'

I could make out enough of their conversation to realize the full scale of the blackout. That's when I finally put two and two together and realized I'd done more than just popped a few breakers.

I grabbed some Munchkins and made a bee-line for my apartment.

Now, I've been told it's fairly standard for New York, but I grew up in a sprawling country farmhouse, so my apartment feels really freaking tiny in comparison. The whole place is basically a rectangle with sheetrock dividing walls that obviously weren't part of the original design. At least I have a separate bedroom and enough space in the bathroom for a stackable washer/dryer, so I can't complain too much.

Well, I *can* complain but other New Yorkers just give me The Look.

I went to my phone first. I had missed a call from Stacey, my BFF. She also left me like six texts. They could be summed up thusly: *You're an idiot, call me.*

I tried to think of a witty response and ended up with: "Something, something, I'm not an idiot."

No, that's literally what I wrote.

Three other missed calls were from Phil, my coven leader. The voicemails were broken up pretty bad with static, but I got that he wanted me to check my sender and call him right away. Why would Phil try to get a hold of me three times on something as unreliable as a phone? I figured it had to do with me blacking out the city and took solace in the fact that he hadn't actually shown up at my door. I mean, if it wasn't important enough to drag his butt all the way over from Brooklyn, then it couldn't be *that* bad.

Which, now that I think about it, should have been my second clue something serious had happened. You would think New York City losing power would be a pretty big deal.

His messages in my sender didn't really give me much else to go on.

What's a sender? Oh, well, I guess I can try to explain. I'm not really the best one to answer magic questions. I was an okay student. I mean, I didn't *accidentally* rip a hole in the fabric of reality or anything. They were controlled experiments, and my mom helped.

Now, a sending spell is where you write down a message and literally send it, via magic, to the intended recipient. Ideally you know their personal sigil, but if you can visualize them, then the note should get there. It can appear in a mirror, in dirt, whatever's around. Most wizards have a specific book, called a sender, where their messages come to. What I'm really saying is that wizards pretty much invented emails and texting.

I'd also say wizards invented Twitter, but I'm pretty sure that was the Romans.

And yeah, I use witch and wizard interchangeably. Technically the term wizard is gender neutral while witch, warlock, sorcerer, and sorceress are gender specific. Everyone likes to use wizard these days because it sounds grander, thank you, Gandalf. Personally, I like being a witch.

Anyway, what was I talking about? Right, senders. I keep mine on my book shelf. It's just a cheap journal I picked up on clearance somewhere. I've etched some serious magical runes into the faux-leather cover which basically act as my SIM card. I keep the book in a dust jacket for the novel *Utopia* by Thomas More. This is my security measure to keep people from reading it. No one is going to pick up *Utopia* when they could read *500 Movies to Watch Before You Die*—half of which I disagree with, by the way.

Flipping to the last used page of my sender, there were three separate notes from Phil. I can't remember exactly what he wrote, but they went something like this:

Minni, You're not answering your phone. I scryed you, you're not hurt, so I'm guessing asleep. Call me <u>*immediately*</u> *when you get this. – Phil*

Minni, I'm getting reports of some serious magical mishaps. I'm pretty sure the blackout is a part of it. I need you to call me as soon as possible. This is important! – Phil

Minni, Seriously? You're jogging? CALL ME! – Phil

I grabbed my phone and dialed Phil's number.

"What happened?" was his greeting.

"I don't know," I told him and realized that was a bald-faced lie. "I mean, when the lights went out in my apartment I thought I only blew a breaker. I didn't even realize how much energy I was draining."

"What? Marcel break up with you?" his words were a note

below pure sarcasm.

I grimaced. "I broke up with him."

There was a pause; apparently he regretted the joke. At least I hope he did. "Sorry to hear that, but you seriously didn't notice the extra surge of power?"

"I was crying and tired." No point in pretending I know the meaning of stoicism in the face of relationship troubles. "I fell asleep only moments after the lights went out and slept till this morning."

"You drained New York City of most of its power grid... while you were sleeping?" he squeaked, causing static to crackle in the line. I may have the latest smart phone, but he used an old '70s style phone connected to an actual landline.

"Yeah, I guess I did…" I replied meekly even though it *was* pretty impressive. "Listen, it wasn't intentional, believe me."

"I know, Minni," he said softly. "It could've been a lot worse, so let's be thankful for that."

"Yeah." It was at that moment the revelation truly hit me. Within the space of twenty-four hours, I had broken up with my boyfriend of three years, blacked out New York City, *and* was nearly mugged. It always comes in threes.

"I've talked to several others." Phil took the hint and moved on from the subject. "A bunch of strange stuff happened around the time of the blackout. Eli went to light a candle but produced a fireball instead."

"What?" I blurted out. "He okay?"

"Yeah, Vivian was there and he managed to direct the fireball into a pool," he said as if it wasn't that big a deal. To be fair, it was Eli, and fireballs are kind of what he's known for. "I've gotten a lot of reports of similar events."

"How'd this happen?" That's me, asking the hard-hitting questions. "Do you think a wizard was doing something they shouldn't?"

"That would be my best guess." I could hear the wheels turning in his head. "You were home, right, when you zapped the power grid?"

"Yeah." I had a good idea where Phil was going with this. "You're gonna see if you can triangulate the point of origin?"

"That's the plan." Ah, yes, Phillip McCree, a good man always finding his way into the middle of whatever is going on, for better or worse.

"Well, be careful then," I said, thinking that this was probably the end of the conversation. I glanced around my apartment and spotted one of Marcel's rust-colored scarfs hanging over the back of the sofa. "Do you need any help?"

"Actually, yeah." The line started to break up. Phil could only use the phone for so long until his magic mucked it up. "Can you bring your laptop over?"

"Can do," I told him, but then looked down at myself still clad in my running clothes, complete with layers of dust and sweat. "Give me a chance to take a quick rinse in the shower. You at the shop?"

"I'll be at my apartment. Ryan is watching the shop."

"Alright, see yah in a bit." I hung up before we could accidentally get disconnected.

A smiling Marcel stared up at me from my phone's home screen. It was a selfie we took together in Central Park earlier in the year. The lighting was absolutely gorgeous. Marcel's dark features practically shimmered as perfect laugh lines framed his face. The copper tones in my auburn hair really popped, and you could even see my sectoral heterochromia.

Sorry, that's the technical term for these rust color spots on the brown of my iris. No one ever notices it until I point it out. Well, Marcel noticed it the first time we met.

I wish I could show you the picture because it was an amazing piece of photography. But in that moment, all it did was mock me.

It was so stupid, what Marcel and I argued over. He thought we should move in together, but I can't risk him learning I'm a witch. Living together would make it so much harder to hide it from him. Of course, I couldn't exactly give that as the reason for why I didn't think we should become roomies.

Words were had: some angry, some childish, most strangely incoherent. Marcel stormed out. I threw a sofa pillow at the door. Then I went to my room, collapsed onto my bed, and out of habit, I started absorbing energy. It's kind of my thing. All wizards have their specialty area, and while I'm not particularly strong offensively, I can channel, redirect, and reshape energies. Electric, thermal, kinetic, magic… if it's energy, I'm your gal.

Anyway, I started to pull in electrical energy as if I was inhaling Munchkins. The donuts, not the… Anyway, I don't know exactly why I do it. It just makes me feel better. Makes me feel whole. But that night, I somehow ended up absorbing more energy than I had any right to. Which meant I basically broke New York City for a couple of hours.

Not the worst thing I've ever done.

Not today anyway.

TWO²

Okay, most of New York City's magical community lives in Brooklyn—and don't ask me why because I have no clue. I took the subway, then hopped a bus. It dropped me off just down from a brown brick apartment building that I'm pretty sure was used in at least eight episodes of *Law & Order*. Phil lives up on the third floor, ninth apartment. His magic has only broken the keypad entry six times in the ten-ish years he's lived there. He never uses the elevator unless I'm with him, so at least that's remained unscathed.

I knocked loudly. "Phil, it's Minni."

"Come in," a muffled voice called out. "It's unlocked, I think."

The man puts industrial level security wards on his apartment, but he can't remember to lock the door.

Ugh, *wizards.*

So anyway, Phil's apartment. Have you ever walked into an old bookshop? That pretty much sums up the place. It's dark and dank with piles of hardbacks, paperbacks, scrolls, and random leafs of paper on every available surface. Crates stood stacked one on another against the wall. Half the couch was piled up with a complete set of monster manuals. The real kind, not the D&D ones.

Those are on the dinner table.

"Over here," Phil called out, and I followed his voice through the maze. I found him standing on a chair while trying to pull a hardback from the top of a bookcase, à la Jenga.

"If you fall, I'm just gonna laugh," I said as I started looking for a clear surface to put my laptop bag.

"Of this I have no doubt." He does know me fairly well.

You probably don't remember Phil. He was the guy who looked more like a surfer than a wizard. He has lightly shaggy brown hair standing on end with styling gel. Strong, straight brows complimenting a baby face incapable of growing a beard despite being in his late thirties. That day, I believe he wore a pair of dark grey cargo pants, flip-flops, and a distressed Mountain Dew t-shirt. It's all nice and ironed and pressed though. He uses a laundry service.

Moving some papers to the side, I pulled out my laptop and placed it on a small table. I then ran my fingers over the sigil carved on the laptop's battery casing. It's the same image I scratched onto my iPod. The base of the design is a circle the size of a silver dollar which has a floating vertical line inside, just off center. Three lines, two from the right, one from the left, flow into the circle and stop at that center line. This is my personal symbol, a simplified diagram for a transistor. I've burned layers of instructions into its image in my mind and carved it onto every piece of electronics I own.

Any items with this sigil on it, when they are close to me, become linked to my special electro-magical field. This way they will never be affected by magical static.

Oh, I'm sorry, I assumed that you knew. Magic users and technology do not get along. Because we get our power from bending and breaking the laws of physics, there tends to be this residue of magical energy that permeates us. You can think of it like static electricity or a large Earth-magnet because it presents in a very similar manner. Anything with a circuit board becomes susceptible to this magical magnetic field.

Phil really shouldn't be living in an apartment building with non-magical individuals. He's a pretty strong wizard, so he has a large magic footprint. But there is always a work around. His wards basically act as a Faraday cage, locking his magical magnetism inside the apartment. It's not foolproof. His neighbors are a bit confused as to why they can't get a phone or cable signal in certain parts of their apartment. They simply blame their carrier and shrug it off.

Now, energy is my thing; it's what I do. I control it so well I don't get magical static.

"Internet?" I asked as I powered up the laptop.

"Yeah." Phil brought over the chair he'd been standing on. "I need to look up some geographical and historical data."

I turned my phone into a wifi hotspot and sat it on the windowsill. The reception can be a bit dodgy, but a weak signal is still a signal. Then I opened the browser and let Phil at it. The man is horribly slow, but I learned a long time ago he's a an even worse back-seat websurfer.

"I'm stealing your food."

"Help yourself." Phil absently gestured to the small, attached kitchen barely visible behind some crates labeled for the Smithsonian. Don't ask. Plausible deniability.

After finding a can of grape soda in his ancient refrigerator and an almost empty box of Cheez-Its in the pantry, I made my way to Phil's balcony, aka the fire escape. It was still early in the afternoon and the sun hung over the tops of the buildings. I sat on the metal grated steps and popped open the can. I almost blended into the city-scape with my jeans, Purdue t-shirt, and sneakers.

I checked my phone, and there was a new text from Stacey. We were in agreement—I am indeed an idiot. The only reason she hadn't come over already was because she had to work a Saturday shift. So instead, she was taking me to Paradiso, a nightclub, and I was to meet her there at nine.

"Another?" Phil came to the window, a replacement grape soda in hand. I hadn't even realized I downed the first.

"Thanks," I said as I took it. I never drink carbonated beverages except when I'm with him. He's totally a bad influence.

"You shouldn't drink so much soda," he commented as he straddled the open window.

"Says my enabler." I tipped the can at him before popping the top.

"Gotta bribe you somehow."

Being the only wizard able to use a computer for longer than five minutes meant I was often being asked to share. I don't mind. It helps me be a part of the magical community. Sometimes I wondered if people like Phil would have anything to do with me if I wasn't useful or if they didn't have to.

"Want to talk about it?"

My eyes snapped up. "About what?"

"Marcel," he said politely, neutrally.

"We broke up because he wanted me to move in with him." The words tasted metallic in my mouth. It was the first time I had said it out loud.

"So?" Grand wizard he may be, sage relationship advice was definitely above Phil's pay grade. "You two seemed like a good couple."

"Yeah, maybe." I became very interested in the slightly warped tab of the aluminum can. There are many people in my life who don't know I'm a witch. I try to keep them separate from those who do. It's easier that way. Well, that's my working theory.

Phil let out an exasperated sigh. "Why don't you just tell him you're a witch?"

It was no surprise that Phil figured out the real root of what our fight was over. It was the same old argument. "So I tell him, and then what? How long before the fear sets in? The awe, the suspicion, the opportunity?"

"The understanding and the respect?" Phil could be horribly optimistic at times. I looked away, hoping he'd drop it, but nope, he pressed on. "Yes, secrecy is part of who we are because bad things can happen when people know the truth. But you'll never know for sure how someone will react until you tell them. You can't assume everyone will respond negatively."

"I can't tell Marcel." The words came out before I could even think them. "He wouldn't understand."

Phil frowned. "You're absolutely sure of that?"

"Too late now." I made absolutely sure of that, didn't I?

"You know what, Minni?" Phil sighed, scratching at his temple. "If I actually gave a damn, you'd probably drive me to drink."

I rolled my eyes. "That's just heartwarming, really."

The laptop made a beeping sound, and Phil glanced in its direction. "One of these days you're going to have to take a chance."

I groaned. "But I suck at Entropy magic."

Phil shrugged. "Maybe you should practice more."

I yelled at him as he padded over to the computer. "Why is your solution for everything practice, practice, practice?"

"Eh, it takes practice." He grinned and started to punch at the keys.

One of these days I'm going to cold-cock him, but in that moment, it would have taken far too much effort. Instead I asked, "Did you ever figure out what happened last night?"

"Think so." He pulled a yellow legal pad from one of the shorter stacks of books next to the table. "I'm pretty sure someone cast an overpowerment spell and it got out of hand."

"An overpowerment spell?" The name sounded familiar. Did I mention I was not the most attentive magic student? "Someone wanted to cast a really big fireball?"

"Not likely." Phil shook his head as he scribbled on the notepad. "The spell is too volatile to be used in conjunction with something as unstable as a fireball. It's best used with a simple spell to make it stronger."

"That takes all the fun out of it." There are no shortcuts in magic. Well, no shortcuts that aren't the equivalent of walking down a dark, blind alley at 2 a.m. with a big neon sign reading *I have questionable judgment*.

Phil craned his neck, squinting at the screen. "The spell is traditionally used to summon or bind a creature stronger than the usual fare."

"Like what?"

"Ancient demons. Old magic." Thanks Phil, that doesn't narrow it down at all. "I believe we're dealing with a wizard of fairly high skill to have even attempted the spell. I can't guess as to their end game though."

"Well, no reports of Stay Puft Marshmallow Men running amuck." I tried to make light. "I think we're good."

"Can't be too careful," he mumbled as he went back to writing. A moment later he looked up at me. "I couldn't get an exact triangulation on ground zero, but I think the spell was cast somewhere in the Washington Heights area of Manhattan."

"That's a lot of ground to cover." I crawled back into the apartment, shutting the window behind me. I knew that tone. Phil was on the trail, and he was totally going to forget to lock up on his way out.

He stood and started to move about the room, gathering things. "I figure a spell this powerful is going to need some kind of natural ley line, magical convergence, or wellspring to draw from."

"You're going to investigate them right now?" I don't even know why I bothered asking. Of course he was.

"The sooner, the better," he said as he grabbed a courier bag which was tucked behind some crates. His satchel held everything a wizard needed for magic on the go: you know, candles, chalk, twine, duct tape.

"Suppose that's fair," I said. I put my laptop away.

"Come on, cheer up," he told me with a nudge of his elbow. "You can hunt this mystery down with me."

I gave him a sarcastic double thumbs-up. "Ah yes, Shaggy. Nothing like a potentially unstable demon spawn to help one get over the post-break up blues."

"Well, when you put it that way, now you have to come." Kicking off his flip-flops, he moved to the half-covered sofa and snatched up a pair of sneakers.

"Come on, Phil." I leaned against the table. "You know you don't have to do this. Report the incident to one of the magic council-thingies and be done with it."

"And what if they think you're at fault?"

Well, okay, he had me there.

Some of the official magic groups can get mighty crazy when it comes to the whole 'do no harm' or 'do not reveal' shtick we've had to endure for years. I caused the blackout, sure, but only because someone else had cast an overpowerment spell. So while it was techincally my fault, I hadn't stopped to consider someone might actually blame me for it. That guilt could carry any sentence from death to much, much worse. "Damn."

"I'm going to make sure *everyone* who got caught in this is protected." Phil stood up and slung the satchel over his shoulder. "I wouldn't mind someone watching my back."

I rubbed the crease between my brows. "Why does this feel like a guilt trip?"

"Isn't meant to be one. You know you're handy to have on an investigation." By handy, he meant he could ride the subway and buses without worry, which cut his travel time down. "Do you have something to feel guilty about?"

"Today? Probably." I shut my eyes and took a deep breath. Well, I did plunge my adopted city into darkness temporarily. I suppose the least I could do was help hunt the rogue wizard down. It was only proper. Also, what else was I going to do? Call Marcel and apologize? Yeah, no.

"Ready to go?" Phil stood at the front door, tucking his beige hoodie over his satchel.

"Sure, Holmes, lead the way."

THREE[3]

Two subway rides later, we were in Washington Heights. The A-Line dropped us off close enough to walk to The Cloisters, which is part of the famous Metropolitan Museum of Art. It's more commonly known as the MET, not to be confused with the baseball team The Mets, which are also based in New York. Because reasons?

I don't know. I don't get this city most days.

As for The Cloisters themselves, in the 1930s, John D. Rockefeller, Jr. donated a bunch of spectacularly gorgeous medieval art and land to the MET (I especially admire the unicorn tapestries). Somewhere along the way, it was decided several European abbeys and buildings would be shipped over brick by brick in order to house the collection. I can kind of see the chain of logic there, but I still can't quite make the leap on that one. Guess I'd have to been there.

I'm sorry, you know all this. I slipped into tour-guide mode there.

But hey, did you know the art and buildings of The Cloisters create a powerful mystical field? It hums outside the senses of normal individuals, but not magic users. It's an old energy, imbued energy. The kind of stuff even I would think twice about touching or forming, and energy is my jam.

Yeah, feel free to punch me if I say that again.

Anyway, what this means is that The Cloisters is the perfect place to lay down a juiced up spell. But that kind of havoc would leave scars on the building's aura. No such luck here.

Wait, is not finding the dangerous wizard's lair a good thing or a bad thing?

"I would've thought this was the place." I nudged Phil, who

was appreciating a tour group of college-aged Brazilians walking past. "It's chock full of all the essential vitamins and minerals needed to carry off a major spell."

"I didn't think about how public it is." He tore his eyes away from the men and glanced around. The area was swarming with tourists, staff, and the occasional security guard. "The wizard would need a lot of set up time. They'd get caught with this size of an audience."

I gave Phil a pat on the shoulder. "Worth checking out."

"Yeah. Well, on to the next stop on our tour." He gestured down the hall.

I turned and nearly ran into someone because I am completely oblivious to my surroundings. I think we've established that. "Whoops, sorry."

"It's okay ma'am," the man, a guard, said as he brushed past.

"Come on." Phil took me by the shoulders as I reeled from someone calling me 'ma'am.' I'm not even thirty yet! That's just cold! "We're heading to Jeffery's Hook next," Phil said as he pushed me towards the exit.

"Aww." I completely forgot about the guard as the thought of the lighthouse brought a twelve-year-old's smile to my face. "I love the Little Red Lighthouse."

He laughed at me politely. "It sits atop a natural wellspring where the Hudson's mystical energies pool up."

Okay, so the Hudson River, like all rivers, has its own aura given to it by the way it's perceived by others and the creatures living in it. Being a natural landmark and a notable symbol of New York City meant the Hudson had become a force of immense power over the last two centuries. The only U.S. river stronger is the Mighty Mississippi, though don't let the Hudson hear you say that.

The Rio Grande and Red River are also up there in the rankings, but they're too busy fighting with each other to care.

"The lighthouse is also right next to a running water source," I pointed out. Every wizard knows running water is a natural dampener or grounder for magic, unless you're a water-based magic user. "Even if it's a wellspring, wouldn't casting there be so difficult it would negate an overpowerment spell?"

"The thought had occurred to me," Phil replied as we stepped outside to see the sun hitting the horizon. "It's gonna start getting dark soon."

"Want to pick this up tomorrow?" I asked, but I had a feeling I knew the answer.

"Nah, the Lighthouse isn't too far, and it's on the way to the third location." Phil slipped off his bag so he could put his hoodie on. "They'll both be quick to check, and if nothing doing, I'll rethink my search grid."

"Sounds good," I said as I pulled out my phone. No messages from Marcel. I chastised myself for being disappointed and jammed it back into my jeans pocket. I had opted to leave my laptop at Phil's since I didn't want to lug it around on a walking tour. "Where's the third spot?"

With his hoodie sliding down over his head I heard a muffled, "Trinity Church Cemetery."

I had to think about that for a second. "You do know that's in Upper Manhattan, not Washington Heights?"

Phil shrugged. "Margin of error."

From The Cloisters, we caught public transportation down to Fort Washington Park. We walked the rest of the way to the Jeffrey's Hook Lighthouse, aptly nicknamed the Little Red Lighthouse. The bright red, circular body of the lighthouse stands at about two stories tall and holds a white lantern room with vertical panes of glass and a black roof. It sits perched on an outcropping of rock in the shadow of the George Washington Bridge, isolated from the world by the massive trees growing in the park.

The whole scene was the inspiration for a children's book from 1942, *The Little Red Lighthouse and the Great Gray Bridge* by Hildegard H. Swift. In the late '40s, the cast iron lighthouse was decommissioned and scheduled to be scrapped. Thanks to the book, and the efforts of many New Yorkers, it ended up being saved. It now sits as the only remaining lighthouse on Manhattan

Island.

And I'm doing it again. What can I say, it's a habit.

"Where are all the tourists?" I glanced around the strangely quiet area. The Lighthouse isn't open to the public, but you could easily snap selfies and admire the building's height—of the lack thereof—against the backdrop of the bridge. It would be typical even at this time of day to see a few camera happy individuals milling about, perhaps even a vendor or two.

"Something is really wrong here," Phil muttered beside me as we got closer, passing one of the support legs of the bridge.

"Yeah." There was a chill in the air that wasn't from the cool river breeze.

Eventually, we could see that the railing around the external platform circling the lantern room was mangled on one side. It was as if it had been pulled out of place. There were these wide, long scratches to the paintjob of the roof of the beacon housing.

"Public vandalism?" I hoped.

Wow, what a crappy thing to hope for.

"No, I don't think so." Phil crushed my optimism as he blinked and focused, his brow pinched. He was using his Third Eye to survey the area. "We need a look inside. The magical harmony here is in chaos."

"I'll take your word for it," I told him because I don't like to use my Third Eye.

Third Eye? Well, it's a fancy way of saying you focus all of your senses on the visible and invisible magic around you. This allows you to see things you would normally ignore as white noise. You might have heard it also be called Sight, or Second Sight, and it often gets confused with the Sixth Sense.

I can't really know for sure, but I imagine using your Third Eye is probably akin to tripping on acid. Now, I've never done LSD, but I hear you see lots of beautiful and scary things in various shapes, sizes, and colors. When you use your Third Eye, free-flowing magic often presents the same way and you sometimes end up seeing more than you bargained for. I had a really bad experience once. I won't bore you with the details right now, but just know it involved Dire Penguins.

When we got to the Lighthouse, there was a laminated sign zip-tied to the black, eight foot tall iron fence that surrounds the structure. It proclaimed that there were no public tours at this time. I jutted a thumb at the notice. "Hate to say this, but I think we're both having illegal thoughts right now."

"Yeah." Phil ran a hand through his hair as he checked every entrance into the clearing. "Don't see any other options. It's either find out who did this so we can keep it from happening again, or commit a felony."

"I think it's only a misdemeanor." Yay for optimism!

Phil ignored the comment. "Think you can pull some E.M.P. magic on it?"

"Sure, but it could trip an off-site alarm when the power goes dead."

"A risk we'll have to take," he said as he gestured to the building and took a step back.

Okay, an electromagnetic pulse, or E.M.P., is a wave of energy which disrupts all electronics in its path for awhile. Since I can focus energy, I can disperse it in the required wavelength to create an E.M.P., or emp as I like to say. I'm from the Midwest, we don't do multi-syllables if we can avoid it.

The emp is one of my best spells, and perhaps my most powerful. Some days, I worry that maybe the military would like to get their hands on me because of it. But at the same time, I'm not sure they want the hassle of dealing with magic users. For one, we do not mix well with their fancy electronics. Secondly, they can barely keep a lid on their own super-secret, mundane weapons and aircraft testing facilities.

I have a sneaking suspicion that when magic gets officially revealed to the world, it will be done in the form of government documents being posted on Tumblr or something.

There didn't seem to be any outside cameras to catch us looking all suspicious-like. Glancing around, I still didn't see any tourists, either. They must have felt the eerie vibe and had sense enough to keep away. I preferred it that way because what came next always made me feel like a bad actor in a cheesy '70s fantasy flick. I lifted my left arm and held it straight towards the lighthouse. My fingers were balled into a fist with my copper bracelet wrapped around my wrist.

Yay, look at me, I'm Native American Wonder Woman.

My bracelet is my personal focus item, which means it's basically a magical cheat sheet. Wizards imbue focus items, or foci, with the instructions for spells they've mastered. This way, instead of starting the spell from scratch each time, they can simply throw some magical energy into the foci and let it to do the rest for them.

I've carved several spells onto my focus bracelet, including instructions for forming energy into a localized electromagnetic pulse. I simply have to dial the power up or down manually. It had taken more effort to decide what I wanted to wear that afternoon than it did to send the pulse.

"Good job. I saw the security lights blink out." Phil pulled some glowstick necklaces out of his bag. "It's probably going to be dark inside."

"Thanks," I said as he handed me one of the necklaces. "I don't know how much time we'll have, so in and out."

"Right." Phil snapped his glowstick to life and threw it around his neck. He kept digging through his bag, only pulling out one pair of black latex gloves. "Apparently I forgot to restock. This is all I got."

"No worries." I know better than to get my grubby fingerprints on everything. Not my first rodeo, real or metaphorical. Did I mention I'm from Nebraska? I did? Oh, well then, Go Huskers!

With me playing lookout, Phil picked the lock on the gate. No fancy magic required there, just a set of locksmith tools. It only took a little longer to get past the lock on the lighthouse proper.

Before stepping inside, Phil pulled out an engraved piece of polished, stainless steel about a foot and half long from his bag. It was covered in small, chiseled markings. This is commonly known as a blasting rod and, as the name suggests, it's Phil's foci for blowing things up. A rod is separate from a wand as it's usually longer and thicker, while wands tended to be shorter and thinner. It's not really the size that matters, in this case, but how you use...

You know what, ignore me.

I'd never been inside the lighthouse before, but I'd seen pictures. The walls were a milk chocolate brown, if I remembered correctly, but in the light of the glowsticks, they were a sickly gray. This did little to soothe the growing uneasiness and generally creepy vibe the whole area gave off.

A staircase snaked around the wall with a pillar driven through the heart of the building. There were a few scary shadows but everything was calm and still. Light bled through the watch room door above and from a couple of port hole windows. With the current angle of the sun, the light did less to illuminate and instead cast long shadows.

Phil let out a low whistle.

"Woah," I muttered when I saw it. Ancient runes, possibly of the Norse tradition, were laid immaculately in concentric circles, six deep, around the base of the pillar. Residue of wax lay in clumps every few feet, and there was a distinctive smell of charcoal, sulfur, sage, and… mint?

"Look." Phil moved to the bottom of the stairs and walked up two steps. Using his glowstick, he lit the area to show a similar but smaller circle painted on the wall.

"What was that drawn in?" This was the least of my questions, but the only one I decided to voice for some reason.

Phil leaned forward and sniffed the wall. "Charcoal paste. Is this due east?"

"Didn't you bring your compass?" I asked as I pulled out my phone.

"Demagnetized it exorcising a poltergeist last week." He gave a short, unfortunate chuckle. "I forgot it was in my pocket."

"Nice." I smirked as I brought up one of the three different compass apps on my phone. I have no idea why I have so many. I stepped carefully over the circles to get as close to the pillar as possible without touching it. "Wonder why no one's noticed this?"

"Who knows. It no longer functions as a lighthouse, and it's not open to the public." Phil's voice was slightly disembodied as it echoed softly off the walls. "You felt that vibe; no one wants to get near it. There's been no tourists to report the external damage."

"I guess. Man, some poor trust worker is gonna have to clean all this up." I felt their pain, I really did. I mean, if you're going to break into a place and perform some ritual magic, you might as well clean up after yourself.

It's only polite.

"Yep, due east," I told him.

"Is there any writing on the west wall?" Phil asked.

I shined the glowstick against the opposite wall. "Nope."

"Interesting." I could hear his footfalls on the stairs. "It looks like a summoning ritual. Probably what the overpowerment spell was used for."

"Summoning what?" I knocked my phone slightly on the pillar and listened to the hollow metal resound. "Lots of cast iron in here, enough that most shadow creatures and fae would avoid it no matter how strong the summon."

"Yeah." He appeared around the pillar, scratching his chin, his arm blocking the glowstick and giving him a bit of a haunting silhouette. "An overpowerment spell could force a creature to come to this place, maybe. But why perform such a tricky spell here when they could pick a better, more magic and demon friendly locale? Running water, cold iron—this is a total fail of *Witchcraft 101*."

"So either our wizard is a complete idiot or this narrows down the suspect creature list." I started to compile a list of possible suspects in my head. Nothing seemed to fit the profile. "Something that's okay with iron but needs to be near water to summon? Some kind of fish orientated creature. Mermaid?"

"Possibly. This could also be considered a crossroads, the bridge connects New York to Jersey. And there's the damage to the roof." He pointed upwards. "Not many creatures could do that."

As I stood there trying to figure out what could have been summoned, I remembered something. "Oh hey, the cops could be on their way if the power outage tripped an alarm."

"Can you snap some pictures first?" He asked as he moved

towards the door.

"Sure." I switched over to camera mode and got what I could. "All right, done."

Phil opened the door, paused, then slipped out. I gathered it was safe and followed him into the daylight, or what was left of it. The sun had long disappeared behind the skyline across the river, but New York City never truly goes dark. I checked my phone to find a message from Stacey reminding me about tonight. I still had a couple of hours left to get ready.

"Want to swing by my apartment on your way back?" I asked as we swiftly walked away from the lighthouse. "I can print those pictures for you."

"Great, thanks." We stopped a good distance from the lighthouse, enough to feign ignorance if the cops came. "Glowstick."

I slipped it off my neck, and he tossed it into his bag along with his blasting rod and gloves. I took one last look at the Little Red Lighthouse, so lonely and small against the big, gray bridge without admirers milling about, smiling and laughing. "How long until it recovers?"

"Hard to say." He shrugged and gave a sad shake of his head. "Once they clean up the ritual circle that should help."

"Good." The wind picked up again, and I wished I'd thought to grab a light jacket that morning.

There was a loud rustling in the trees lining the entrance to the park, followed by a long, jagged wail. We both looked at each other and any hope we were hearing things was dashed. More rustling preceded a piercing howl. Phil fumbled with his bag as a large branch snapped and a demon crashed down from the trees. It was roughly the size and shape of a grizzly bear, but its matted and coarse fur was dark green. Its face held more of a resemblance to a beaten goat than a bear.

Instinctively, I lifted my left hand, thinking of the high voltage symbol carved onto my bracelet and the instructions embedded within it. The image glowed, and in true Sith fashion, a lightning bolt shot from my hand, striking the demon in the chest.

It didn't even flinch.
Yeah, so… running, lots of running.

FOUR[4]

Backpedalling like a drunken frat boy, I made for the only cover in the area: the Lighthouse. Phil was on my heels with the demon not far behind.

"Inside!" Phil shouted as we wrenched the thankfully still unlocked gate open.

We nearly fell through the Lighthouse door, slamming it shut behind us. At this point we didn't care about any forensic evidence we might be leaving behind as we took refuge. The lights were still off, and the adrenaline pumping through my body caused all the dark shadows to deepen and move.

"Okay." I tried to slow my breathing. "What the hell was that?"

"Any number of things." Phil pulled out a still active glowstick. "But we'll know soon enough if it's a shadow demon."

Yeah, so, iron is as harmful to a shadow demon as bleach is to a human. This is why iron is one of the most effective weapons against them. Seeing as the Little Red Lighthouse is one big cast iron cylinder, no way was Goat-Grizzly going to get through it. If Goat-Grizzly was a shadow demon.

"I can hear it wailing," I said. It was kind of hard to miss, but I doubt those on the bridge could tell it from all the traffic passing by. "It didn't plow in after us."

"Likely a shadow demon then." Phil held his glowstick high, looking up towards the watch room. "I don't think it was what was summoned. This way."

"You sure?" I followed him up the stairs, using my phone to better light the steps.

"The demon outside has four front claws." He stopped half way up at a port window facing the tree line. "The marks on the roof are from a three-clawed creature."

"When the hell did you have time to count claws?"

"When you zapped it." He craned his neck back and forth trying to get a good view out the porthole. "You've been practicing by the way."

"Oh, don't make me hurt you." I took a few short breaths and cleared my mind to send more energy to my bracelet, ready for the next go around. Even though I can control energy, I have a bit of a amperage issue. I can't seem to output more than the five billion-ish joules found in lightning. Which sounds like a lot, but, "I barely singed it."

"Happens," he said before becoming completely still. "Uh oh."

Phil pulled me down right before the building shook, ringing out like a struck church bell but not nearly as pleasant.

"So it's not a shadow demon?" I shouted into the noise.

He shook his head. "Tree."

"Tree?"

"A whole tree!"

I realized he meant Goat-Grizzly had thrown a whole damn tree at the building. "Shit."

Another strike sent the lighthouse trembling, the ringing at a higher pitch this time. Phil grabbed my hand and herded me up the steps through the watch room into the lantern room. One of the glass panels was knocked out by a large branch wedged through the railing, torn from its trunk.

"That thing's gonna smash this place to bits." That really upset me because the Little Red Lighthouse is too darn cute to be destroyed. Not that possibly getting skewered myself wasn't also an unsettling notion, but I prioritize.

We edged our way out onto the viewing platform, or gallery I think it's called. There was only a metal railing there, hardly any protection. We tried to stay in the shadow of the warped branch as the demon pulled another tree out of the ground in the distance.

"Same time." Phil extended his blasting rod and began to mumble in some archaic language. I twisted my bracelet around my wrist and readied myself to let out another burst of lightning.

The creature held a new tree over its head, getting a running start for his next throw. Phil yelled and a lightning bolt with tendrils of pure energy shot from my hand, clipping the ground as the full force of the blast focused on the creature. A pinpoint stream of mercury plasma accompanied the strike, courtesy of Phil and his blasting rod.

When the energies hit the demon, its heavy mass lifted from the ground. Goat-Grizzly was thrown back against the immense support beam of the bridge, knocking down the fence guarding it. There was a slightly panicked moment when we realized the demon hit the support with such a tremendous force it could have damaged the integrity of the structure. We then completely panicked a few seconds later when Goat-Grizzly picked itself up, snarled, and went for the tree again.

"Damnit!" Phil said as we ducked back into the lamp house just in time to have glass shatter over us from the tree hitting the tower.

"We need to get out of here," I shouted over the din, checking my body for damage. Only a few scrapes thankfully. "Maybe we can find a way around into the park?"

"Sounds good to me," he said as he opened the trap door, descending back into the lighthouse. Another tree was hurled against the iron building. I feared one more high pitched clang like that and I'd go deaf.

Phil stopped abruptly on the stairwell and I ran into him. "Hey!"

"I have an idea." He narrowed his eyes as he peered out the porthole.

"Better than the last one?" The words came out a bit more sarcastic than I meant, which is like my default, but whatever.

"Yeah." He bounded down the stairwell. "I'm gonna need you to distract it."

I'm pretty sure I heard the words 'you' and 'distract it'. "Wait, wut?"

"I think it left blood on the fence surrounding the support

beam," Phil explained as he opened the door a crack. "If I can get to it, I can use it to banish the demon but only before it dries."

"You *think* it did?"

"Uh, pretty sure."

Apparently, that was good enough for me. "How am I supposed to distract it?"

"I dunno, but you're a faster runner and I'm a better spell caster." He opened the door wide enough for me to get through. "Just keep it busy."

"Busy, right." I almost laughed. "Maybe it'll be interested in a round of *Angry Birds*?"

"Just give me a couple of minutes," he shouted as another howl filled the air.

Unfortunately, I couldn't argue with him. It was a decent enough plan. But still. "This is gonna suck."

As I slowly crept out the door, a tree lay up against the fence, the gate itself still open. I could feel myself being watched even though Goat-Grizzly was out of my line of sight. I could see the mangled fence Phil mentioned, the support beam of the bridge looking undamaged. Did I mention the lighthouse sits on a jut of land with the bridge support column between it and the tree line? Nothing but rocks and water behind me.

There was a large snap and the demon came running towards the lighthouse with a slight limp, tree in hand. What did Goat-Grizzly have against trees? Seriously, did it get summoned by the Arbor Day Foundation one time and it didn't end well?

Taking a deep breath, I jogged out a few paces and lifted my arm, a sizzling arch of electricity striking the creature. Goat-Grizzly stopped for a second, then snarled at me, its mouth opening to show hundreds of sharp, shark-like teeth.

Yeah, so, more running.

There was open land to the right of the lighthouse and I hoped to maybe skirt around the creature enough to lure it into the wooded area. As I hoofed it, I came to the realization that Goat-Grizzly was no longer damaging the poor Little Red Lighthouse. Instead, it was now throwing the trees directly at me.

I'll take it as a win.

The trunk overshot but I had to dive and duck to avoid the branches. Skidding across the grassy area, I landed on my back. I coughed a few times before seeing the creature loom over me. Lifting my arm, I leveled it at Goat-Grizzly's head, letting go with another blast of lightning.

The demon momentarily stunned, I got back on my feet. The tree blocked most of my exit route and I ended up heading straight towards the rocky outcrop that was the river's shoreline. The wind was heavier, swifter, the closer I got to the water. The rocks became more worn, smooth, and wet. Running out onto them in sneakers wasn't the best idea, so I came to a halt. I glanced back to see the creature stalk forward.

Phil was taking his sweet, merry little time.

I did the only thing I could and brought my fist to bear against Goat-Grizzly. I just kept pumping energy into the high voltage symbol on my bracelet. Instead of one blast, I held the surge of power steady, tapping into what was left of the city power grid inside of me. Sparks and tendrils shot off in every direction, lighting up the darkening sky.

I knew the bolt struck hard against the creature's chest but that didn't stop it, only slowed it down. I forced myself to focus the electrical beam, keep it strong and solid, even as the edge of my vision went dark. We're talking blotting out the sun kind of dark.

Goat-Grizzly howled inhumanly loud and I forced myself to look up, squinting against the light. The darkness wasn't in my vision. Something physically muted the world, or at least our portion of it. I lost concentration and the stream of lightning stopped, plunging us both into absolute darkness.

Seconds later it was over. The darkness and the creature passed into the night, taking with it the general air of uneasiness which had been plaguing the area.

Took Phil long enough.

I fell to my knees in exhaustion, rolling over onto the ground. I closed my eyes and took stock of myself. Nothing was broken, just some bruising and a few minor lacerations. I'd be fine.

"Minni." Phil decided to grace me with his presence. "You gonna live?"

"Only long enough to kill you." I started to laugh for no other reason than I could.

FIVE[5]

The first thing I did once we got back to my place was make a beeline for the fridge. I could feel a dehydration headache coming on. Occupational hazard. "Want a drink?"

"Sure." Phil tossed his bag onto the kitchen island which doubles for my dining table. "I'm gonna borrow your bathroom."

"Give it back when you're done," I mumbled, pulling out a pitcher of lemonade I'd made the day before from the powdered stuff. I grabbed two glasses from the dish rack and started to pour. That's when I could no longer ignore the trembling of my hands.

I balled my fingers into fists, pressing my forearms onto the counter, willing my body to stop shaking. My eyes screwed shut and I let the pain and fear wash over me, leaving my system as the natural adrenaline high hit its low.

Mentally, I understood this wasn't the first or last time I'd ever be attacked by a magical creature. To dwell on such facts would drive me crazy. That didn't stop my body from reacting to the incident as evolution dictated.

Beep.

My arm jerked at the sound and I knocked one of the glasses across the counter into the sink, shattering it. "Hell."

"Minni." Phil's soft voice came from outside the kitchen boundary. "You okay?"

"No." I pulled a trash bin out from under the sink and started to throw the larger shards of glass into it. "But I will be."

He didn't move. "I'm sorry, I didn't know—"

"Don't you start." I washed the small bits of glass down the drain. "We both knew there was a possibility of danger. We were attacked, we lived, it happens."

Phil might have wanted to say something but instead he

only nodded and I silently thanked him for it. When he asked me to distract the creature, he knew how easily it could have killed me. He hadn't even blinked. Maybe he had that little regard for me, or maybe he had that much faith in me. Either way, it wasn't something I wanted to discuss at the moment.

"I'll be right back," I said quietly, heading to the bathroom.

While I was washing my hands, I finally got a good look at myself in the mirror. I was a mess with nearly bloodshot eyes and a bruise travelling from above my temple into the hairline. When I lifted my hand to prod at the discoloration—as one does—I saw grass burns and little cuts lining my forearm and shoulder. My Purdue t-shirt was torn, a chunk missing out of it which kind of sucked. It was one of my most comfy shirts.

But yeah, I looked like I had picked a fight with, well, a grizzly bear.

I smiled. I'm either a hero, or insanely stupid.

I'll take either as an acceptable answer.

I cleaned up the cuts, but nothing looked band-aid worthy. When I was done, I headed back into the little kitchen area. Phil had already poured new drinks and made pb&j sandwiches.

"You are a wise, wise man, Phil," I said by way of thanks.

"Get your own," he teased. "These are for me."

"Bah." I stole a sandwich off the plate, grabbing a glass of lemonade before heading to the tiny computer desk stuck in the corner. "Still want those pics?"

"Yes, please." He settled in at the kitchen island.

Nibbling on the sandwich, I sent the pictures to the printer via wifi. As I waited for them to print, I remembered I left my laptop at Phil's. I figured I'd get it later. I think it's still there, actually.

"So, if that wasn't the summoned demon..." The question loomed in the air, slightly muffled by the peanut butter stuck to the roof of my mouth. "Then where did it come from?"

Phil took a long draft of lemonade before answering. "Could be the demon latched onto the summoning, riding it into our world. It could have already been in the park, drawn to or aggravated by the magic. Or it could have been a sentry left there to cover the wizard's tracks."

"Lots of 'coulds' in there."

"Yeah." The word was quiet, filled with more questions.

Beep.

I got a text from Stacey telling me she'd meet me at Paradiso. I checked my watch, it was seven thirty. "Frack."

"What?"

"I forgot." I slouched in my chair. "Stacey wants me to go with her to Paradiso tonight."

"Gonna cancel?"

I gave it a long hard thought as the last picture printed. "I might as well go. If I don't, she'll think I'm being mopey about Marcel and come drag me out. Can't rightly tell her I'm exhausted from fighting a Goat-Grizzly-Shark-Demon from the Shadow Realm now can I?"

"You never know." He gave a light shrug. "She might believe you."

"I am so not going there with you right now." I grabbed the sheets off the printer. "But you know what? I could really go for some dancing right now, some non-magical normalcy. You wanna come?"

He choked on his drink. "Me, in a night club?"

"You had fun last time." I grinned at the memory.

Phil gave me that look—you know the one—eyes wide and forcefully telling you to never ever speak of said events ever again. He took the pictures from me and said, "No, I think I'll spend my night researching this summoning circle."

"Alright." I wasn't going to push it. "Good luck with that."

"You could sound a little less sarcastic?"

"Nah."

Phil stared at me for a good minute before giving up. Wise choice. "Well, I'll get going," he said as he extended his arm towards me. "You have fun tonight."

"That's the plan. Well, Stacey's plan." I shook his hand which was more symbolic than anything. I drained away the magical static that had built up around him. Well, I had already been siphoning it off to keep the subway from breaking down on the way home, but this was a full-on empty of the tank. "That should get you back to Brooklyn, just try not to cast any spells or else your aura will build up static faster."

"I know the drill." He gave me a little salute. "Thanks again for your help tonight."

"It's what I'm here for," I said unenthusiastically.

Phil nodded slightly and headed to the door. I saw him out and, honestly, I thought that was going to be the end of it. When I'm wrong, I'm really wrong. I mean, I don't half-ass these things.

I pulled myself together for a night of dancing. I used makeup to hide the hairline bruise and styled myself in a pair of nice jeans and black thick-heeled boots. I went with an unbuttoned long-sleeved men's dress shirt with a shimmering gray tank underneath. I held the look together with two miss-matched, burnt orange colored belts, a heavy necklace, and a few bangles on my other wrist to match my foci.

I never take off my focus bracelet, even if it causes a fashion faux pas.

Since I didn't have time to do my hair, I piled it up in a messy bun and went for it. Fashionista I ain't, but it's not like I care. Okay, maybe I care a little. Grunge is back, right?

I took the subway down to 5th Avenue then walked the rest of the way to Club Paradiso. The place was new. Stacey had found it through a friend and it was now her favorite haunt. I didn't mind; these places are all pretty much the same to me. When I rounded the corner, there was a line of maybe forty people deep standing in the light of too much neon.

"Minni!" I barely heard the word over the din of the club and passing traffic. Stacey was standing half-way down the line, waving frantically at me. She was hard to miss in a black mini-skirt and pink top made of several layers. It draped over her like a biker-Grecian goddess, her dark hair in dozens of curly tresses.

I waved, then waited for the traffic to stall before crossing. It would be embarrassing to narrowly defeat a shadow demon only to get flattened by a taxi.

I have an image to maintain.

"Hey," I called out as I approached, hoping not to annoy too many people as I cut in line.

"Girl!" She grabbed me in a bear hug, causing the bruises on my arm to ache. "I'm so sorry about Marcel! What happened?"

I tried not to let the grimace show on my face. "I'm really not in the mood to talk about it."

"Nonsense!" She crossed her arms and stared down at me. "Spill."

Have you ever heard the term Amazonian? Next to the word in the dictionary is a picture of Stacey Sanchez. Impossibly long legs went with seriously high cheekbones and brown hair so dark it might as well be black. She was second generation Puerto Rican immigrant and contained enough self-confidence for the both of us, and then some. It's hard to say no to her.

I gave her the short and sweet explanation. "He wanted me to move in with him, I said no, we argued." Well, short explanation.

"Seriously?" She looked as if she was about to slap me. "Girl, I don't know what I'm going to do with you."

Now, let me explain something. Stacey is my best non-magical friend. She doesn't know anything about me being a witch.

After I graduated from Purdue, I… decided to move to New York. I didn't have the funds I have now, so I answered an ad for a roommate. There were four of us in the flat, all different in our backgrounds and personalities. Stacey was the only one I got along with and I honestly couldn't tell you why. While I started working at an engineering firm, she was into design and marketing. She wants to start her own clothing line.

Of course, I don't really have much in common with Phil either, except for the fact we're both wizards. So I guess that's what me and Stacey have: we're both normal. Or at least I pretend to be.

I like being able to hang out with someone who doesn't think of me in terms of magic, especially when they have none. Regular people tend to look up at wizards in awe or fear, or both. Even if they've known each other for years, grew up together, there's still that level of 'wow, this person could turn me into a newt if they really thought about it.'

Often this doesn't end well.

"Why couldn't you help them?"

"Why can't you help me?"

"Why didn't you do something?"

"Why didn't you save them?"

These are the questions that start getting asked. Questions whose answers always end badly.

Think I'm being cynical? Maybe I am.

Doesn't change the truth.

"Yeah, well." I tried to shrug it off. There was nothing I could do except, you know, tell Marcel the truth about me and magic. And that's not going to happen.

Stacey sighed and put her hand on my shoulder. "Minni, I could tell you you're crazy but it wouldn't do any good."

"Probably not." After all, I did take on Goat-Grizzly for no better reason than it seemed like the thing to do at the time. "I don't want to talk about Marcel."

Stacey moved to wrap her arm around me. "Alright, tonight we PARTY!" The shout returned a few exclamations as well as a couple of odd looks. Stacey didn't care. She never does. "But this conversation isn't over."

"'Course." I let myself smile and relax a bit. I figured the worst that might happen was I sprain an ankle on the dance floor.

Oh, that's what happened. I jinxed myself. I totally should have seen the rest coming.

As we stood waiting in line I was happy to let Stacey do most of the talking. I was tired and feeling on edge. Then ten minutes in, I seriously got the 'I'm being watched' vibe. I fidgeted with my copper bracelet and sensed out for any pockets of magic in the area using my sixth sense.

This is pretty easy, actually. If you know what magical energy feels like, which I do, it's a simple matter of using all your senses to locate any magic nearby. You know how you might listen for a particular voice in a crowded room, or you're looking for a certain image in a collage? Same thing.

Failing to sense anything, I checked out the emotions of everyone around me using empathy magic. Empathy is my eldest brother's specialty, but I have a decent enough grasp of it to sense if any negative emotions were being directed towards me. Other than Stacey and a woman who did not like my outfit, I was being ignored by everyone in a three square block radius. As I seemed to be safe, I took a deep breath and let it out slow.

Have I mention wizards are notoriously paranoid? We're basically genetically disposed to be suspicious of all the things.

Anyway, twenty minutes later we were still standing in line when yet another fancy car pulled up. This one was a Bentley, though I can't tell one model from the next. The driver rushed around to the rear passenger's side, opening the door swiftly. A Dorito emerged. You know, the wide at the shoulders, narrow at the hips, ex-military body-guard type.

A tall man with slicked back, blond hair and a short trimmed, full beard stepped out next. He wore a charcoal grey suit with a powder blue undershirt. All Gucci, if the group behind me was to be believed. No one knew who he was. He kind of looked like a young Antonio Banderas but with dumb frosted tips.

He might have been handsome if it wasn't for the air of extreme self-confidence and self-importance hanging around his person.

Tipping the bouncer, he made his way into the club while we plebeians had to stand out in the cold. To be honest, I didn't give him much thought after that. Just another rich doucheboat who thinks he's better than the rest of us.

In my defense, I wasn't that far off.

Five minutes later we were finally ushered into Paradiso and the noise level made the ringing lighthouse sound like a hand bell.

Paradiso was originally a three-story office building. The center atrium, once the lobby, now had a dance floor with wall-to-wall bodies. Off to the right was the bar. A bag & coat check area had been made from some offices. The rest of the place was gutted to fit a stage in the back. Load bearing pillars still held the floors above.

Dozens of faces peered down from balconies decorated in every neon color you could imagine. The entire place was coated in lights and signs showing various flora and fauna of Paradise, I think. Maybe you had to be a little drunk to truly appreciate it.

"Dance!" Stacey let out a whoop and dived into the fray.

I followed the path she cut. I mean, what else could I do? They were playing *Uptown Funk* and it's one of Stacey's favorites.

But you know what? I wasn't going to complain. Among the mash of dancers, I could forget crazy wizards, shadow demons, public vandalism, and simply feel the music. There is a different kind of energy found in a situation like this. It was very rejuvenating.

I did have to lightly zap three guys who tried to grind too close me and Stacey without permission. Hey, someone tries to grab my ass on the dance floor and they're going to get the static discharge from hell.

"Drink?" Stacey shouted into my ear after about twenty minutes of dancing

"Huh?" Once I got going I didn't really want to stop, but they were playing a particularly bad mix of *Toxic*. "Sure."

"Upstairs," she nearly yelled as we exited the dance floor.

"Okay," I shouted back, not sure if she heard me.

The third floor of the club contained another bar with tables and sofas. We made a quick stop at the bar first. Stacey never has to wait for a bartender to serve her. Her drink of choice was a vodka and Redbull. Personally, I can't stand Redbull. I feel like I should enjoy it because of the whole energy motif I have going on, but it's just not for me.

I ordered a Cape Cod: basically just vodka and cranberry juice with a lime wedge. Managing to find an empty table, I sipped at my drink. I'm not a heavy drinker, and that night especially I wasn't feeling it.

"Soooooooo," Stacey drew the word out. "Marcel?"

"Was that..." I shouted, then realized I didn't have to this high up in the club. "Was that why you brought me up here?"

She blinked a couple of times. "You broke up with your boyfriend of what, three years? It's okay to be upset."

It's also okay to be upset about almost being eaten by a goat-headed shadow demon. You don't see me complaining about it, oh wait... "Look, I've had a long day and I don't want to deal with this right now."

There it was, the stare down. I knew I was about to lose; it's hard to win against Stacey. But she blinked again, sitting back in her chair. I really should have figured out what was going on. I was a bit self-absorbed at the time, I'll admit it.

No words passed for what seemed like several minutes as we nursed our drinks. Not the worst night clubbing ever, but it definitely sucked.

"I'm tired," I finally said out loud. "I appreciate it, what you're trying to do."

"Yeah." Her features turned soft. "Want me to walk you home?"

"Nah." I gave a tweak of a smile in thanks. "Might take the long way."

Stacey chuckled lightly. She knew of my love of walking and jogging. Of course, she didn't know it was because of my constant need to do something with all the magical energies inside me. "Might knock some sense into you."

"Only if I fall down." Man, I regret those words.

Stacey's phone beeped and she dragged it out of her clutch. "It's Chelsea. She wants to meet up. You sure you'll be okay?"

"Yeah." I tipped the drink I was nursing. "I'll finish this then do a walkabout."

She stood, reaching over to give me a hug. "You text me every hour until you make it home. Things have been kinda crazy since the blackout. Don't take any chances."

Oh yeah, the blackout. Another reason to sit there and feel crummy. "I'll be fine, but I'll text you."

"Good." Stacey hugged me, again, then made her way to the stairs. She waved at me before she descended into the club.

It was only while I sat there, nibbling on the lime wedge, that I started to think something was a bit off in our conversation. I figured I was probably being paranoid, as usual.

"May I join you?" A shadow fell across the table and his tone of voice was not exactly asking. He couldn't have waited five minutes after my friend left to attempt to pick me up?

Ugh, *men.*

"You can sit there if you want." I didn't bother looking up from my drink. "Doesn't mean I'll keep sitting here."

"Surely you'd give me a moment of your time?" His accent made him British-adjacent, but he hardly sounded like James Bond. He pulled the seat out, smoothly sliding into it. "Especially after all the trouble I went through to arrange this? Your friend has a considerably strong will, for a mortal."

My hands clenched around my drink, alarm bells going off in my head. I raised my eyes to see Gucci-Bentley from before, his face a mix of suspicion and smugness. He reached into the breast pocket of his suit and I tensed, wondering how much collateral damage a lightning strike might do in the crowded club. Smiling, he slowed his movements and produced a little zip-lock baggy which he tossed onto the table between us.

The bag contained the ripped piece of my shirt from earlier and I could see dry specks of blood on it. I assumed it was my blood and he had used it to track me down. There were too many possibilities to consider as to how and why he obtained the piece of fabric in the first place. I couldn't even remember when my shirt ripped during the fight.

All Gucci-Bentley did was smile. "You're sloppy."

I took a quick moment to assess my situation. For one, he used the word mortal, which no one uses these days. No one human anyway. He spoke of willpower as if it was a quantifiable form of energy; which it is, if you know magic. And he tracked me down after finding a piece of my clothing at a supernatural crime scene where an unknown quantity had been summoned.

But none of this told me anything substantial. I needed to get more information before I jumped to any conclusions. I decided to go with a more diplomatic approach to the situation.

"Congratulations." I smiled. "You know a tracking spell."

I'm sorry, did I say diplomatic? I meant sarcastically antagonistic.

"Indeed I do, among other things." He ran his finger around the rim of Stacey's abandoned drink. "Suggestion spells can be tricky. You have to be subtle and clever, or else the subject won't acquiesce."

Suggestion spells are neat little party tricks. And by neat I mean so not cool. It's basically like becoming the devil on someone's shoulder. It makes the victim do things they aren't completely against, such as heading upstairs for a drink then leaving to hang out with someone who actually wants to party. While not technically a Black Listed spell, its use is generally frowned upon.

"I would take it as a kindness," I said slowly, deliberately, throwing my Midwestern drawl on thick, "if you left this table and never, ever, came near me or my friends again."

"Would you now?" A smirk tugged at the corner of his mouth.

"Indeed I would." I was not going to back down. No wizard wants to fight with someone more stubborn than they are. I may not be very powerful, but stubborn I can do.

It did worry me that if he was a wizard, then why hadn't half the club exploded by then? I couldn't see any obvious magical dampening talismans. Though it would have been rather stupid of him to bring any if he was expecting a possible fight. So was he not going to be confrontational or was I in over my head? The more I thought about all my options, the less sure I felt about everything.

"Do you know who I am?" Gucci-Bentley questioned. I instinctively reached out to get a better feel of his aura. It was strong, very powerful, and quite strange. I hadn't felt anything like it before, so I made a guess.

"A jerk in a suit. Sorry, a really nice suit?"

"Yes, it is a nice suit." He unconsciously smoothed out invisible wrinkles. "But I believe we got off on the wrong foot."

"Ya think?" I deadpanned. "I'm beginning to suspect you're not very bright."

"Antagonizing someone who has shown an obvious aptitude for delicate magic and the will to use it?" His light colored eyes twinkled in the neon as he smiled. "Who's the questionably intelligent one here?"

"Oh, it's you." I grabbed the baggie and shoved it into my pocket as I stood. "Since you seem to want something from me, but you spectacularly failed to get it the moment you messed with my friend."

He narrowed his eyes. "Did I now?"

In the cheesiest accent I could muster, I said, "Cheerio."

I didn't want to get into a magic battle at the top of the club where so many people could be hurt. But if gloves were going to be thrown down, I wasn't going to be intimidated. And to prove I was wasn't afraid of his power, I turned my back on him.

I might have also poured all my energy into the shielding instructions on my bracelet. You know, just in case.

"My father was taken," he said bluntly.

I admit, I didn't know what to make of that little piece of information. I tucked it in with what I already knew, which was Gucci-Bentley had obtained a piece of my shirt from the attack at the lighthouse. The same location where a major summoning was performed. It's feasible his father was a victim of whatever happened and he was tracking evidence, which admittedly did lead to me.

Of course, it was possible Gucci was the crazy wizard and this was some elaborate scheme to do something, um, elaborate and scheme-y?

Well, only one way to find out.

I turned and stared down at the well-dressed man. "You have a funny way of showing bereavement."

"My apologies." His mouth tightened around the word. "I'm not used to requiring help from maidens."

Odd choice of noun, but whatever, he's British. "How beautifully archaic of you."

He grinned slowly at me. "You have no idea."

"And I never will if you keep wanting to dance." I crossed my arms and did my best to look bored. "One chance to give it to me straight or I'm walking."

"Look at me, really *look* at me." He spread his arms in a peace gesture. "And tell me what you see, Son of the Master."

He actually referred to me as a Son of the Master, and this was the moment I really should have just called it a day.

SIX[6]

Okay, so why did the use of a simple four-word phrase nearly give me a panic attack? Well, as I said before, I'm a Masterson, but more specifically, a descendent of the First Master. My father's family line traces back to the Sixth Son of the Master, or Master's Sixth Son. The surname became Masterson somewhere around the Invasion of Normandy in 1066 (not to be confused with the Normandy Invasion of 1944).

The First Master was an insanely strong wizard, a contemporary of Merlin actually. But unlike that crazy old bat, First Master wasn't nearly as personable—a family trait no doubt. He's not really remembered anymore. He didn't get poems and stuff wrote about him. Some, even my own family members, think he could have been a myth.

But there was something in the way Gucci said Son of the Master. It was as if not only did he believe in First Master, but he had a personal beef with the man.

I focused my Third Eye on Gucci-Bentley. He still sat in his chair, completely relaxed with a patient tint to his features. Behind him, though, stood one of the most beautiful and yet terrifying creatures I had never seen before. Its power pulsed in rhythm to its smoky breaths and I found myself lulled by the sensation of rise and fall.

With a jolt, I snapped my eyes shut and tried not to think about what I'd seen. It was difficult, tormenting, and I'm sure I looked a fool standing there shuddering for no apparent reason. When I finally worked my eyelids open, the man was fiddling with his phone. That's when I learned his kind doesn't have the same problems as wizards do with electronics. How handy for them.

"Who are you?" I tried to keep the awe out of my voice.

He tipped his head in greeting and gave me a toothy smile. "*I* am Aiden Drake, CEO of Pennington-Kettering Enterprises."

"Of course you are." I gave him a dour look.

"And you are a Masterson. Dominique, right?"

I tried not to look flustered. "Pull that out of your bag of magic tricks?"

He pointed at his phone. "I Googled you."

Of course he did.

I needed to take control of the conversation. "Now what's this about your father?"

That wiped the self-satisfied smugness off his face. "He was the one summoned at the lighthouse, but I don't understand why he hasn't escaped yet. A single wizard, five wizards, ten, they wouldn't have stood a chance against him."

"Maybe." Actually, he was likely right in his assessment but I wasn't about to point that out, all things considered.

"I tracked him to Jeffery's Hook," Drake continued as he put the phone back in his jacket pocket. "The trail dead-ended at the lighthouse, but then what do I find? The tell-tale traces of a Masterson."

And it was at that moment I remembered something very important about his kind and the Masterson clan.

"I've got nothing to do with your father's disappearance," I told him firmly.

"I can see that." He snorted and waved broadly around. "You're barely a witch."

"That's a good insult." I nodded appreciatively. "I'll remember it as I'm walking out the door."

He again held his hands out in apology. I was pretty sure it was just for show. "Gaerwen, Son of the Master, was a friend of my kind. I had hoped one of his descendants would also see fit to aid me, especially as she seems to be already involved."

"Stumbling onto the summoning was a fluke." Which was essentially true, but more importantly: "and Gaerwen was a whole other branch of the family, from the Second Son. Also, doesn't the Book of Gaerwen teach a wizard how to easily bind your kind to their will?"

Some friend Great(+infinity)-Uncle Gaerwen was.

"Yes." A tight smile formed on his lips. "Gaerwen was privy to many things, most of which he saw fit to put to parchment. It was another Son of the Master who destroyed the manuscript in later years. Surely you've heard the legend of the Copper Knight?"

I could tell the story of the Copper Knight in my sleep, and I probably have. My mother used to tell it to us all the time. Depending on the situation, she either spun an epic tale of adventure or an endearing ballad of romance.

"The Copper Knight was sent to find the Book of Gaerwen," I rattled off the short sweet of it. "He found the book and gave it to his king so he could use it to force your kind into helping him win a war. The king turned out to be an utter douche about the whole thing. So the knight mounted a rebellion, stopped the king, and the book was destroyed."

"Maybe." It sounded a bit like an accusation.

"Trying to say something?"

He relaxed into the chair. "You did bring up the book."

"You brought up Gaerwen." I mean, honestly dude.

Drake stared at me for a long uncomfortable moment. "You don't trust me."

"Yah think?" I laughed at the incredulousness of the whole thing. "You don't trust me either, so I guess we're even."

"Well, if it is any consolation, I don't believe you are involved with my father's abduction." His eyes narrowed. "But you *are* involved, and you know we can help each other."

"Can we now?"

Help a monster find his equally monstrous father? Meh, I've had worse propositions.

The truth is… his kind isn't exactly evil, they simply suffer from extreme arrogance and superiority complexes. This means they are as equally likely to help you as let you die if it suited their needs. I guess you could say they looked down on humans as we would a rat. Pet, test subject, vermin, food: all these names apply.

"I've come to a dead end," he stated simply as he held my

gaze. "Evidence at Jeffery's Hook has been destroyed, tracking has failed, and the last time I visited New York parachute pants were in style."

"I feel your pain." I tried to put as much disinterest in the words as possible.

Though I was legitimately sorry for the parachute pants.

"I'm sure you do," he replied dryly. "I have found myself at an impasse with you as my best lead."

I didn't exactly believe him. His kind aren't the type to have a single transparent motive. Unfortunately, there wasn't much I could do about it right then. I figured I might as well play the long game and see if I win a prize. The prize being I rake him over the coals for pulling a suggestion spell on Stacey.

Oh, I have not forgotten about that.

"Overpowerment spell," I said once I made my decision, for better or worse. "Thought it might have been used for the summoning, but now I guess it was for binding your father."

Drake nodded slowly. "Yes, the lighthouse is a perfect place to summon my father. Our unknown wizard would be able to save his main reserve of magic and focus it on keeping him there."

"Yeah, I imagine the whole 'not getting eaten' part of the plan would be a priority."

"Indubitably." He chuckled, probably remembering some disembowelment done to an unlucky wizard. He glanced up at me thoughtfully. I hoped he wasn't considering how I'd look with my insides on the outside. "What's your stake in this?"

Well, in for a penny. "The overpowerment spell went a little crazy. Caused havoc with spells being performed at the same time. It's bad for business."

"Yes, I see." Again he narrowed his eyes at me. He may have already put together that the blackout was related to the abduction. I mean, it would be a pretty interesting coincidence if it wasn't. "I'm assuming you have no leads since you took the time to come here. What about the second wizard who was with you?"

I tried not to frown. I was hoping to keep Phil as a backup. I suppose I could have lied, but I wasn't sure it would be worth it.

"Working on it."

"Then shall we go?" he said as he stood.

"I never said I'd help you." I tilted my chin up in defiance… and because he's a good head taller than me.

Drake leaned forward, his smile all teeth. I could easily imagine them turning into sharpened weapons. "You never said you wouldn't."

I walked into that one, didn't I?

"It's not my call." I nearly growled in annoyance.

"Of course." He pulled his phone out again. "Does your wizard friend have a working phone? If not, I'm quite adept at improvising sending spells using cocktail napkins."

I stared down at the slick black box, wheels turning in my head. He would know wizards don't carry cell phones. But did he know I had a special ability that let me use one? I mean, it's not exactly a state secret or anything. Would it be a problem for me if he knew?

And that was my paranoia kicking in, for realsies.

"It should have had time to degauss," I said as I took the phone from him. "Aren't you afraid I'll fry it?"

He waved me off. "Please, it's not as if I can't afford a hundred more."

"Right." I rolled my eyes at the show off and proceeded to type in Phil's number, pausing as I tried to remember it.

Phil answered after a couple of rings. "Hello."

"Hey, it's me."

"You calling from the club?" Phil nearly shouted. "I can hardly hear you."

"Yeah, I'm at the club." I stuck my finger in my other ear. "Got a lead on the case."

"Really?" I don't think he believed me.

I glanced at Drake. "I know who was summoned."

When I told Phil everything that had happened in the past twenty minutes, he practically choked. "Okay, so, that was unexpected."

"Tell me about it." At this point I was still deciding how I was going get back at Drake for Stacey. "Anyway, he wants to come visit. Pool our resources."

"Until we're no longer useful."

"Your investigation, your call," I said as I sized up Drake. "We can trust him to work towards getting his father back. But I'm sure he'll not think twice about us being collateral damage."

Drake gave a not-even-going-to-try-to-refute-that shrug.

There was a moment of silence from Phil as he thought it over. "Well, he's a good a lead as any. And maybe we can keep him from literally tearing New York apart looking for dear old dad."

"Yeah." It was a legitimate worry. "I'll see you in a bit."

"I'll be waiting."

"Kay, bye." I took the phone from my ear and ended the call. What happened next totally wasn't spite at all. As I handed back the phone, light wisps of smoke started curling from it. It's amazing what a little current can do.

Drake frowned at the smoking device.

"Sorry." There wasn't an ounce of remorse in my voice.

"No bother." He slipped the phone into his abandoned high-ball glass, the displaced liquid nearly splashing over the sides. "Shall we go then?"

"Said the spider to the fly," I mumbled under my breath.

Drake raised one eyebrow. "I assure you, at this moment it is in my best interest for you to be alive, therefore you are likely the most protected you have ever been."

Unfortunately, he was probably right. "This day just keeps getting better."

As we walked down the steps, Drake's bodyguard appeared and followed quietly. Seriously, what would a monster like Drake need with a bodyguard? Was he a glorified personal assistant?

Outside, a few individuals were still waiting to get in and the road was lined with traffic. We stood on the corner patiently as the guard called the car around. I tried to figure out what was happening, really happening. You don't summon a monster of that caliber, go through extreme measures to bind it, just so you can have it over at a birthday party.

Whoever was behind this was up to something big, and that usually went hand in hand with nothing good. This line of thinking wasn't me being paranoid for once, which made the whole situation, like, a zillion times worse.

A breeze shot down through the buildings and I unconsciously shivered. I almost jumped as Drake laid his jacket over my shoulders.

I blinked at him, twice. "Seriously?"

"You know." He looked at me thoughtfully. "Your gender used to be more of a gentler lot, appreciative even."

"How gentle were they when they were being sacrificed to *your* lot?" I countered, keeping my voice low.

He grinned. "Not very."

And this is why I'm not allowed to carry sharp objects. I literally would have stabbed him. Several times. In front of witnesses.

I scowled at him instead. He ignored me and his eyes shot up, followed slowly by the rest of his face as he straightened to full height. "Miss Masterson, you rightly have no reason to trust me as I would sacrifice you in a moment to save my father, but would you be so kind as to walk into the dark, blind, alley behind the club with me."

"Uh." Is it sad I actually had to think about that? "No."

He grabbed me gently by the elbow. "It seems I'm not the only one who knows a tracking spell. This way."

Drake pulled me with him as he took long, measured paces towards the alley, trying not to be suspicious. I was going to protest but thought it would be more productive to use my senses to figure out if there really was a threat other than Drake. Sure enough, while I was lost in my own thoughts, an oppressive aura had started to coat the area.

"Goat-Grizzly," I hissed the name.

"Pardon?"

"Shadow demon who attacked us at the lighthouse." My eyes flitted around the alley which was blocked half-way down with a chain-link fence. A few dingy dumpsters lined the walls and music leaked from the club. "It's him, or it, whatever. But we banished it?"

"You merely sent it back where it could be recalled," Drake pointed out as we reached the fence. I couldn't see a way around it. "Or I suppose it could be another of its kind."

A howl filled the air, eerily floating on top of the pulsing bass coming from inside. We looked up to see the demon fall from the roof of the three story club. Asphalt cracked beneath its feet as it landed with a powerful thud. Its beaten face snarled showing hundreds of shark-like teeth.

I'd almost forgotten that part.

Almost.

"That's definitely Goat-Grizzly," I managed to say with a straight face.

"Same beast?" Drake asked casually.

"You know, it was dark," I snapped, not taking my eyes off the demon and raising my bracelet on instinct.

"Pity." There was a touch of real remorse in his voice. "It would have been nice to know."

Goat-Grizzly, Part Deux, stalked a few paces forward and I frowned. I hadn't even scratched the last one with my electrical blast so I lowered my arm. "You gonna do something or just stand there and look pretty?"

Drake stared down at me, smiling. "But I am doing something."

I got a terrible sinking feeling in my stomach. Drake finds me and then so does a supposedly banished demon? And the man drags me into a place where I have little options of escaping said demon?

"Drake," I said the name warningly. "You're a *dragon*, do something!"

He laughed, a right chuckle even. "Do you honestly think I bother to get my hands dirty anymore? At my age?"

Dragon or no, I was pretty sure I was going to murder Drake before this was all over.

You know, if the second coming of Goat-Grizzly didn't get me first.

SEVEN[7]

"Drake!" I shouted the word as a warning.

Another howl filled the air just above the din of the club. This time it sounded different. It was full of pain or fear, maybe both. Turning my attention back to Goat-Grizzly, I saw Drake's bodyguard standing over the fallen demon. A sword the length of a claymore was in his hands. I was fairly certain it was made of pure iron.

The demon trembled slightly then melted into ectoplasm.

"Wait." I threw my hand up to stop Drake from moving forward. "We were bait? You willingly put yourself in harm's way just so *he*," I pointed at the guard, "could stab it in the back?"

"Yes." The dragon replied as if there was nothing wrong with that.

I addressed the bodyguard. "Are you human?"

The guard nodded yes as he wiped down the sword which he apparently conjured from out of his ass. Okay, he got it from of the trunk of the car. I just didn't know that at the time.

I turned back to Drake. "You let a non-magical, mundane, human being dispatch a shadow demon while you just stood there doing absolutely nothing because… what? You're lazy?"

He was a little taken aback. "It is what I pay him for."

"But…" I nearly flailed at Drake, "you're a dragon!"

He frowned at me. "And I pay him quite well."

I'm pretty sure there are some serious OSHA violations going on here.

Shaking my head, I followed Drake out of the alley where his car waited for us. I was way too tempted to curl up and go to sleep on the plush leather seats. Honestly, I should have been home, sleeping off the hectic day. It seemed like a reasonable request before I knew the crazy wizard we were chasing was the proud owner of a bound ancient dragon.

At least I assume Drake's dad was ancient. What other reason would someone have to try to capture him? The older a magic user, human or otherwise, the stronger they are. And with dragons, ancient scales and blood are more potent for spell components. Or at least, that's the accepted belief.

The subject of dragon organ harvesting is rather hazy because the Book of Gaerwen contained the correct formulas and lists of what all does what. Of course, no one bothered to properly copy the book before the Copper Knight destroyed the original. After that, everything fell into myth and legend, kind of how gorilla parts and ivory are treated in more modern times.

What we do know for sure is you can't get true dragon's blood, claws, or scales when the dragon is in human form.

The transmutation spell for becoming human is something only dragons who are at least a hundred or so years old can cast. Unlike a lycanthrope or skinwalker, shape-shifting is not natural to a dragon. It's a spell like any other and takes a lot of experience and knowledge to be able to cast effectively. Once cast, the dragon is kind of stuck as a human. If they go back to their true form it takes a long time before they are able to cast the spell again.

That's one of my favorite parts to the Copper Knight story. He waited for her.

Anyway, I zoned out on the drive to Phil's apartment. When we got there, the bodyguard stayed in the car despite his non-verbal objections. He didn't seem to trust me, which I thought was hilarious given the circumstances. I was wary of Drake myself, but figured I was safe as long as he needed me to help him on his quest. Once I became useless, then my well-being would no longer be his concern.

I was sure he wouldn't kill me right out though.

Pretty sure.

I knocked on Phil's door three times. I could feel his wards were reinforced. This essentially made his apartment near-impenetrable against anything not human.

The door swung open and Phil stood baring the entrance, blasting rod held loosely at his side. "Dominique."

I flinched at the use of my full first name. "No tricks, Phil. He wants our help."

"As much as it pains me to admit," Drake added dryly.

Phil's eyes darted to me and with a sigh I stepped across the threshold. His wards didn't react, so his shoulders relaxed and he turned to Drake. "You may enter but any hostile act will be met with force."

"Of course." Drake gave a slight nod of his head.

Dragons don't live as long as they do without being smart about picking their battles. One place you never want to duel a wizard is behind his own threshold. I would bet even money Phil was thinking the same thing as he stepped aside and let us both enter the room properly.

Then it got real awkward as the three of us stood there, staring at each other. I decided to do proper introductions as is polite in these kinds of social situations, or so I've been told. "Phil, this Aiden Drake, dragon. Drake, meet Phillip McCree, coven leader."

Drake gave a slight nod of his head. In the glow of standard light bulbs (as opposed to neon), I could see the tips of his hair weren't frosted. Instead, the roots were the color of burnished gold and the ends became more polished. His eyes were similar to unprocessed ore. His tan was literally golden.

Of course, he was a gold dragon.

In a world of hair dyes and contacts, no one would have given him a second thought. And the whole effect was actually quite stunning. His striking visage nearly making up for that cloud of smugness which hung over him. And by nearly I mean not even close.

But you know what, that's one thing I love about Marcel. He makes confidence seem so effortless. Never smug or haughty. And that smile… talk about pure gold.

Right, sorry, I'm getting off track.

So, Drake. He started to walk around the room, taking a

critical eye to it. "Good to see some things never go out of style."

"Did you come here for help or to insult my choice of decor?" Phil didn't bother to hide his annoyance, his curious eyes taking in every detail of his guest. I don't think he'd seen a real dragon, either.

"My apologizes," Drake responded before creasing his brow in thought. "No, I meant what I said. No use for civility where there is none. It does pain me to ask you for assistance, but now and again even a lion needs a mouse to remove a thorn from their paw."

"Real charmer you are." Phil rolled his eyes before heading over to his desk. "You want to fill this mere mouse in on what you know?"

"Certainly." The dragon straightened his suit, looking for a place to sit. Thinking better of it, he stayed standing. "My father was at our estate. We discovered him missing when he did not appear for breakfast this morning. The summoning maw which took him left traces and at first I wasn't too concerned. It's not the first time this has happened. I expected contact once he dealt with whatever foolish wizard had sent for him."

"Where is this estate?" Phil asked as he started to open some books. Drake remained quiet until Phil sighed. "Look, I need to know as many facts as possible. Magic is six-dimensional, you know that. Any detail could be important."

He considered this for a moment before finally saying, "About thirty minutes north of Swansea, Wales."

"Alright." Phil nodded and closed one of the books and set it aside. "Then what?"

Drake sighed as if he was bored already. "I set up a tracking spell and followed it to Jeffery's Hook. I lost track of my father, but then found trace of Miss Masterson."

"Minni is from the Sixth Son," Phil quickly defended.

"Yes." Drake smiled far too broadly. "We've had this conversation."

"Did you now?" Phil asked as he glanced over at me.

"Great-Something Uncle Gaerwen was a bit of a dick," I said, leaning back against a book shelf. "Let's move on."

"Lets." Drake's grin turned into a grimace. "I believe a blocking spell was cast on my father."

"Smart thing to do," Phil agreed as he started to flip through another one of his books.

I wondered out loud. "What would someone want with an ancient dragon?"

Two sets of eyes stared blankly at me.

"Besides the obvious," I amended.

Drake decided to address my rhetorical question. "Well, if the wizard in question wanted dragon blood and scales, then he picked the... cream of the crop, as it were."

Phil set his book down and went to grab another. "Gold dragons are the top of the European Dragon hierarchy, right?"

"We are the leadership, the strongest of all our kin," Drake answered proudly.

"But that's not right," I said, something shaking loose in my memory of the Copper Knight story. "You may be the leaders, but you're not the strongest. You're not the warrior class."

"You are half right," he replied, his face a mixture of annoyance and curiosity. "Copper Dragons are the warrior class, the fiercest and strongest of the European Dragons. But my Copper-kin have been extinct for some time. Gold has picked up the slack, and are now the strongest."

"You do realize how dodgy you made that sound, right?"

"Copper's extinction was the fault of humans," Drake got a tad bit snide with me.

I nodded sagely. "Sounds like us."

"Okay," Phil interrupted, "why don't we focus on the living? Minni, you have it right. If we figure out exactly why his father was taken then we might get the who."

"I think we can rule out Pete Townshend," I quipped, but was met with more blank stares. "Really? Nothing?"

Phil ignored me and turned to Drake. "What do we call dear ol' dad?"

"Ignatius," Drake answered. You'd think dragons would be more original with their nomenclature. I guess you get old enough and you're just like 'screw it, I do what I want.'

"Alright." Phil's cheekbones tightened as if he was holding back a comment. "Let's work on the assumption the wizard wants Ignatius alive as it's the most likely probability. Even if this is a harvest, dragon blood has to be obtained while the heart is still beating. Which brings up another question. Was he a dragon or human?"

"Human," Drake spoke the word as if it made of acid, which was hilarious considering it was coming from a man currently wearing a human suit, by choice. "If the wizard wanted blood, father would have to revert to his natural form."

"Going back to dragon is easier for you than turning human, right?"

"Gaerwen was said to have asked much the same questions." The dragon tilted his head slightly. "You're very inquisitive."

"Oh yeah." Phil nodded and crossed his arms, leaning forward slightly on the balls of his feet. "Did Minni not mention this is an elaborate plot to get all your mystical dragon-y secrets? You asked for our help, remember? But, you know, the fact you came to us so easily is pretty suspicious itself."

"Yes." His eyes narrowed. "Perhaps it was a mistake to cohort with wizards."

"Oh, my, god," I involuntarily shouted. "A pissing match, really?"

What can I say, something in me snapped.

I pointed at Drake. "You're here because you're covering your bases of whether or not we're involved. You also want to keep an eye the only Masterson in the Five Boroughs." My hand swung accusingly at Phil. "You're scared witless and trying to make up for it with bravado. Chill! He's not going to eat you... at least until he finds his dad."

Both Phillip McCree and a gold dragon stood speechless in my presence. I'd give myself a self-satisfied pat on the back if I wasn't so tired and slightly terrified.

I cleared my throat. "Now that's resolved, I really have to

pee. Try not to kill each other before I get back."

Rubbing my temples, I headed around a stack of books and disappeared into the bathroom. It wasn't just an excuse to get out of there; I actually had to go. I did my business and when I was done I splashed water on my face. My skin was hot to the touch—I mean really hot—and I had no idea why.

I pulled off my over shirt and checked my cuts. Nothing looked infected so I was sure it wasn't a medical thing. Most of the power grid energy I had absorbed was gone, but I still had my reserves so I wasn't jonesing for energy. I barely drank half my Cape Cod, so it wasn't the alcohol.

I figured I must have been more exhausted than I realized. It's not every day I face down a shadow demon—twice—and meet a dragon.

Yay me, trying new things, making new friends...

I put the over-shirt back on, leaving it open, belts hanging on my hips. While I was at it, I pulled my hair into a cleaner ponytail. I doubted the two men in the other room would care about any fashion faux-pas I might make.

Stacey!

I texted her that I was okay and I had gone to Phil's. She sent back a semi-manic text apologizing for leaving me like she did. I told her not to worry about it and have fun.

The problem with suggestion spells is when they wear off the victim is often left with guilt for not listening to their better angels. This is why wizards with some kind of moral compass don't use them. Also, several variations of the spell are considered Black Listed spells. So what did that say about my new dragon friend?

I put the phone on vibrate and stuck it in my pocket. When I got back to the living room, Phil sat at his table shifting through papers, a map of New York City laid out in front of him. Drake stood, quietly reading a leather-bound book.

"No blood," I mumbled as I made for the couch. "I'm honestly impressed."

Drake glanced up. "Is she always this way?"

"Off day," Phil replied before I could open my mouth.

"Boyfriend broke up with her yesterday."

"Ah," Drake said as if that explained everything.

Okay, maybe it did a little.

I decided not to justify their comments with a response and instead asked, "Find anything?"

"Not yet." Phil turned one of the papers sideways. "Since we can't narrow down the motive yet, I've decided to try and identify which summoning spell he used. If he uses the same tradition for all his magic then I might be able to find a way to get a tracking spell to work."

"Good strategy." I curled up on the end of the sofa that wasn't piled with books. I dragged the throw blanket down to cover me even though I was burning up, 'cause logic. My belts were jabbing me in the sides so I tossed them to the floor.

Drake started to look over Phil's shoulder. "How did you manage to get digital pictures of the summoning circle?"

The papers in Phil's hand were the printouts I'd given him earlier. "I have my ways. Gotta keep with the times."

"Of course." Drake didn't sound like he bought it. He turned the book in his hands around so Phil could see. "I knew I had seen the design before, only with different symbols."

"Interesting." Phil took the volume and laid it on the table next to the photos. "But who mixes prehistoric Oasisamerican and medieval Scandinavian traditions?"

"Nothing says one can't."

"Yeah, but..." Phil rubbed his perpetually smooth chin. "Why?"

"Circles have always been used in magic as a potent symbol," Drake pointed out, leaning against the table and crossing his arms. "Perhaps the wizard did not know his use of six concentric ones was a predominate trait of your early native people?"

"Yeah, possibly." Phil stood up and headed over to a stack of books. "Doesn't help us identify him, but it's a start. Let's go back to the Germanic and Scandinavian symbols. Maybe we can find a variant with the type of ruins he used."

"Very well." Drake shrugged.

I tossed my necklace onto the side table as I tried to get comfortable. At this rate I'd either be asleep or naked in ten minutes. Snuggling against the cushions, my eyes drifted shut of their own accord.

"Hey," Phil asked with a grunt, accompanied by a thud of books hitting a table. "When did you come across Prehistoric Hohokam rituals?"

Drake chuckled. "Not sure you'd believe me if I told you."

I fell asleep before hearing the story. I'm sure it was cool.

As for the impromptu nap, I didn't feel bad for passing out. I'm pretty much useless when it comes to researching magic. Phil has spent years learning the different traditions, sects, and clans. I spent maybe four hours when I was eight. His grimoire encompasses two hefty volumes filled with spells, thoughts, and observations. My grimoire is twelve pages stuffed inside an old *Gargoyles: The Animated Series* school pocket folder.

Yeah, I should probably update that.

I left the research to those much more skilled at it than I and slipped into a coma, or, you know, thereabouts.

Now, have you ever thought about how weird sleep is? Your body shuts down like an office building overnight. Sure, the emergency lights are on, the A/C is running at a minimum, and there's the light hum of computers on standby… but it's just empty. Everyone has gone home to do hopefully more productive things with their lives. Meanwhile, the building just sits there, waiting for the people to return.

While you sleep, your body restocks your immune system and aura while your consciousness is out having a life of its own. Your subconscious is like the janitor dancing through the place thinking no one is there to see them do it. Dreams are an involuntary use of your Mind's Eye and you see all sorts of crazy and wild things: part memories, part attempts at understanding the universe around you.

And when you're an active magic user… there is a whole other level of W.T.F.

In my dream I found myself sitting on a stool in a retro 1950s dinner. Next to me was this guy who kind of looked like Dominic Monaghan. Yes, Merry from *Lord of the Rings*.

He was eating pumpkin pie. I was holding a sunflower.

"Don't you have some place to be?" he said as he took a big bite of his desert.

Glancing past him, the diner was fairly busy with your usual trucker types, but no one I recognized off-hand. They didn't seem to be fussed about the fact that half of the diner was simply gone. It was replaced by a field of sunflowers which were bowed since it was pitch black outside.

The dream didn't go on for much longer though, as I was rudely awaken by acid reflux. Ever had that problem? I have it from time to time. It literally feels like your throat is on fire and you want to hurl.

My eyes popped open and I sat up. Drake was now sitting at the table and Phil was searching through a Smithsonian crate. They both noticed my movement but made no effort to stop me as I raced into the bathroom, making a beeline for the toilet. I could feel the burning tickle the back of my throat as I quickly raised the toilet seat I'd left down. Not wanting to get puke all over my button-up shirt, I slipped it off and tossed it into the sink, leaving me in the shimmering tank.

Like I said, I hadn't eaten or drank much so I figured the day's anxiety had churned up my stomach pretty bad. As I readied to expel the burning from my throat, the most curious thing happened.

Fire. I breathed fire.

What the hell?

The toilet paper was on fire.

EIGHT[8]

A blast furnace opened up in front of me and I broke into a sweat. The golden hues of the flames I spewed were pure and gleaming. They curled around the toilet looking for someplace to go. Most of the torrent crawled up the wall, taking the wallpaper with it.

It only lasted a second or two before I slammed my jaw shut. I fell back, scrambling away only to hit the wall. As I coughed, black sooty smoke escaped from my trembling lips, wafting up to make my nose itch.

A towel lying across the rim of the bathtub smoldered while the plastic shower curtain lay half-melted on top of it. The side of the sink cabinet was blackened and burned, the wallpaper peeling off in chunks. The toilet brush was a melted lump along with the seat. Thankfully, nothing seemed to still be on fire, except for the toilet paper.

Now, as for myself…

Worse. Sunburn. Ever.

My arms and chest were red and I could feel my lips were dry and chaffed. Pain was starting to register from the burns. I tried to think of some numbing spells but nothing came to me. I'm sure it was plain old adrenaline that got me through the next five minutes.

Trembling, I climbed over the edge of the tub to reach the faucet. Turning the dials, I didn't care what the temperature was as long as I got a heavy stream going. I popped the little metal thingy that redirected the water to the shower and was instantly drenched in cold water.

Gripping the showerhead for support, I tried to stand in the path of the stream. My body felt as if all the blood had drained out of it. I either slipped or simply fell; either way, I ended up at the bottom of the basin.

As I lay there in pain, water beating down on me, I was totally confused. Fire is just another form of energy; I had plenty of experience with controlling it. I can even light a candle at thirty paces if you asked me to. But I've never breathed fire before. No one I know of can breathe fire without casting a spell.

Other than dragons, of course.

"Minni." I heard Phil come in. I wondered what the scene looked like to him. Oh, crap—I wonder what he told his landlady. "Minni!"

I tried to open my eyes. It wasn't a smart idea as my face erupted in a sizzling torrent of agony.

So. Much. Pain.

"Huh, interesting." Drake sounded genuinely surprised as I felt the water shut off. "Only first degree burns. Let me get something from the boot."

"Minni." Phil took my right hand and whatever he did hurt like hell. "I'm going to send some healing magic into you, but I need you to focus on stabilizing your aura. Can you do that for me?"

I gave a grunt as I felt Phil cast a numbing spell over me. The pain ebbed and I tried to focus my Mind's Eye on my aura. It was hard to do with so many questions rolling around in my head. Why did I randomly breathe fire? Why was the inside of my mouth not burned if my body was? Why was the surface of my aura sparkling the golden hue of a thousand firecrackers going off?

It, um, doesn't usually do that.

When I metaphysically reached out to touch my aura, I expected my mind to translate heat or a prickling sensation from the tiny explosions. Instead my aura felt crumbly. When I lifted away my hand, rich soot smeared across my fingertips.

This was not a spell. It didn't have the markers of one. This was a direct energy transfer. Somehow I absorbed draconic magic into my aura.

This made no sense. I mean, obviously I must have received it from Drake. The thing is, I'd been in control of my abilities since

I met him. This wasn't an accidental power drain. I didn't draw from anything else, so it couldn't have been another overpowerment spell either.

I heard Phil lean over the tub and open the small window, night air drifting in. He muttered a few words in Latin. I think he was clearing the smoke out of the room.

"Is she still living?" I heard Drake reenter the bathroom.

"Your concern is touching," Phil muttered back.

There was the distinctive sound of a metal lid getting twisted off glass.

"What's that?" Phil asked.

"Balm." The tub squeaked right before I felt something cool on my shoulder. "Special formula. Give it half an hour and it will take care of these burns by promoting natural but accelerated skin regrowth. No harmful side effects."

"You just happen to keep that in the trunk of your car?" Phil asked warily but I felt another hand starting to smooth the liquid over my face.

"I breathe fire," Drake deadpanned.

"Right," Phil said as he continued to rub the oddly sweet smelling balm across my face. "If this stuff is as good as you say, then why isn't it on the market?"

It's common nowadays for magic users and monsters alike to use their abilities to create sellable items, anything from spells to medicines. Since they can't hold down normal jobs, it's a great way to make money. In the old days, it was more of a barter system. Today, there are whole corporations and pharmaceutical companies built around selling repackaged magic to consumers.

"It's been considered." Drake rubbed down my arms. It must have been him because he wasn't as gentle and damn, it stung. "But the product can't be synthesized and it's not easily stockpiled from its natural source. Miss Masterson is lucky I still believe I require her help."

"What's in it?"

I imagine there was a very large grin on Drake's face when he spoke the next words. "The main ingredient is dragon bile."

Eww.

But, you know, it worked. After fifteen minutes I could move without severe pain, but I didn't dare open my eyes or mouth until I washed that gunk from my face. The men passed the time with idle chat regarding Ignatius. I could feel the tension in the air as I laid there in the tub, sopping wet and hurting all over. Actually, it kind of reminded me of my twenty-first birthday.

Phil started to clean up the mess I made of his bathroom He left and came back a few times. I definitely heard him messing with a plastic trash bag at one point.

"Well now." Drake's voice echoed softly off the tile after Phil walked out to get me a change of clothes. "Dragon fire. Isn't this interesting? Fear not, I want you to survive in good health long enough to explain to me how this happened. The balm is perfectly safe."

I wasn't sure if that was supposed to be general discourse or a veiled threat.

Phil returned and Drake had nothing more to say to me.

"Let's see how you're doing." Phil lifted my arm up to rub a cloth against it. I tensed but there was no pain. "Amazing."

"Was there any doubt?" Drake scoffed.

Phil slipped his arms under me and I followed the motions as he helped me to stand. "Now, this is gonna be cold."

I nearly shouted when a rush of freaking-cold water hit my face. I clenched my jaw shut feeling the slithery bile slip down over my lips. A small towel touched my fingers and I snatched it up. Trembling, I wiped the balm from every inch of my skin and hair. The fire hadn't singed my hair, which I was simultaneously grateful for and confused over.

"I think that's all of it." Phil shut the water off.

I opened my eyes slowly to see him standing with a fresh dry towel. Drake leaned against the doorway. Phil looked a bit worried while the dragon seemed decidedly curious, a slight smirk to his lips.

Phil helped me out of the tub. "You okay?"

"Yeah, I'm fine." I tried to smile encouragingly as I could

see the questions in their eyes. "Can I change first?"

"Of course." Drake disappeared with a slow saunter.

Phil pointed to some sweat pants and a t-shirt laying on the non-blackened side of the sink. "Not fashionable, but clean."

"Thanks." I smiled the best I could. "I'll be right out."

"Take your time." He pulled the door closed behind him as he left.

I ran my fingers through my hair, not wanting to see myself in the mirror. But of course that's the first thing I did. Vanity gets the better of everyone eventually. That's why even wizards still keep a mirror or two about the place, even though they can be dangerous.

Okay, so, dragon bile may be slimy and gross, but I'll take a dozen jars. Drake said it promoted new skin cell regrowth, but in doing so it cleared out all my splotches or blemishes. Even the cuts and bruises from earlier were gone, leaving the smooth, perfectly toned skin you only find in airbrushed magazines.

It was amazing. But since the bile was an ointment, not a spell, its effects wouldn't be permanent. It figured it would only last until these skin cells died and new ones formed. Until then though... holy shit.

If I were insane enough to want to harvest a dragon, I would totally go after the bile. Could that be why Ignatius was taken? Probably not. I mean, I doubted the crazy wizard was after the secret to eternal beauty… unless maybe he worked for a cosmetics firm?

Going to file that in the 'maybe' folder.

I checked my focus bracelet and was glad to see it unharmed due to the magical protections I placed around it. However, the bangles on my right wrist were cheap aluminum. They'd been fused together. Damn, how hot was that fire?

Phil had pulled the melted part of the metal away from my skin earlier and stuck some toilet paper between it and my wrist. I guess the bile took care of any nasty scarring that should have occurred, but that area was still a little red and sore. Probably should have left the bile on there a little longer. I tried slipping off the mangled mess but it was now too small to get around the bones of my hand without some serious dislocation. I left them as they weren't that high on my priority list.

I emptied my pockets and laid everything out on the sink to dry. As for my phone, it was completely waterlogged. I slid the cover off the battery compartment, took everything apart, and laid the pieces out to dry the old fashioned way. I didn't see any rice in Phil's pantry earlier. I thought about using thermal energy to dry the phone, but why risk it? I was already having an off day.

My boots where fake leather, thank goodness. I turned them upside down on a towel on the floor. The jeans and tank top came off next and I draped them with my socks over the bathtub to dry. Phil had definitely cleaned up during the wait. The shower curtain and other items were gone.

The blue sweats Phil left for me didn't exactly fit. Even though he's lanky for a man, he still has a bigger waist than I do. The t-shirt was plain grey, military surplus style. It must have been on the smallish side for Phil because fit decently enough. I borrowed his comb to only moderate effect, my hair draped around my head in flat wet clumps.

Taking a deep breath, I made my way into the living room. Phil sat at the table and Drake stood a few feet away. They both stopped talking when they saw me.

"Why didn't my skin burn off?" I always ask the important questions first.

"It's one of the unique properties of draconic fire." Drake smirked at me. "It does not harm the wielder. However, being human, you were still susceptible to the heat it produced."

Phil glanced between both of us. "That was draconic fire?"

"And I breathed it no less," I said without taking my eyes off Drake. "Something is wrong with your aura, isn't there?"

"Wrong is an incorrect assessment," Drake spoke the words slowly, carefully.

"Explain." It was mostly a demand rather than a request. When I realized he wasn't going to talk, I let out an insincere, "Please?"

Drake gave me a sour look but said, "My kind are not natural shape shifters. When we become human, our aura does not want to reform and some of it becomes displaced."

"Displaced?"

"I assure you, we are as deadly in human form as we are in our dragon skin." Drake narrowed his eyes at me. Apparently that's his favorite past time now. "There is simply too much aura for our metaphysical form to marry to our new physical form. Part of the aura..." He shook his head. "Auras are hard enough to explain without adding our particular intricacies."

"Try." The word came out harsher than intended.

His jaw tightened.

"If what I think is right," I explained, "then I may have a way to find your dad."

While I got the feeling he was again wondering what my insides would look like tied in knots, he continued. "When dragons perform the spell to take a human form our auras become... displaced. Still attached, still able to draw upon, but partially displaced is the only way to describe it. It's a shadow image that is a part of us but not..." His words died in frustration.

"You're right." I tried not to frown and failed. "That's a horrible explanation."

"Auras are not defined by shape or size." His nostrils flared, which made me flinch. "For natural shape shifters, it adjusts to the new form. With dragonkin, our auras split into a kind of photographic negative. Gaerwen theorized our auras are too powerful, too full of magic, and that while we are in our natural dragon form it's not as easy to notice the effects of such a strong aura. In less powerful creatures, it's not an issue when they shape shift unnaturally."

"That's why you can use technology." Finally things were making sense to me. "The displaced aura acts like a lightning rod, drawing away any excess energy."

"Yes, but how does that help us?"

It was my turn to grin. "Because nothing is ever simple when a Masterson is involved."

Drake judged me for a moment. "When I read up on you, it mentioned your guide and transit services. I was unsure what to make of the claims put forth by your employer, Mystical Moments Tour and Travel."

I mentioned before that I moonlight as a tour guide. Well, specifically I work with magic users who want to visit tourist traps like Time Square, Broadway, Hollywood, Silver Dollar City, you name it. I've seen *Wicked* so many times I could probably understudy for Elphaba. One family even pays me a considerable bonus to go with them to Disneyworld every spring break. It's basically how I afford my apartment.

Best babysitting job ever.

"I admit," Drake continued, "the claims seemed fanciful, mythical even."

Mythical? That's hilarious coming from an honest-to-goodness fire-breathing gold dragon. I coughed to keep myself from laughing. "I'm an energy conduit. I can transfer and transform magical energy, electrical, thermal... you name it. I don't necessarily need a spell or foci. I only have to concentrate for the big stuff."

He drew his lips into a straight line. "You destroyed my phone, on purpose."

"Let's focus on the important things right now."

"Yes," he said the word slowly. "How is your talent going to help find my father?"

"Well, normally I don't draw in energy unless I want to." I could still feel the gritty taste of charcoal on my tongue. "But because your aura is a lightning rod, it's somehow discharging energy through the path of least resistance: my aura."

"That's what you believed happened?" Drake tilted his head curiously.

"Why else would I breathe fire?" I replied sarcastically.

"Fair," he acquiesced.

"Alright." I sighed and gathered my thoughts. "I have a plan, though it assumes your dad is still alive."

Drake didn't even flinch. "I'm listening."

I tried to keep my words as impartial as possible. "The way I figure it, if all the wizard wants is blood, scales, and whatever else, then he would have killed Ignatius by now. That way, he could avoid the risk of the binding wearing off."

"I believe you are right." Slight touch of emotion there from Drake. "However, there are plenty other reasons to keep my father alive before harvesting him."

"Yes, there is." I gave him an encouraging smile. "But a full-sized dragon is going to be hard to move. He'll want to keep your father in his human form until he needs him to change."

"That's what I would do," Phil agreed. Drake shot him a look, so he quickly added the amendment, "If I was, you know, suicidal enough to try to bind a dragon."

"You said you couldn't track Ignatius by usual means," I continued. "The wizard would have to put up barriers to prevent blood tracking, the usual, but I bet he didn't consider masking Ignatius' aura or energy field."

"That's because all energy fields look basically the same," Drake stated the obvious. "And you can't do tracking spells on auras."

"*You* might not be able to." I let myself smile broadly. "Me on the other hand..."

Phil snapped his fingers. "You're going to search for the displaced energy."

"Exactly." Now I was feeling productive. "But I'm still picking up magical energy from your displaced aura. I'm going to need to learn how to block myself from doing that so I don't go all fire starter again. This means I'll need your permission to poke around your aura."

Not that I actually needed permission, but it's only polite to ask first. Consent matters.

Drake gave me a shrewd smile. "And once you know what a displaced aura looks like in real time, the type of energy it outputs, you can use your special understanding of energy to search for that image using what, astral projection?"

"Pretty much, but I'll only be seeing the displaced energy,

not the aura." Which was the downfall of my plan. The energy coming off an aura is invisible to the naked eye. I can use my Third Eye to view aura and energy fields, but as the man said, all energy pretty much looks the same. Fire looks like fire, electricity like electricity, magic like magic. It doesn't matter if the fire is from coal or alcohol, it's still fire in these instances.

Imagine a military sniper with a thermal scope. They can see outlines but they're just blobs. Other indicators are needed to tell if the target is friend or foe. If my plan worked, I'd be seeing the same kind of blobs. I'd then use the small differences in them to determine which one was Ignatius.

"I mean, how many other creatures could there be in the five boroughs with a partially displaced aura giving off a unique double energy signature?" I'm really good at this optimism thing.

"It would be highly unlikely," Drake agreed, nodding his head in approval. "And I know of no other dragonkin in New York City at this time. We tend to stay in our natural habitats of Europe, Asia, and South America. Though I do know of one currently residing in Washington and one at Fort Sill."

"Fort Sill?" One of the U.S. military's major training centers for artillerymen, aka the people who blow stuff up for a living. "You know what? Never mind."

I wanted to go with plausible deniability on that one.

"First things first." I looked around the room, deciding how I wanted to play this. "I need to block your aura so I don't set the rest of Phil's apartment on fire."

"That would be appreciative," Phil added dryly.

Drake spread his hands. "What would you like me to do?"

I pointed to the chair Phil was using. "Grab that and come over here." I went to the sofa, snatching up a throw pillow. "You'll have to sit in front of me because we'll need to hold hands."

"Charming," he mused as he waited for Phil to vacate.

Ignoring him, I sat down, getting comfortable against the pillow. Drake then situated himself in front of me. The chair was short for him, so he scooted his legs to the side to avoid stepping on my toes.

I took a deep breath and hoped I was right. Otherwise I could end up setting Brooklyn on fire. "Alright, put your arms out, palms up. This could take a while, so you might want to rest your arms on your knees."

He did as I asked, his fingers naturally curled as they tend to do. I hovered my hands over his, palms down, as I didn't want to touch him just yet. I took another deep breath, the aftertaste of burnt matches on my tongue. Closing my eyes, I opened up my Mind's Eye to view the metaphysical world around us.

My aura still sizzled, crackling in my ears. It smelt of spent bottle rockets, tasted of charcoal, and crumbled at my touch. They say you can only mentally comprehend about a fraction of your aura, and what I saw was astounding.

There was a flicker of yellow and my head swung over to locate the offending color. Drake's dragon form aura shimmered pure gold. Dazzling firecrackers of energy pulled me to him, his aura a pulsating star of energy. It was the most beautiful metaphysical form I had ever laid my eyes on.

I became acutely aware of the power I siphoned from Drake. A glittering mass of golden dragonflies poured from him. They flittered around me, wrapping me in a strangely comfortable cocoon of sparks.

A humanoid shape formed before me. It was Drake's human form's aura, faded and grainy. The spectral image smirked, placing its hands out, palms up. I put mine over his, letting the action register in my physical body, and our hands grasped in the real world.

I peeled back layers of his aura, first ridding it of the excess and wild magic discoloring it. His human form's aura crackled with fireworks of its own, each explosion so bright it blotted out every trace of color. What lay underneath was the dull golden shine of a well-worn, thousand year old piece of jewelry.

The sizzling of energy around us was deafening. His raw power swirled like a typhoon waiting to return to a harbor. Any harbor, be it Drake, his dragon aura, or myself.

"I am glass." I repeated the words like a mantra. "I am

wood. I am porcelain."

I named off every insulator I could think of, each time imaging being wrapped in layers of the substance. Drake's human form began to pull away, repulsed by my lack of conductivity. Over his shoulder, the head of the dragon aura appeared and gazed at me with glittering gold eyes. It said something in Draconic, a guttural language based off the subtle tones and pitches of a dragon's growls and snarls.

Shockingly, Draconic is not an option for the Foreign Language credit at Purdue.

Both dragon and human tilted their heads in the same exact way. They stared at me curiously, then intently. I'm pretty sure they were sharing a joke at my expense.

Ugh, *dragons*.

I mentally backed away from both of the auras and focused on myself. I still had some draconic fire attached to me, so I attempted to shed it, letting it float back to Drake. I couldn't quite rid myself of all the energy as it clung to my aura like a stubborn child. Eventually I gave up, figuring what was left wasn't enough to be problematic and I'd work through it in time.

I opened my eyes to I find myself lying on the sofa. My arms were across my chest, my feet propped up on some books, and a damp rag lay on my forehead. My body was paralyzed but this didn't worry me as I knew it would wear off quickly. It was a common after-effect of spending a lot of time in the metaphysical world. In other terms, my aura had to do a reboot to accept all the changes I had made.

"How long was I out?"

"Not long." Phil checked my pulse before also examining the lymph nodes on my neck. "Thirty minutes. Give, take."

Didn't seem that long, but then it usually doesn't. "I think it worked."

"You think?" He gazed at me quizzically, eyebrow raised.

"Pretty sure." I gave a weak smile.

"We will find out," I could hear the smirk in Drake's voice. "Will we not?"

Phil frowned. "Just… give us a warning if it's going to happen again?"

"You'll be the first to know." There was a tickle in my throat and I coughed, gritty charcoal still on my tongue.

Yeah, that got old real quick.

"I'll get you some water." Phil headed into the kitchen as I sat up.

Drake was flipping through another of Phil's books. He barely glanced at me while saying, "Find what you were looking for?"

I sighed, stretching a bit, my back popping audibly. "At the risk of stroking your ego, dragonkin are extraordinarily magnificent creatures."

"True." He turned a page and smiled. "But did you find something more useful than basic facts?"

"What time is it?" I asked Phil as he handed me a mug of water.

"About three a.m." And on cue, he yawned.

"We keeping you awake?" I teased before taking a gulp.

"Nah, I'm good." He gave a little wink. I figured he'd probably use an energy boost spell if he needed to, or chug a Red Bull. "You want to wait before you astral project?"

That would be the smart idea, allow time for my aura to recover and settle. However, "I want to do this while it's all still fresh in my mind."

"Okay," he didn't sound happy but he wasn't going to argue. He helped me get comfortable on the sofa, moving more of the books and bringing another pillow from his bedroom.

Once I was ready, I closed my eyes again. Only this time instead of going into my subconscious via the Mind's Eye, I did the reverse. I cut my conscious mind off from my body, thereby leaving the subconscious in control. It would take care of all those needy little involuntary bodily functions, like, you know, breathing and blood pumping.

It's usually a good idea to keep those things running while you're away.

I wrapped my consciousness into a protective cocoon of energy and jumped it out of my body. I looked down at myself which you never, ever, get used to. A person performing an astral projection sees the world in a first-person perspective able to go anywhere, through any non-magical barrier, at any height and any depth. I had to get myself out of Phil's apartment if I wanted this to work. His wards would only get in the way.

Once I was floating in the alley, I mentally blinked a few times to see the world as energy, not a solid mass. A blast of color assaulted me as the energies surrounding, well, everything, came into view. Like that sniper's rifle, I had to figure out what I was looking for based on contextual clues.

Generally it all looks the same, but energy is my thing. It's what I do. I can tell the subtle differences between certain groups of energy. I sifted through the images, dropping the power cables, phone signals, radio signals—everything that wasn't in the general vein of what I was looking for.

I could see the glowing magic surrounding Phil, Drake, and myself. My energy field was thin, tame, and controlled, which is not typical of wizards. Phil's was as wild and spiky as his hair, which is typical. As for Drake, my eyes kept sliding off his energy signature. It appeared as a white shadow hanging just out of view no matter which angle I tried. This was because of the shadowing effect from the two auras overlapping each other.

Now that I was sure of what I was looking for, I hoped Ignatius was still in town.

I floated up until I was high enough to see the twinkling lights of New York City. Not the street lamps or office buildings, but the pulsating energy surrounding all living beings. And considering this was New York, it was more than a simple sea of stars. It was galaxies ground up into cosmic dust.

This was starting to feel like it was going to be impossible, so I started looking for anything I could use to narrow down the field of view. First, I got rid of the fish and other small animals such as birds, cats, rats—basically anything with a really small signature. With those gone, the outline of Manhattan Island came into view.

The Hudson was a black void against the glow except for the occasional bright dot of some kind of large or magical aquatic dweller.

Merfolk do exists… but do any of them go by Aquaman? I have no idea. But they totally should, copyright be damned.

Next, I removed all the plants and trees. While they aren't living beings in the same sense we might think of humans, certain plants do contain their own amount of mystical and magical energies. Peeling away the vegetative layer, Central Park became more defined along with other green areas.

I narrowed my focus further to encompass only the human and humanoid. Mundane individuals with no magical propensity have generally the same amount of natural energy. This comes from their conscious and subconscious mind, neurons firing back and forth. It was the trickiest layer to remove. I focused on the intensity of the energy blobs. Hours seemed to pass as I worked, subtracting those stars that didn't shine quite as bright as the rest.

The world became blackness except for a few random dots scattered here and there. I searched for the shadowy echo that defined a dragon's aura and wiped away everything else. Below me, I could see Drake's energy signature clearly but not Phil's. So, any other pulsating dots following a specific rhythm and a certain intensity should be Ignatius.

And I could see two of them, not including Drake.

Ain't that just peachy.

Drake said there weren't any other dragons in New York. Was he mistaken, or had he lied? Neither possibility was an appealing notion.

I still needed to find Ignatius, but I wasn't sure who to check first. I realized that if Drake was below me, and Central Park was over that away, then the glowing blob near to my left would put it in Washington Heights. Or close enough.

I focused on that aura and flew towards it. When moving quickly in an astral projection, it can be difficult to keep up the perception filters. In my peripherals I could see buildings flying by, random people, places, things. I kept my central vision clear, focusing on the beacon of light that was the aura. I could have been passing through anything, even people. Most would register it as a 'chill' or as one of those shudders old people like to call 'someone walking on your grave.'

It's kind of creepy if you think about it, so I don't, you know, think about it.

As I got closer, it *felt* right. I could tell this new aura had a familial relationship with Drake's. The residue of dragon energy inside me pulled towards the glow, echoing against it. Soon I'd be close enough to get a location.

But then I felt like I hit a brick wall at a dead run.

If I had teeth on the astral plane they'd probably been knocked out of my head. Some serious wards were going on. Coming to my senses, I started removing filters. Sure enough, there was a massive sphere of spirit blocking, magic repelling barriers in my way.

Stepping back, metaphysically speaking, I let the solid world come into focus, hoping I wasn't inside a wall or an occupied bathroom. Thankfully, I saw all I needed to see.

The quickest way back to my body was basically to click my heels like Dorothy and think of home. I instantly returned to the apartment to see Phil and Drake were still hovering over me. I dived into my body—best way to describe it—and met up with my subconscious. I'm pretty sure it didn't notice I was gone. That kind of hurts me a little bit, you know?

I opened my eyes but my body was momentarily paralyzed again. When sensation returned, I felt pins and needles setting in something fierce. I felt drained, like I'd ran a marathon.

"Ugh." My throat was dry. "How long was I out this time?"

Phil raised his eyebrow, momentarily speechless. "Um, five minutes, maybe six?"

Yet it felt like hours.

Magic can drive you crazy. Trust me on this.

"Was it a success?" Drake asked.

"I know where Ignatius is." I considered drawing out the reveal but didn't feel up to playing 'annoy the fire-breathing dragon.' "He's at The Cloisters."

"Hah!" Phil basically shouted. "I knew my instincts weren't wrong."

"The Cloisters?" Drake wasn't impressed.

"Museum of old medieval art built from real European abbeys," Phil explained as he started rummaging for a book. "Lots of powerful artifacts. The place is swimming in magic."

"Our wizard is planning one dandy of a spell."

"Yeah." Phil found whatever he was looking for—an almanac, I think--and flipped through it. "If he hasn't already performed his spell, then the next best time to do it is at dawn. This time of year that's about 6:30. That gives us roughly three and half hours to prepare and get over there to stop him."

Drake raised an eyebrow. "Us?"

Phil gave the dragon a 'don't be crazy' look. "You can't go in there all fire blazing. You'll cause a lot of damage, especially if the wizard is already setting up his spell. We have some strong wizards of our own in our coven. I'll call them and we should be able to take the rogue wizard down without destroying another local landmark."

Drake thought about this for moment then smiled approvingly. "Very well." He probably figured he could act the king to our pawns and not get his hands dirty. It was his style after all. Hell, he wouldn't even have to pay us.

I tried sitting up but my blood decided not to rush to my head, or anywhere really, and I fell back onto the pillow. "Woah."

"Hey." Phil checked my pulse again. "You've been overdoing it on the magic all day; you need to recharge the old fashion way. Take a nap, we got this covered."

I wanted to argue with him but decided if he was offering, what could it hurt? Besides, I did the leg work and found Ignatius. Phil didn't need me during the administrative task of gathering the coven's able-bodies. "Wake me in an hour-ish."

Turning to my side, I passed out on his sofa for the second time that night. As I drifted off I hoped I wouldn't be woken up with really bad heartburn again. Seriously, I've always had problems with acid reflux, but this just takes the cake.

And in my dream a faceless waitress brought me a piece of pumpkin pie.

"You gonna eat that or what?" The man next to me asked as he sipped on what I think was coffee. I was back in the diner from earlier, sitting at the counter.

I frowned as I picked up a sunflower that was lying next to my plate. "I hate pumpkin pie."

"Then why did you order it?" He tore into his own dessert, a piece of pecan pie with a healthy amount of whipped cream on top. Wasn't he the one with the pumpkin pie earlier? I honestly couldn't remember. Was there a reason I should care?

Glancing around the diner, it was more of the same: truckers, a family or two, all sitting around enjoying their meal. It was bright and sunny outside the windows, but the missing half of the diner was a moon lit field of downcast sunflowers.

The diner… and a sunflower field…

"It's rude to order food and not eat it," he admonished me as I stood up.

"I didn't order it." I moved past him, heading down the aisle towards the open end of the diner. I stood at the edge of the tiled floor before it broke away into soil. I reached up and ran the yellow petals between my fingers.

"You don't want to go in there," the man warned softly.

Tears streamed down my face. Why was I dreaming of this, of all things? Why was I being reminded of what happened? What did magic know that it felt the need to show me this?

I stepped into the sunflower field, the diner disappeared.

I started running.

NINE[9]

"Minni." A hand pushed at my shoulder, but I ignored it. "You ain't no sleeping beauty. Get up."

Groaning, I popped my eyes open to see Eli Lange standing over me. A scruff of a grey beard and deep set wrinkles showed him to be the hard working gent he was. He's retired now, so he spends most of his days working on what I can only call a kosher barbecue pop-up shop.

"I'm awake." I sat up, stretching out the kinks. Power napping for the win.

I couldn't shake the dream, though. You see, weird stuff happens when you mess around with a lot of magic at once. Barriers in the subconscious, consciousness, aura, soul, etc, all become a bit thinner and… stuff begins to leak through.

I looked around Phil's apartment and realized the whole gang was there. Eli's granddaughter, Vivian Lange, stood next to him. Her mass of curly brown hair was held back with, I don't know, magic? It broke the laws of physics and looked really cute, so I'm pretty sure magic is the only possible answer here.

Sitting on the windowsill was Ryan Thompson, who I lovingly refer to as the coven mascot. A few years ago he ran away from his home in Utah. He got himself into more trouble than a bad after-school special before he found the Mercury Shop. Phil gave him a job and lets him room there on the third floor.

"Alright." Phil grabbed everyone's attention. "We know this wizard has to be both brave and stupid enough to bind a dragon. He could be capable of anything."

I missed the 'previously on' phase of the discussion.

"Eli, Viv, Drake, and myself," he continued, "will be on point to take down the wizard. Let's try to subdue him first. We don't know how far the wizard is into casting his spells or how our own magic might affect what he's doing. Also, he has a bound dragon he could set against us."

"Don't even think you can take on my father," Drake added lazily. "He will eat you alive, and I do mean that literally."

"Yeah." Ryan ran his hand through his pixie cut hair. "Can I already call dibs on *not* fighting the dragon?"

"You'll only need to get us through the wards," Phil told him. "After that I expect you to take a back seat. You're not ready yet to get that close to the action."

"No argument here." Ryan held his hands up. At nineteen he's still considered a child as wizards go. He's really good at his specialty, he just doesn't have a lot of real world experience yet. I guess Phil thought inviting Ryan to help battle a rogue wizard who has a pet dragon would be character building.

"Minni." Phil turned to me. "You feel up to running defense?"

"I'm good," I said as I did a quick check of myself. My aura seemed to have settled down. My magic was at optimum levels. I couldn't help thinking I was forgetting something though.

"Shall we go?" Dragons apparently aren't a patient bunch. Though I suppose we should be happy Drake didn't go off and tear through The Cloisters like it wasn't full of priceless artifacts.

Phil ignored the dragon while also addressing him. He's talented that way. "So we're clear, our goal is to subdue, not rip to shreds."

Drake's eyes flickered with flames. Not literally, but it was heavily implied by the look he gave Phil. "Whoever kidnapped my father, their life is forfeit."

"They will not go unpunished," Phil told him, keeping eye contact. "If it's a fellow wizard, we'll take care of it."

"Justice will be served and all that?" Drake was not at all impressed. "You'll go soft on him."

Phil scoffed. "An evisceration is the answer?"

"To almost anything."

I laughed because apparently I found all this hilarious.

Everyone just kind of looked at me, so I explained, "Dragon justice is a bit… draconian, don't you think?"

Drake gave me a glare that foretold of my impending dismemberment if he had any say in it. "Draco of Athens. He created the Athenian's first written law code in the 7th Century BC. It was a rather harsh, cruel system, and *that* gave rise to the term."

Draco meant dragon, like the constellation.

"So, happy coincidence then?" My tombstone is totes going to read 'should have known better.'

Drake's eyes flicked away and settled on Phil. "Fine, we'll do it your way, for now. Though, should he give me cause, I will feel justified in any action I deem to take."

Phil took that as a win and we gathered our stuff to leave.

Vivian pointed at my feet. "Toes."

I looked down at myself still in Phil's clothes and sans shoes. "I'm gonna change. I'll be a sec."

I didn't wait for a response and ducked into the bathroom. I was reminded again at how much damage I had done in there. I wasn't sure how I was going to make it up to Phil. I'm pretty handy with a paintbrush, though. Well, in a Jackson Pollock kind of way.

Anyway, my socks were dry but my jeans had a ways to go. While I appreciated Phil helping me out, I didn't want to go into battle with oversized sweatpants. I grabbed the cuff of the denim and sent a light wave of thermal heat through the strands. Steam rolled off the fabric.

Voila, insta-dry.

I gave the same treatment to my boots then turned to the sink. My phone was still lying in pieces and I doubted it had had enough time to dry properly. I could have attempted the same heat spell on it, but electronics take a more delicate touch and I didn't really have the time. I had people waiting on me.

After slipping on my jeans and boots, I grabbed my ID and some twenties from the sink. The money was in case I ended up taking a cab or other transportation. The ID was if my body needed to be identified when everything went wrong. What can I say, I'm an optimist and a realist. When one messes around with magic and monsters, they aren't too surprised if one day they find themselves flayed, sautéed, and served with a side of parsley.

Personally I think I'd go better with parsnips.

When I left the bathroom, everyone was gone. I locked up and skipped down the stairwell instead of waiting on the elevator. Outside, the group was standing next to a black transport van like the ones hotels use.

"Minni," Phil asked as he opened the front passenger's seat. "Do the honors?"

"But of course," I said and hopped inside. Drake's bodyguard was at the wheel. I had wondered where he went.

Placing my hands on the dashboard, I felt the hum of the electronics. I isolated the different energies, placing a protective barrier around the vital systems. I tied it to my focus bracelet which I basically turned into a magic heat sink. The melted bracelets still dangled pointlessly from my other wrist.

Everyone piled in and I looked back to see Phil and Drake sitting on the front bench seat. Drake was on his phone again, the light from the screen making his features sharper. Phil kept glancing at him, like he didn't really trust him. Or maybe he was just checking him out. Sometimes it's hard to tell.

The bodyguard pulled out into the road and sped off. Traffic was near non-existent at that time of night, or morning, whatever. If it hadn't been a Sunday, I'm sure we'd probably have been screwed.

When we approached The Cloisters, we could see lights coming from the tower which rose above the tree line. As you know, The Cloisters complex sits on its own little piece of Manhattan. It's surrounded by a lawn and micro-forest as if it was still back in Europe.

We ended up parked along the road. Standing there in front of the van and staring at the tall stone fence, we must have looked like a very suspicious bunch. Well, we were about to break in, so, yeah.

"How you think he got in there?" Vivian asked, then put her hand up. "Better question, how do *we* get in there?"

"I have an idea," Drake said with a grin.

"Let's try to avoid the wanton destruction of property," Phil replied dryly, pulling his courier bag from the van. "There has to be a night guard, security cameras, maybe even motion sensors and lasers."

"Lights are on." I pointed out. "Don't think he emp'd it."

Drake's eyes went a little wide. "You think imps are involved?"

"Do what now?" It took me a second to realize what I'd said. "Oh, no, E.M.P. Electromagnetic pulse. One of my specialties. I just hate superfluous syllables."

"I know what I'd do." Ryan stepped forward, holding up a visitor's guide map. I have a vague recollection of Phil having picked one up when we stopped by earlier. "With a place like this, I'd go with a snow spell for the cameras. And either a sleep spell or billy club for the guard."

Billy club? Does anyone even use that word anymore? Apparently, Ryan does.

"Snow spell?" Phil asked the more productive question.

Ryan grinned. "It makes the screens go snowy and pours white noise through any communications devices."

"Nice." Now why didn't I think of that? "You'll have to show me."

"It's a bit tricky," Ryan admitted. "But you'd probably have an easier time of it."

"How'd you learn the spell?" Phil asked.

"Figured it out myself." He shrugged and lowered his voice to a near mumble. "There may have been a version of it in a grimoire at the shop, which I totally didn't touch, not at all."

"This is all very enlightening." Drake rolled his eyes. "Now how are we getting in?"

"Check for the snow spell." Ryan gestured at me, totally ignoring Phil's questionably raised brow. "You should be able to feel it as some kind of electrical interference."

"Right." I moved forward and shut my eyes, reaching out for the familiar sensations of energy and magic. The formed electro-magical field lying across the complex wasn't exactly trying to hide itself. I drew away before disturbing it as I didn't want to tip our hand just yet. "Yep, snow spell."

"Impressive," Ryan said thoughtfully. "I can only keep mine up for twenty minutes, max, before the magical static shorts everything out proper."

"We already knew this wizard was powerful." Phil's eyes flickered over at Drake. "This confirms it. We follow the plan."

"Alright." Ryan shoved the map back into the black athletic bag he uses to carry his wizardly stuff, slinging the whole thing over his shoulder. "Follow me."

Not even the dragon argued as we crossed the quiet street. There was a locked gate and Ryan set to work with some locksmith tools—who do you think taught Phil? It was only seconds before we were safely inside the complex.

Point of interest, we were now that much closer to the crazy wizard. Funny how these things work out.

"I'm not sure where he is exactly," I admitted as we stalked across a grassy area to the main building.

"Don't worry," Ryan said as he picked the lock on the service door. "I can smell the wards from here."

"Wait here," Drake told his bodyguard once we were all inside. Phil eyed Drake warily but he ultimately knew the benefit of having someone watch your escape route, or the potential entrance for an armed response.

Ryan led us through a maze of rooms and doors. No alarms, no wandering guard, it was all a bit anti-climactic. Eventually we found ourselves in the museum's main hall. I could see the security cameras but felt the buzzing energy washing out their signal. While Ryan played guide, the rest of us prepared for battle, checking our foci, mumbling words under our breath, gathering energies.

"Saint Guilhem Cloister," Ryan said quietly as we were walking down a vaulted hallway. "That's where he's held up."

"Who's Saint Guilhem?" Viv asked.

The kid shrugged. "Dunno, it's the name on the map."

"Ah." Viv nodded and they continued down the hallway

into what I think was a chapel.

"Taking the long way around on the approach," Ryan whispered. "Don't want him to see us coming."

We exited through a gallery into another hallway. This one also had a vaulted ceiling but with arches and pillars cut into one side. There were noises echoing off the stone: lots of muttering, water bubbling, bustling about, etc. A faint shimmer reflected in the air, a sure sign of the wizard's warding spell.

Ryan held his hand up and we stopped. He sat down on the floor and pulled out some chalk. Drawing a circle on the floor, he added a five-sided star. The pentagram is an old magical symbol that's gotten a bit of a bad rap recently. The design itself is a quick and easy way to draw and form magic, which is a good when you need your focus someplace else.

He retrieved an old style skeleton key and a pair of wire cutters from his bag. These are his foci and they're etched with small print Latin words. Placing them in the center of the design, Ryan began to mumble in Latin, I think. I don't know, all Romantic languages sound about the same to me.

Now, there are a lot of ways to break spells, and most of them are a bitch to pull off. Brute force is always an option but it's not exactly subtle. Ryan likes to trick wards into thinking their task is complete so they shut down naturally. Not exactly sure how he does it, but he's never failed us.

As he worked, we stood at the ready. Phil, Eli, and Vivian had their blasting rods in their hands. The shield symbols on my bracelet were lightly glowing. Drake was... being a dragon, I guess. His hands twitched at his sides. I was pretty sure smoke was coming out of his nose like one of those cartoon bulls Bugs Bunny likes to annoy.

It was hard to tell in the light.

"*Decido*," Ryan called out softly. It was our cue that his spell was almost done. "*Decido*." On the third repetition the ward would topple, but this would alert the wizard. There would be no way to sneak up on him after that. This was an all or nothing kind of deal. "*Decido*."

Before the word finished passing Ryan's lips, we surged down the hallway. There was a slight spark as the ward simply turned off. We didn't get zapped, so kudos to Ryan. Now we actually had to face the crazy wizard.

Yay?

As I discovered, Saint Guilhem Cloister is a stone atrium open to the sky via a glass roof. The walkways on each side are lined with pillars. You can't walk between them due to the raised stones, but there was an entrance around the corner. The atrium itself is a cold, open area, but quiet and serene. Just the kind of a place a monk might go to simply sit and contemplate the meaning of the universe.

Or where a crazy wizard might go to end the world, or maybe just destroy Manhattan. Still not clear on that one.

"What's going on?" A voice bellowed, echoing off the stone. At least he didn't start with 'hey, dragon, kill the intruders.'

In the center of the atrium was a plastic card table. Something large and papery was laid on it, held down with pieces of quartz. A tv-dinner stand sat off to the side. It held a portable stove with one of those huge pots you cook corn on the cob in. Bluish black smoke rose from it. There was another card table behind the wizard which looked to hold a variety of things used in magical ceremonies.

The mad wizard himself was dressed as a lawyer, or maybe a banker. He wore a nice gray suit. Not as expensive or well-tailored as Drake's, but definitely not off the bargain rack. His black hair was clean cut, he obviously moisturized, and he had that air of importance around him that one associates with that kind of tradesman.

He also had on a pair of thick rubber gloves, the type used for messing with major chemicals. That kind of killed the whole dapper look.

For a moment, I thought he might have been Ignatius, but I spotted the elder dragon standing a few feet away with a severe look of annoyance on his face. He wore one of those light brown 'guru' outfits: long, loose, and comfortable. There was no mistaking him for anyone but Drake's father. His gold hair had flecks of silver which I assume is the dragon version of gray hair. When he saw his son, a snarling smile formed on his lips but he did not speak.

"Clint?" Phil said as he hoped over the stone that barred our way, Drake following. "Clinton Canton?"

Really, his parents named him Clinton Canton?

I think I found his motivation for being a crazy wizard bent on destroying the world… and I'm okay with it.

"Stay back." Canton reached into the pot and pulled out something I couldn't make out from my vantage point.

I moved down the hallway with Eli and Viv. They were going around the atrium to the other entrance to flank Canton. I figured I'd get between both groups before I started to climb over the barrier.

Phil tried the diplomatic approach as he slightly raised his blasting rod. "Clint, help me understand what's going on here."

"I'm tired of people saying that!" The words came out loud and strong, Canton's body visibly trembling.

I hopped into the atrium as Eli and Viv entered from the side. Canton's eyes darted back and forth between all of us, jaw clenched. It was a large knife he held in his hand, pointed downwards. He was sweating, his whole appearance just a shade of wild.

"Alright, no problem." Phil gave an uneasy smile as he inched closer. "I see you still have the dragon bound. That's impressive."

Yes, flatter the madman. That always works out great.

I glanced over at Ignatius, wondering why he hadn't said anything. I figured Canton had commanded the dragon not to speak unless told to. It would be the smart thing to do. Even though the dragon was bound, there are ways around every spell if you're clever enough.

"Stay back," Canton shouted. Everyone paused.

Drake growled menacingly and raised his hand towards Canton. "It's almost sunrise. Take him down or I will."

Phil ignored him and kept on task. "You don't seem the type

to want to hurt anybody, Clint. Tell me what you're doing so I don't have to worry that it's something bad."

Canton glanced up to the sky, beads of sweat now dripping from his face. "I'm putting everything back the way it's supposed to be."

Okay, that didn't sound dodgy *at all*.

"Release my father," Drake nearly yelled. "I might even be charitable enough to let you live with most of your limbs."

"Not helping, Drake," Phil said out the side of his mouth.

"I can't." Canton said, glancing up again.

The sky had gotten a little lighter, almost straight up dawn. Eli and Viv had taken positions on the other side of the atrium. It wasn't a big space so they ended up putting the elder dragon between themselves and Phil. This whole thing was about two degrees from due south.

"Stay back!" Canton shouted and trembled as Phil took another step closer.

"You need the first rays of daylight, Clint." Phil slowly moved forward. There was still a chance to subdue Canton instead of getting into an out-and-out fight, but sleep spells have a short casting distance. "You can stop this before anyone else gets hurt."

"I'm trying to make it right." The statement would have been melodramatic fluff if not for the dead seriousness in the man's eyes. Whatever was going on in that twisted noggin of his, I wasn't sure I wanted to be privileged to it.

Drake growled and a wisp of fire rolled across his fingers like a silver dollar. "This really is boring. Release my father, *now*."

"Drake," Phil gritted his teeth.

"You're outnumbered," Drake haughtily told Canton.

"Shut up, Drake," Phil nearly shouted.

Rolling his eyes, Drake completely extended his arm, palm flat to the ground. Fire began to spew from his fingertips in a nice controlled arc that shot directly at Canton.

"Attack them!" Canton shouted as I lost sight of him through the flames.

The screech of a thousand fingernails on a chalk board

accompanied a release of energy powerful enough to knock me flat to my back. I blinked away the dots to see a gold dragon standing on its hind legs, wings folded awkwardly in the enclosed space. It was larger than a grown elephant, give or take a giraffe, with rose-vine spikes covering its tail. The girth of which was thicker than my whole torso, ending at a point about as round as my thigh. The tail thrashed, looking for a place to lay its twenty foot length, and ended up crashing down beside me.

"Eli, Viv," I heard Phil call out as I scrambled to my feet.

Ignatius had turned his attention to the two wizards. That's the fun part about bindings. All Canton said was attack, he didn't say who. Obviously he wouldn't attack his own son, so that left us.

"We got this," Vivian shouted as she dived out of the way of a snap by the dragon's toothy maw. In an open arena, I imagine Ignatius would be quite agile, but not so much in the small confines of the atrium.

Phil and Drake ran past the table and supplies, chasing after Canton. I knew Phil could take care of himself against another wizard, so I made the quick decision to help hold off Ignatius.

Wait, did I consciously decide to fight a dragon?

What's the standard for legal insanity?

Asking for a friend…

TEN[10]

Ignatius' tail thrashed between me and the others. With no place else to go, I ran toward the semi-wall. Hopping the divider into the hallway, the tip of his tail snapped around and barreled into a stone pillar beside me. Chunks of rock exploded from the impact. The shrapnel was mostly negligible, but one large piece struck my shoulder blade hard.

With a loud yelp, I spun with the impact and skidded across the floor.

"Minni!" Ryan shouted as he was hiding farther down the hallway, eyes wide.

I waved at him to stay back and raced down the hall. I started sliding on the marble floor, bouncing off the far wall. Getting traction, I bounded through the opening into the atrium, coming to an awkward halt just behind Eli and Vivian.

"So, hey, dragon," I said helpfully.

"Is that what that is?" Viv managed not to roll her eyes at me. Instead, she raised her blasting rod towards the beast.

Eli and Viv shouted incantations in tandem and released havoc on the dragon. Their trademark fireballs might be lavender and banana yellow in color, but they're lethal to most organic beings. Ignatius batted them away with his curled wings, howling as he did so. The air sizzled and filled with the smell of burnt metal, like when you boil water out of a pot. It was amazing they managed to do any damage to Ignatius at all. Dragons are, well, dragons.

Ignatius' tail swept the room again and we all dodged, regrouping to the left of him. Viv made a growling sound of her own. "These small orbs aren't going to be enough. Cover me."

Viv stood tall and gathered her magic about her. Eli threw off some quick fireballs to keep Ignatius' attention. I stood ready to absorb any fire the dragon might unleash. I wondered, somewhere in the back of my mind, why Ignatius hadn't tried fire-breathing yet. Perhaps he thought the area was too confined for such a thing. Or maybe he was trying his best not to actually kill us. Canton hadn't specified our deaths.

With a shout, Viv released another fireball, this one about three feet wide. Ignatius managed to deflect some of it with his wing, though he snarled in anger. The remnants of the flaming sphere hit the wall, instantly blacking it to the point that a spider web crack formed, chunks of stone falling from its center. The resulting shock wave shattered part of the ceiling causing safety glass to rain down.

Ignatius ducked, hunched over on his front legs, wings flapping open. We dived to avoid the span, but Eli wasn't quick enough and got clipped, the force sending him backwards against the pillars.

"*Zeydi!*" Viv yelled and moved towards her grandfather.

I was about to join her when I stopped in my tracks. Maybe it was because I could sense the buildup of energy, maybe it was because I had firsthand experience with this type of magic, but I could feel it. I knew Ignatius was finally going to use his fire-breathing.

Arm raised in what might have looked like a futile effort to stop the dragon, I shut my eyes and felt the wall of thermal energy hit my shield as Ignatius let loose. As the fire struck, I started to pull it in, absorbing the heat and quelling the chemical reaction as I would any other type of fire-based spell.

But I didn't think it through.

I felt the slime hit my arm and torso, clumps of it going into my hair. I knew that smell. Dragon bile. Like a flame-thrower, the dragon spat the bile out, somehow catching it on fire. This would guarantee distance, better accuracy, and continual damage as the sticky substance burned through clothing and skin. It would have been interesting to study if not disgusting and lethal. I threw up a physical barrier, but it was too late to save myself from being covered down one side.

Ignatius stopped when he realized I wasn't turning into a potato chip. I stole a chance to get a good look at the elder Drake. The dragon tilted his head and his nostrils flared slightly, almost as if he was sniffing at me. Did he perhaps sense that last bit of Drake's aura that I couldn't quite get rid of? Whatever it was, he stared at me for entirely longer than I was comfortable with.

The dragon quickly whipped his head to the side, looking at something. With a grumble that shook dust from the walls, Ignatius jumped and climbed to the opening above. The massive tail whipped around like a mace, knocking into one pillar and cracking it while more glass fell from the ceiling.

I back peddled, slipping on the smooth, bile covered stone. I fell to my side and rolled away in case the tail whipped back. Thankfully it didn't and I looked up to see the dragon take flight, disappearing into the sunrise.

As I got to my feet I tried to decide if this was a win, a loss, or a draw. I settled on just being happy I wasn't dead.

"Minni," Vivian called out. Eli was propped up against the wall and she tended to him. "I think he broke his leg."

"How bad is it?" I rushed over as quickly as I dared, not wanting to fall again. It was becoming a very bad habit.

"No bone showing through," she said. Eli sat with his eyes closed, using his subconscious to help with healing.

I was about to state the obvious of needing to get him to a healer when loud bickering voices started to bounce off the walls. Phil and Drake jumped over one of the dividers on the other side of the atrium.

"You should have taken him out when you had the chance," Drake scolded.

Phil rounded on him, his finger in the man's face. "And what did your methods achieve? Nothing except a hell of a lot of damage. Clint and your father are gone, no idea where, and it's all your fault. You should have trusted me and stuck to the plan!"

Drake pulled off a perfect glare of disdain. "Humans, to think I thought you might be useful."

"Yeah," Phil shouted back. "Why is that?"

"An obvious lack of judgment on my part." Drake said dismissively and Phil looked like he might deck him.

"Guys!" I shouted before we had another fight on our hands. "Eli's been hurt."

"How bad?" Phil immediately asked.

"Broken leg."

"Concussion too, I think," Vivian added.

"Stabilize him. I'll be right with you," Phil told us and jogged over to the table Canton had vacated earlier. Vivian started a bracing spell on Eli's leg when Phil shouted. "Damnit. Minni, I need you here."

I hurried over to find a rather ordinary Rand McNally map of New England laying on the table, held down at the four corners by some quartz crystals. One of those nice ceramic knives you see in the late night shopping ads was stuck in the table, point first. It was the knife Canton had taken out of the pot earlier. I had assumed he ran off with it.

"What kind of spell is this?" I honestly couldn't remember anything in my lessons about maps and knives being used together in spells. It's possible I wasn't paying attention though.

"Inelegance." Drake snorted. "That's what it is."

Phil tightened his jaw but otherwise ignored him. "It's a, well, it's designed to rip a hole between our world and the Shadow Realm to the point where they become one and the same, then co-exist."

Drake waved his hand dismissively. "It's a cheap and dirty way travel to the Shadow Realm without a natural gate."

"Yes, it is." Phil glared at Drake. "But with this much magic he would've been able to open a rift the size of Manhattan."

"Wait a second." I raised my hand to keep Drake from speaking. "If you put that big a slice of the modern world on the same plane as the Shadow Realm, they'll tear each other apart."

With the iron content of most buildings and every-day items being so acidic to shadow-stuff, this could destroy that part of the realm, and the resulting cascade effect...

"I'm afraid that might have been his plan." Phil glanced

over at Drake. "Thankfully he wasn't able to get very far, no thanks to numbnuts here."

Drake looked thoroughly put out. "How was I to know this wizard's insanity knows no bounds?"

"Shut up before I punch you myself," I told Drake then turned to Phil. "Okay, what do you need from me?"

"We lost Delaware."

"Kay, wait, wut?"

"Clint didn't finish the spell properly, so the odds are it was only momentarily displaced." Phil finger traced Delaware's geographical boundary. The perception of a state, or a country, can sometimes be strong enough to act as a mystical barrier. "As a whole it should be fine now, but there may be a rift somewhere near Dover, Delaware. If we don't close it then it could spread or cause other problems."

Drake dismissively waved at the map. "Is Delaware even a real place?"

"You caused this mess," Phil snapped, glaring at the dragon. Drake pursed his lips but they curled slightly at the edges as if he couldn't wait to see what Phil would say next. Not taking the bait, Phil turned back to me. "What I need from you, Minni, is to remove the dagger. That should close any possible rifts. But because we're not closing it properly, it'll cause a backlash of magic."

"Right," I said as I twisted my focus bracelet.

Attempting to take the full brunt of a magical whiplash was downright deadly to most wizards. I had to trust that my power siphon instinct could handle the intake, no matter how rapid or unstable it might be. But hey, energy is what I do, and there's always Plan B.

Getting into position, I saw the blade was sticking into the D of Dover, Delaware, making the town name look like Over. Great, just what I needed to see at that moment.

I closed my eyes, took a deep breath, and opened myself to the flow of energies around me. Catching a magical discharge was like taking off a band-aid, best to make it swift and quick. With a sharp tug, the knife easily released from the table, a spike of magical energy exploding against my senses.

I channeled it into my aura, but Canton's spell was dark, sad, yearning for self-destruction as if that was the only path to renewal. I wasn't sure if this was the purpose of the spell or the afterthoughts of the wizard who had created it. What I did know was that every inch of my body felt leaden and I wanted to curl up and die. Somehow that would make everything right...

Put everything back the way it was supposed to be.

"Guys!" Ryan shouted as I heard him hop the barrier.

My eyes snapped open and I had to do something with the magic. I couldn't keep it inside me, not like this. I saw the cooking pot lying on its side on the ground. It was the point where the spell was originally bound together. It sang to me like a siren.

Raising my left hand towards the metal container, Phil and Drake both stumbled backwards as a spike of dark energy flowed from my fingertips. It curled around the cylinder shape, wrapping it in shadows. There was a burst of light and a sizzle as what little liquid left in the pot evaporated. The distinct smell of burnt metal filled the air again, only this time it was far more putrid.

All and all, didn't go as bad as I thought it would.

"You okay?" Phil asked.

I took a long deep breath to clear my head. Most of the darkness in the spell had gone but something was left lingering, like the aftertaste of a diet soda. Nothing that couldn't be cleared away with a good mental scrub later. "I'm fine."

"But we're not." Ryan rushed his words. "The snow spell collapsed and the silent alarm tripped. I give it five minutes—ten tops—before the cops will be all over this place."

"Time to go." Phil took the knife from my hand, wiping it down and laying it on the table. "Drake, help me with Eli."

Drake looked like he was about to argue but Phil gave him a death-worthy glare. Sighing, Drake followed Phil over to the elder wizard. I think Phil's plan was for both of them to carry Eli. Drake gave a rather cultured grunt and scooped up Eli's decently sized frame into a bridal carry as if he was holding a small child.

"Alright then." Phil didn't question it. "Let's go."

I started to follow, getting one last look at the poor Saint Guilhem atrium. Various cracks, burns, and chunks of stone made the place look like a bomb had gone off in the room. It was enough to make an architectural history student cry.

A glint of metal caught my eye.

"Phil!" I jogged after him as the group rounded the hall. "What about the cameras?"

He frowned at me. "I doubt they would've survived the magic being used in there."

"And the rest of the building?" I pointed to a camera that was at the end of the hall, covering the doorway into another section.

Phil frowned. "Ah, Ryan?"

The kid shook his head. "No way to know for sure if the whole system was affected. And there's not enough time to recast the snow spell before the police arrive."

"I could emp the building," I suggested.

"That won't guarantee any footage would be erased."

"Did any working cameras catch us?" Phil asked directly.

"I dunno, maybe?" Ryan shrugged helplessly. "Fifty-fifty."

Vivian looked like she was ready to take her grandfather out of there herself. "We're wasting time."

I turned to Ryan. "So the servers are onsite, right?"

"Yeah, should be."

And this is why I should not be allowed to come up with the plans. "Phil, get everyone out. Ryan can show me where the recorders are. I'll erase them and we'll find our own way out."

Phil shook his head. "It'll take too long."

"Not if it's just me and Ryan." I glanced over at Eli. "We can move faster."

"I'm game," Ryan piped in.

"Fine." Phil realized there was no point in arguing with us. "We'll take the van, you'll have to take the subway or something, and meet back at my place."

"Will do," I quickly agreed, then chased after Ryan who had

already started bounding down the hallway. As I moved, I could feel the bile from Ignatius' attack drying and sticking to my skin through my clothes. I hoped we wouldn't pass any mirrors because I really didn't want to know what kind of state I was in.

Ryan turned down a different hall from before and made his way across one of the main gathering areas like a bloodhound on a trail. A couple of hallways later and we entered an office area with a heavy door marked 'Authorized Personal Only.' The lock was one of those numbered keypads, nothing he could traditionally pick.

The little thief pulled out a small ziplock baggy from his tote. It contained a fine silver dust. Taking a pinch, he threw it against the keypad as he mumbled some words in Latin. Different numbers began to glow, though in different intensities. Starting with the brightest one first he pushed the five numbers in order and the lock indicator turned from red to green.

"Nice." I stood in awe.

"Own personal blend." He winked as he turned the handle and pushed the door open. The lock then sparked and went dead.

The security room was fairly typical: a wall of monitors, another of servers and DVRs, a table and chair with coffee maker, and a small fridge. In the middle of the room a guard sat on a chair, his head lolled back and mouth gaped open in sleep.

"Check the guard." I motioned to Ryan while I made my way to the server rack.

I placed my hands over the individual servers one by one, only taking a second to send enough electromagnetic energy to erase the drives. It was always possible they might be able to retrieve something later, but it was a risk we'd have to take.

"Done." I turned back to see Ryan checking the pulse of the guard at his wrist, a frown on his face. "What?"

"This isn't a sleep spell. I think it's a type of Siren Calling."

"Damn," I reflectively muttered. "How much longer do we have?"

"A few minutes, not much. Enough to get out."

"Alright." I am very good at making rash decisions. "You

go ahead, I'll see what I can do for him."

"No, no no no." Ryan held his hands up and tried to ward me off. "Even if you could break the spell, the cops will be here any second now. They'll take him to the hospital. You can sneak in and help him there."

"After how long?" I said as I grabbed another rollie-chair. "A Calling gets stronger the longer it's in place. The victim loses parts of themselves. He's already had it for, what, a couple of hours? Another several hours and it's possible no one will be able to break it."

Ryan pointed to the clock. "The police—"

"Aren't here yet and we're wasting time." I situated the chair next to the guard but faced the opposite direction. "Go!"

Ryan looked between me and the guard, then shook his head. "Good luck."

"Thanks," I said as unsarcastically as I could and sat down in the chair. Ryan went to the door, slipping out after one last glance in our direction.

Siren Calling spells are pretty much what they sound like. Part sleep spell, the subject goes into a coma-like state while in their mind their fondest wish plays out. Their body then withers and dies, if it's not eaten by something else first. So why would Canton use this kind of spell? Why not use a basic sleep spell or any number of non-lethal subdue spells?

That was just one of many questions racking up in the wake of what happened.

I took the guard's hands in my own and with slow, even breaths, I let his energy flow through me as if I was completing a circuit. I let my consciousness follow that path, slipping my way into his mind as I would during an astral projection. Normally it's bad form to get into someone else's head without their permission. Being able to do so without having to go through a bunch of spell casting would have likely gotten me killed back in the day.

The natural barrier the mind puts up against mental invasion is like a fog bank and white noise machine combo. I should probably explain that this is only a visual representation for the benefit of the conscious mind. It may also not sound like much, but plenty of wizards have gotten lost in the fog. They are unable to find their way back to their own mind, let alone the one they are trying to visit. This is why most wizards prefer to cast physical or surface thought spells; it's a hell of a lot safer for all parties involved.

But thanks to my special ability, the energy of a person's mind becomes a beacon, a lighthouse as it were, in the fog. It's a perk I don't like to advertise and very few know I can do it. Dangerous slippery slope and all that.

Within moments I was face to face with a soft glowing orb that signaled the entrance into the guard's mind. Each person is different, no two have the same entrance as far as I know. It's not like I've done this enough times to have a decent sample size.

Reaching into the light, I grimaced as my hand hit metal, but it was a familiar sensation. Unable to see through the glow, I ran my hand across the surface until I found what I was looking for. Pulling up on a handle there was a flash of even brighter light. I found myself sitting in a typical New York taxi cab, except there was no driver and the meter wasn't running.

To my right, the windows were as dark and foggy as the barrier I just exited. To the left, it was a bright, sunny, gorgeous looking day with trees blowing in the wind and birds sailing by. Scooting across the seat, I pushed the door open. The sun was so bright I had to shield my eyes as I surveyed the landscape.

I found myself in Central Park but the skyline wasn't full of buildings hanging over the tree line. There was a statue next to a bridge which I was pretty sure didn't go together. In fact, the proportions of the entire area seemed a bit skewed. It was like this Central Park was built from flawed memories.

There was laughing in the distance. Since I had no time to spare, I took off at a run towards the noise. Weaving through some clustered trees, I came to another clearing. The guard was playing with a boy of about eight. They tossed around a football, laughing as they mock tackled each other.

"Hey!" I shouted as I jogged across the clearing. The man

ignored me even after I yelled and waved my hands in the air. I grabbed his arm while he attempted to throw the football back to his son. "Hey!"

He gave me a curious look, his head slightly tilted. "I don't know you."

"No, you don't." Because I just violated your mind but let's not dwell on that shall we? "You're under a magical spell. I've come to help get you out."

"Get me out?" He probably thought he was having a wonderful dream and weird stuff happens in dreams. "Thanks, but I don't need your help."

He turned away, so I held my grip on his arm. "This is a dream. It isn't real."

"You think I don't know that?" he shouted as he wrenched easily out of my grasp.

I followed his gaze to a woman in a blue dress sitting at a picnic table. She smiled and waved as the boy shouted for his dad to hurry up and throw the ball. I got in front of the guard and planted my feet. I needed to make him remember reality. "This is just memories. None of it is real."

His eyes flitted back and forth and his jaw twitched. He didn't want to remember.

"Come on, Dad," the kid shouted. "Throw the ball!"

The man tossed the football lazy through the air and his son caught it. He then turned to me and sternly said, "You can leave now."

I gestured wildly in the boy's direction. "He's a shadow. He's not real."

"He's real enough," the man replied sternly.

"Is this what he would want from you?" The words fell out of my mouth before I could even think them. "You're dying. Would he want you to give up on life?"

"He didn't live long enough to know what he'd want, now did he?" The guard downright sneered at me as he pushed past.

I let my shoulders fall in defeat. There was no way I was going to convince him, not in the short amount of time I'd been allotted. There had to be more options, but for the life of me nothing came to mind. I wanted to help him, but he wouldn't let me. Leaving him here like this felt like giving up.

"There's a taxi cab," I hollered after him in a vain hope that maybe he'd figure it out on his own. "Beyond the trees. That's your exit."

He picked up his boy and swung him in circles, laughter filling the air. I know he heard me but he seemed content to die like this. And there was a distinct possibility that he would forget me the moment I walked away. He's reliving memories I'm not a part of, and I reminded him of a reality he wanted to forget. My only solace was that maybe I could help him later when I had more time.

This made me acutely aware of the fact that I had no idea how much time had passed in the real world. I jogged back through the trees into the other clearing. The cab still sat there, illegally parked on the grass. I pulled open the door and slipped inside. Quickly scooting across the seat, I opened the other door into the fog.

I followed the flow of energy and slipped my consciousness back into my body. My eyes fluttered open and I felt heavy from the paralysis. I could see a clock from my position and thankfully only three minutes had passed. Maybe the cops would be slow to respond?

Some pins and needles settled in before I could move again and I slowly stood, rocking on my feet a bit to get the blood flowing. Staring down at the security guard, I whispered into his ear, "Remember what's real."

Then I booked it the hell out of there.

Taking off down the hallway, I wanted to go back the way we came in. I knew everyone would be long gone, but getting lost right now was not the smartest move I could make. Not that, you know, I was having any luck in that department.

"*Halt, police!*"

Speaking of…

I skidded to a stop on the polished floor.

I figured I was going to be labeled a gangbanger or druggie

on site. It probably wouldn't help that my clothes were stiff, grungy, and smelled from the dried bile. I don't even want to think about my hair.

I threw my arms up and took a deep breath while trying to be as non-threatening as possible. I really didn't feel like getting shot right then. I generally don't like getting shot at, period, but you know, it happens.

Hands grabbed me from behind and pressed me up against the wall. The officer had one hand on my shoulder and the other was holding my arm behind my back. "You got needles, anything in your pockets I should be aware of?"

"No." The word came out tired and I collapsed against the wall, letting the tension seep from my muscles. It had been a really long day. I didn't need to top it off by getting into it with a cop.

"What's your name?" He was thorough but not too thorough, if you know what I mean, in his pat down.

"My license is in my back pocket." I decided to save him time and effort. He kept a hand on my shoulder as he fished the ID out.

Two cops came down the hall, one of them asking, "Who's this?"

"Dominique Masterson," my friendly neighborhood arresting officer said. "Well, Dominique, you want to tell us what you're doing here?"

Do you think 'chasing the dragon' would be an acceptable answer in this situation?

The cops certainly didn't think so.

ELEVEN[11]

You want to know a surefire way to anger a detective? Fall asleep during your interrogation. Trust me, works every time.

The cop's hand slammed down on the table with a sharp clang as his ring hit the metal. "Am I boring you?"

A little, yeah, but it wasn't his fault. An hour earlier I had faced down a dragon, so really, on the scale of things, hah, scales, um, wait, where was I?

I lifted my head from the table, rubbing my left wrist unconsciously. I'd performed a lot of magic in the past twenty-four hours. Any other wizard would probably be tethering on comatose by now. I wondered what would happen first: the detective giving up in frustration or me completely passing out.

"You have an interesting rap sheet, Miss Masterson." Detective something-something Gant pulled a file out from under a yellow legal pad he'd been taking notes on. "More than once you've been listed as a person of interest in some very… interesting events."

Yeah, that Kishi I helped Phil and the gang take down in Queens last year was pretty insane. It had two faces, one a human male, the other a hyena. The male face would attract women and then the hyena would eat them. So gross.

His chair creaked as Gant leaned forward and I got a better look at him. A tad shade darker than pasty white, he had an angular face and light blue eyes. He might have been handsome if he wasn't trying to intimidate me into a confession.

Not that anyone could quite match the intensity of Marcel's eyes. They're the perfect shade of chestnut with just that one speck of black on the bottom left of his right iris…

Sorry, I keep getting distracted.

"And now," Gant continued, "we have you at the scene of some kind of occult gathering with untold amounts of property damage."

Best thing I could do was keep quiet. I needed to bide time until the cavalry arrived. So I stared at him with as blank of an expression as I could muster. Wasn't that hard, I may have even dozed off, again.

"What's all this about?" Gant pointed the tip of his pen at the damaged bracelets on my right hand. Now, normally they take everything off you when they book you in, but the melted mass wouldn't budge. The arresting officers decided that the bangles, while garish, were harmless and not worth finding something to cut them off with. "Well?"

"High art," I mumbled.

They did take my focus bracelet. I kept reaching for it. Even though it was gone I swear I could still feel it, which was causing me to have separation anxiety tremors. I'm sure Gant believed it was withdrawal symptoms.

There was a soft knock on the door and I tried not to breathe a sigh of relief when I finally saw someone I recognized. The grandchild of Nigerian immigrants, Detective Laurence Harper is in his late forties and solidly built. You know those types of guys who are like ninety percent muscle mass but they can put on the right shirt and look three times smaller than they are? That's Harper.

He's also a Forsaken.

"Gant," Harper greeted the other detective, passing over one of the two files he carried. "You might want to see this."

As Gant flipped through the papers, Harper gave me an ever so subtle nod that meant the calvary had indeed arrived. You might think it was rather convenient I happened to get booked into the same precinct as Harper. Truth is, all the precincts have at least one person in them that helps us out. I would even be comfortable in saying that New York City has more people who believe in magic than actual magic users.

"Well, no indication of drug or alcohol use." Gant almost

sounded disappointed. "That still doesn't explain what you were doing there."

"This might," Harper added as he passed over the other file. "Anonymous 911 caller saw a woman matching Miss Masterson's description get roughly pulled into a minivan last night. Said it looked like it was against her will. And it was three blocks south from her listed home address."

So yeah, that was Harper's big plan to get me out of there. I nearly face-palmed.

Gant stared intently at me. "You want to tell me the truth, Miss Masterson?"

Harper wanted me to agree but I figured a simple yes wouldn't be enough. I looked the part with my disheveled clothing, but I needed to react like someone who'd been through such an ordeal. But despite everything I have done, I've never been kidnapped. So I was going to have to draw on my extensive knowledge of movies and tv shows to get me through this.

Hoping I was doing it right, I whispered, "I thought it was all a bad dream."

Pretty sure I saw that in a movie once.

I figured I'd break into tears next because that really sells it, you know? To get the waterworks going, I first thought of Marcel. The break up hurt more than my denial would lead you to believe. Regardless, I couldn't muster any more tears for him even though the wound was fresh. If anything, it was too fresh. I was still dealing with those emotions. I wasn't sure where I stood with them. I didn't want to accept my guilt for the breakup even though I was the one at fault.

So I turned my thoughts to David and that night out in the sunflower field. It had rained, it was cold, he'd lost so much blood...

I held him.

Waiting.

Crying.

Screaming.

Nobody heard me.

"Dominique." The tone was unusually kind coming from

the overly suspicious detective. I glanced up as he offered me a box of tissues. My eyes were foggy and glazed with tears, my shirt soaked through. I have no idea how long I had been crying.

"Thank you." I coughed as I accepted the tissues and used them to wipe my eyes and blow my nose. It'd been ages since I really let myself think about that night.

Gant moved his chair around to the side of the table. He leaned into me but at a respectable distance. "Dominique, why don't you tell us what happened?"

I tried not to look too suspicious as I glanced over at Harper. All he did was give me an encouraging smile. I wasn't really feeling the courage. I rubbed my naked wrist and hoped for the best.

"I ah, I was out clubbing." I decided to stick with the facts; it's typically the easiest way to lie. But then I realized I was totally not dressed for clubbing since I burned my shirt after the whole fire-breathing incident. "Then I went home, changed my clothes and decided to go to this bodega a few blocks away. I got about three blocks." I think Harper said three? "And this guy comes out of nowhere and starts talking all crazy, tells me I have to go with him. He… he said he was fixing things."

"Did he have a weapon on him?" Gant asked as he made a note on the legal pad.

"He, ah, had this knife." I relied on everything I learned from binge-watching episodes of *Law & Order* with Marcel. "It was a big knife and… and I don't think he was stable, I… I froze up."

"It's understandable." Gant looked up and assured me with a sympathetic smile. "Can you tell me what happened next?"

I looked to Harper who gave me another encouraging nod. "He told me to get into the passenger's seat of his van." I made myself choke up for the next part. "I don't really remember. He was waving the knife around as he drove. I was afraid if I tried anything, even move for the door handle, he'd stab me."

"It's okay." Gant gave no judgment, accepting every word without question. The man went from bad cop to good cop in like thirty seconds. Such a flake.

"We ended up at The Cloisters. He dragged me across the

lawn into the building." I described a few of the corridors in a haphazard manner. "Then we came to this atrium with all this weird stuff. He kept babbling about fixing things."

Gant tilted his head a little. "He already had his tables and ritual items set up?"

"Yeah," I replied without considering what the best answer would have been.

Harper slid into the conversation. "Means he broke in earlier, knocked out the guard and security system before getting everything ready. Wouldn't be the first criminal to set the stage before gaining an audience."

There was a furrow to Gant's brow, but he seemed to buy the conclusion for the moment.

"He knocked out a security guard?" I asked innocently, hoping it wouldn't be too suspicious of me to ask. "Are they okay?"

"The guard's in a coma at Trinity," Gant answered. "Doctors are working on him. Now, what happened next?"

Good question. Um, he tried to pull New York City into the Shadow Realm and destroy the fabric of reality? Not to mention the ancient gold dragon that I literally faced down. But hey, it's no biggie.

"Ah, he pulled me over to this table with a map on it. I panicked. We struggled. I fell." I have the bruises down my backside to prove it, thank you Ignatius. "And I don't remember much after that."

"You don't remember?" he asked warily.

"I know I hit my head." I reached up and felt the sore spot from when I fell dodging the tail of the dragon. It wasn't big enough to cause a blackout but I figured I could always claim distress along with injury. "The rest was kind of a blur. Next thing I know, I'm in the middle of an empty and seriously wrecked atrium, so I ran for it. Then there were cops."

"Right," Gant said softly. "You know, if anything did happen, if your attacker did anything to you, it's okay to talk about it. It will make you feel better."

You know what would also make feel better? Chocolate

covered raisins and a nap.

Worst. Interrogation. Ever.

Alright, so after Gant was satisfied with my answers he had me sit down with a sketch artist to describe my 'unknown assailant.' The artist used this fancy computer system so it didn't take long to create a fair representation of Canton. Harper already knew who it was, of course, but he had to play dumb. He did the usual cop stuff and rambled off an impressive list of acronyms such as ABP and BOLO.

It would have been pretty handy if the police located Canton for us. That way we'd only have to go in and grab him. Provided, you know, Ignatius hadn't broken his leash and eaten him by then.

My working assumption as I sat there waiting was that Phil would have already contacted the New England Wizard's Council. Hopefully they'd send help, maybe some backup. Not that they ever really have in the past. The council hasn't forgiven Guiliani for driving all the vampires out of Times Square without talking to them first. Which in-and-of-itself wasn't so bad, except he had went and asked the technomages for help.

Ugh, *technomages*.

New York City basically became persona-non-grata to the wizard world after that. Phil doesn't get much in the way of aid when it comes to trying to help the few wizards who choose to live here. But he doesn't get flak for it either because, well, someone has to do it.

Someone always does.

Anyway, by the time Gant was ready to let me go, it was about noon. Slumped in a hardly padded chair at Gant's desk in the station bullpen, I was exhausted. Harper had gotten me a candy bar from the vending machine earlier, which helped, but what I needed was a natural recharge: good ol' sleep.

"You have someone you can stay with?" Gant asked as my personal items were finally returned to me. The first thing I did was put my foci back on. The cool copper instantly began to draw the heat from my skin. I could feel the stress knots in my back uncurl as my anxiety waned.

"I'd rather go home," I answered honestly, fidgeting with the bracelet.

He passed me his business card. "Well, if you remember anything more, give me a call, okay?"

"Thank you," I said as I pocketed it. I kind of felt bad about lying to him, but he seriously wouldn't have believed the truth. And he was kind of an ass.

"I'll have a uniform give you a lift." Gant began to wave someone over.

"I'll take her," Harper offered casually from two desks over. "I'm going on my lunch and was gonna run some errands. Her apartment is on my way. If you're okay with that, Miss?"

I shrugged in disinterest. "Yeah, sure."

Gant didn't argue, and after a compulsory goodbye I walked off with Harper. We headed to the station garage where he kept his personal vehicle. The interior was tidy, clean, and void of the dozens of straw wrappers usually found in the floorboards of people's passenger seats. It wasn't until we were away from the police station that I finally spoke in a calm and reserved manner.

"Kidnapped!?" Yeah, okay, I yelled. "Are you kidding me?" Curse words were probably involved. I can't remember which ones. It could have been all of them.

"Maybe you should've gotten out with Ryan when you had the chance?" Harper remained calm as he navigated out of the parking structure.

I wanted to argue with him, but I guess he did have a point there. It wasn't the brightest move I could have made. Not that I've been really good at decision making lately. I still have no idea what to do with the whole Marcel situation. I know I'm the one at fault. The breakup is on me, I'm big enough to admit that.

Now.

After sulking in the passenger seat, I asked, "How is Eli?"

"Doing fine, he's at home."

This made me feel relieved, but there was still something else that weighed on me. "Is the guard really at Trinity?"

Harper let out a little sigh as he stopped at a red light. "Yeah. Doctors suspect some kind of stroke brought on by whatever Canton did to him."

Ah yes, the stroke, so much magic has been hidden behind that diagnosis. "He's under a Siren Calling."

"Damn," Harper muttered and we settled into another silence as he drove on. In fact, we didn't say a word to each other until we approached my building. "If Gant or anyone else from the station contacts you, keep to what you said in there. Don't improvise, don't add anything. Don't talk to the press."

"I know the drill." Honestly, you'd think this was my first arrest.

I slipped off my seatbelt as Harper said, "I was worried this wasn't going to work, but you really sold it in there. That whole crying bit really got Gant on your side."

"Yeah." I popped the handle and slid out of the car.

I must have pushed the door forcefully or something. To be honest, I was lost in thoughts I had no desire to have. Whatever I did, it prompted Harper to ask, "Hey, you going to be okay?"

"Probably not." I couldn't be bothered to lie.

Harper gave me the concerned policeman look. "Anything you want to talk about?"

I debated for a moment if I should tell him. I was so tired my brain didn't want to do the calculations of what it would mean to say the words out loud. I said them anyway. "I thought about my little brother. He was attacked and left for dead in a sunflower field. I found him. I held him while we waited for help to come."

Pretty sure Harper wasn't expecting that response. With wide eyes he asked, "Did he make it?"

"Yeah, eventually." I shut the door and turned towards the entry of my apartment.

I realize never said thank you to Harper for helping me out. I mean, he didn't have to. He may be a Forsaken, but there is no rule or even guideline that says they have to help us wizards and witches. I'll have to tell him next time I see him.

Why do I keep calling him Forsaken? Well, it's a common

term for people who have the potential to use magic, but don't. These are magic users who have either elected to forsake magic in favor of living a normal, mundane existence, or had ancestors who made that decision for them.

Perhaps you know someone who can't wear watches, who can't keep credit cards in their back pockets, or maybe they make vending machines go crazy when they get near. Since Forsakens don't actively use magic, they don't get as strong of a magical field. If they don't know about their family history then they probably chalk up the weird stuff to, well, plain old weirdness.

Yeah, 'Forsaken' is a bit of a depressing moniker. That's what happens after years of witch hunts and bad press. Our PR department pretty much called it a day about six centuries ago.

Ah, non-magic users? We don't really have a name for them. I mean, they're just normal people. The default, I guess. Which is substantially more depressing, yeah.

Once I crossed my apartment threshold into familiar surroundings, I was very tempted to lay down on the floor of the entry way and go to sleep. I managed to drag myself to the kitchen island where I had left my sender. No messages from Phil. I went to grab my phone to call him and remembered it was still in pieces at his apartment.

With more effort than it really should have taken, I wrote a note in the sender.

Phil — I'm home. Harper got me out of hot water but you won't believe how. Is the whole Canton thing over now? Surely the binding spell on daddy Drake has worn off? I kinda want to take a nap but not if the world is going to end. Let me know what you need me to do. - Minni

Placing my hand over the words, I sent them along to Phil. While I waited for the reply, I headed into the bathroom to strip off my clothes. They say don't put oily fabric in your washer, and especially not in the dryer, as it could be a fire hazard. Does dragon bile count? I decided to throw the clothes next to the hamper and sort it out later.

As the shower heated up, I tried my luck at getting the melted bracelets off but they still wouldn't slide over my wrist. I could have looked for something to cut them but at that point it was too much extra effort. I went to check the sender instead.

Minni – Get some rest. – Phil.

Well, wasn't going to argue with that.

I took a quick shower, shampooing my hair...*twice*. As I toweled off, I could see all the bruises, cuts, and scrapes I'd collected over the past, what, twelve hours? Man, I really did need a nap.

Heading into the bedroom, the midday sun was bright through the light colored curtains and warmed the room. Most of my furniture is cheap, whatever I could afford at the time. But my bed frame I picked up at an estate sale. I was there acting as a magic-sink for a friend when I saw it. It was disassembled, the step-pyramid shaped headboard laying against a wall. Inside the frame, panels of copper fanned out in a starburst pattern.

I may have spent far too much money on it than I really should have. Worth it.

Getting dressed in a t-shirt and boy shorts, I threw my comforter to the side and slid under the sheet. I barely had time to get comfortable before sleep overtook me and my body shut down. I'm pretty sure I skipped the R.E.M. stage and went straight to M.A.W.B.D... i.e. Might As Well Be Dead.

And where there's sleep, there are dreams.

I was running. I'm always running.

Have you ever run through a sunflower field? It hurts, what with the thick stalks and long leaves smacking against you. You come out the other side of the field with your body covered in red whelps and nature's version of paper cuts. Add a drizzle of cold rain and you have the definition of insult to injury.

When I finally stopped running, I was in a clearing of crushed sunflowers.

Yellow stained with red.

TWELVE[12]

"Girl, you still asleep?" A hand started to rock me back and forth setting off pins and needles through much of my extremities.

"Ga wa." I'm pretty sure I said 'go away', but I could be wrong.

"It's five o'clock." It's times like these that I regret giving Stacey a key to my place. She decided to wake me by dragging the sheet off the bed. "Get up… oh."

I turned, trying to get off my right hand. It was now screaming particularly loudly about its blood flow being partially cut off due to the damaged mess of metal. I'm not used to sleeping with bracelets on that wrist.

Rubbing the sleep from my eyes, I saw the gape in Stacey's mouth. She was staring at my hip and thigh. They were the prettiest shade of black and blue you ever did see.

"What happened?" Stacey blurted out.

"I, ah, fell." It was the truth, sort of.

She gave me the most incredulous look. "On to what?"

"The ground." I sat up and stretched, trying to get the blood flowing again. I sounded like a bowl of Rice Krispies.

"Damn girl." She stared at me for a solid minute, then shook her head. "Get dressed. I'll make you something to eat."

"Knew there was a reason I kept you around." I tried to make light but she barely looked at me as she left.

I sat on the edge of the bed, crunching my toes and moving my ankles to help get rid of the prickly sensation. Everywhere ached, especially the bruises, which I poked at, because reasons.

In the bathroom, I washed my hands and instinctively adjusted my copper foci. It caught the light, glimmering prisms against the wall. On my other wrist, the brash piece of modern art still mocked me. I glared at it but that had no effect. I considered possibly sending heat into the bracelet to melt it enough to either warp or break, but nixed the idea. I was too hungry to focus without getting nasty burns again.

I grabbed some sweat pants and a thin sweater. While trying to find the second arm-hole, I remembered I'd left my sender on the kitchen island. What I couldn't recall was whether or not I'd left it open.

When I walked out towards the kitchen, there was the distinctive aroma of eggs in the air. Stacey hummed something I couldn't make out from the noise of the local news station. She gestured with a spatula for me to sit at the island where a glass of OJ was already waiting.

Stacey really is the best. I probably should tell her I'm a witch. I'm not going to, but I should.

The sender was where I left it, thankfully closed. The *Utopia* book cover was still on it, making it innocuous. I sat down and pushed it to the side, trying not to be suspicious about it.

"Have you seen the news?" Stacey asked as she fiddled around with plates.

"Ah, no," I replied, grabbing the OJ and taking a swig.

"You're missing something," she said as she started to scrape instant mash out of a pot. "The last few days have been crazy."

"Ah, okay." I turned slightly on my barstool chair to see the local news returning from a commercial break. An image of Delaware popped up with a red crossed-out circle over it. Pretty sure I forgot to breathe for a minute.

"New information has surfaced regarding last night's loss of wireless, cellphone, and internet service across much of the state of Delaware," the news reporter began. "Experts are now saying it was likely the result of residual energy from a large solar flare and not a terrorist act or related to Friday's blackout. Reports are still coming in about the incident which momentarily left Delaware without everything from traffic lights to 911 service. So far there have been no reports of serious injury due to the event, but it has baffled scientists. We'll have more on this story later tonight as it develops."

The reporter switched cameras. "Speaking of fluke occurrences, did a tornado take out Manhattan's Little Red Lighthouse? We go live to Jerry Sudeki at the scene. Jerry?"

The feed switched to a side-by-side with a parka clad man standing in the shadow of the George Washington Bridge, the lighthouse in the far background. Even at that distance, you could see the damage to the beacon housing as heavy machinery removed the downed trees.

"Thank you, Dana," the reporter said once he realized he was live. "As you can see from behind me, work crews have been working since early this morning to remove the debris left by a freak tornado that passed through here last night. A spokesman from the National Weather Service said the tornado may have started as some kind of water spout which picked up momentum over the unseasonably warm waters of the Hudson."

"And the storm damage wasn't reported until this morning?" the anchor asked.

"I've been told the storm, while powerful, was short-lived once it hit land. Even though it was recorded at the meteorological center, no one knew the extent of the damage until a police patrol spotted what you see behind me."

"This was a fluke occurrence then?" Dana asked as if to assure the audience.

"Very much so." Jerry nodded. "Residents of the area and commuters have nothing to worry about. They won't be getting snatched up and taken to the Land of Oz any time soon."

I bet his producer told him to say that.

Dana let out a fake laugh. "And the cleanup efforts?"

"As you can see, there is a lot of damage to the non-structural elements." The camera zoomed past Jerry for a moment to focus on the lighthouse, including the three claw marks on the roof. Seeing them again made me realize something was off. I couldn't exactly place what it was in that moment, but it would come to me. "Overall, the building is still in very good condition.

Nothing a little paint and elbow grease can't fix, I've been told."

"Good to hear." Dana smiled. "Thank you, Jerry, for that report."

"Thank you, Dana." The reporter smiled before the image cut back to the news anchor completely filling the screen.

"The police are currently investigating a break in at The Cloisters that occurred early this morning," she continued with the broadcast. "Details are few at this time, but it's been reported that while some vandalism occurred and a security guard was taken to the hospital, none of the many priceless artifacts were stolen. The police believe burglary was not a motive for the break in." The sketch I made of Canton popped up. "The police do have a suspect If you know this man or have any information that could help in the investigation, please call the number on the screen."

"See." Stacey brought over the food. "Crazy."

Ah yes, ignorance truly is bliss.

I looked down at the offering she placed before me: a pile of instant mashed potatoes, three over-hard eggs, diced avocado, and sliced fried tomatoes, all smothered in ketchup. "You are the best-est best friend ever."

"You are the craziest best friend ever." She laughed as she sat down to eat a much more moderate helping of toast and two runny eggs. "And that is your favorite hangover cure."

Protein, starch, and salts, exactly what a wizard needs after some heavy spell casting. I dug in and squashed up the tomatoes, mixing them around in the potatoes, and cutting up the egg into little bits. After the last two days, the solid mass of food on my stomach was an agreeable weight.

"So." Stacey held out the vowel. "Marcel."

"What about Marcel?" I asked seriously and without sarcasm. I hadn't had time to think about the situation with him, what with crazy wizards, dragons, goat-grizzlies...

Which yeah, I know, is exactly what I wanted. Go me?

"He called earlier." Stacey sawed through her eggs. "He's been trying to get a hold of you and your phone kept going to voicemail. That's why I popped over."

"Yeah, my phone got a bit wet." Earlier I was interrogated by a cop, now by my best friend. "It's still at Phil's, in pieces, drying."

"Explains why you didn't answer my texts, either." She gave me a slightly incredulously stare that I could only shrug to. "And here I was thinking you were mad at me for last night."

"Mad at you?" I stuffed my mouth with food and let out a muffled. "Why?"

"For leaving you at the club," she said with a 'duh' look on her face.

"Oh, yeah." I bought some time by taking a gulp of OJ. It totally wasn't her fault that she left; it was that stupid dragon. "Don't worry about it, it's forgotten."

I don't think she believed me but her guilt turned to worry. "What were you doing that your phone got wet and you fell so hard you got all bruised up like that? That's no trip on the sidewalk."

I chose to ignore the fact that if I was just honest with Stacey in the first place about being a witch I wouldn't have to worry about telling her the truth. As it stood, I needed a convincing lie.

Yeah, I had nothing.

"I really don't want to talk about it right now." Lame.

She sat up straight on the stool and crossed her arms. "Okay, then how about you tell me what's going on with you and Marcel?"

Stacey probably figured the fall and Marcel were somehow related. Or if not, then she'd use Marcel as the bait and switch. If I don't tell her about one, then I'd give in and talk about the other. Neither ends well for me.

"I thought men preferred the whole 'bachelor' thing." I pushed some of the potatoes around on the plate. The subject of Marcel left a cold spot in my chest I wanted to fill with as much thermal heat as I could possibly draw from the world around me. Though somehow I knew even that wouldn't be enough.

"What is your problem?" The words dripped with exasperation. "A good looking, stable guy, wants you to live with him, prelude to bigger things, and you balk. Are you afraid of, what, marriage? Kids? Joint Netflix account?"

"None of that." I sat my fork down a bit too roughly and the resulting clatter echoed throughout the room, even over the television. "He's just… it wouldn't work out."

"Why not?"

Because I'd have to tell him I was a witch and nothing would ever be the same again between us. Therein lies the Catch-22. I could never sustain a long-term relationship with a non-believer because eventually the secret would tear us apart. It already has. Sure, I could forsake magic, but even though I'm not exactly a pillar of the magical community, I'm not going to do that. I am a witch, a sorceress; it's who I am. It's the one thing no one wants to take away from me. For now at least.

I needed a partner who wouldn't look at me in awe or fear because of what I can do. But I have yet to find a magic user who interested me in the slightest, relationship-wise.

They all pale in comparison to Marcel.

Damn that man.

"I'm too freaking picky for my own good." I shoved the plate forward and stood, grabbing my drink with the intention of touching it up.

"Well, at least you recognize that." Stacey smirked at me. "First step to recovery."

I ignored the jab as I pulled the jug of OJ from the fridge and refilled my glass. I stood with my back to Stacey as I took a couple sips. Eventually I had to ask the question. "What did he want?"

"Hm?" she mumbled as she dipped her toast in egg yolk.

"Marcel." I turned and leaned against the counter. "You said he was trying to get a hold of me. Why?"

"Why do you care?" The words lacked any interest but I bet if I could have seen her face she was grinning like a fiend.

I let out a soft growl. "I hate you."

She laughed and swirled around on the stool to face me. "You'll have to call him to find out, or you can tell me about the bruises."

See, told you. Crafty, that one. "I really do hate you."

"Yeah, I know, sweetie." Her smile was just a tad bit condescending, as if I was acting like a pouting five-year-old. Which yeah, I know I was, so shut it. The only reason I'm telling you this part of the story is because of what happens next.

"Can I borrow your phone?" I sighed, giving in.

"Of course you can." She fished it out of her bag.

"I really, really, hate you," I deadpanned.

"You say that," she replied mock-thoughtfully as she placed the phone in my hand, "but all I hear is love."

Knocking on the front door reverberated throughout the apartment. Stacey quickly held up her hand. "I got it, you call."

"Fine," I whined, a little… a lot.

I stood there, punching in numbers as Stacey went to the door, checking the peephole before she opened it. I wasn't too worried. For one, I trust Stacey's judgment when not under the influence of dragons. And secondly, I have some freakishly awesome wards on my apartment.

"Hey, Phil," Stacey greeted the wizard who was dressed in a dark blue department store business suit. He cleans up nice.

The phone dialed and rang. No answer yet.

"Oh, hi, Stacey," Phil greeted her as he stepped in, a similarly clad Harper right behind him. "Uh, this is Laurence Harper. Laurence, this is Stacey, Minni's BFF."

Harper politely said hello to Stacey and I nearly had a panic attack. I was pretty sure I never told Harper that Stacey didn't know I'm a witch. I mean, why would I have?

Another ring. I really should have just hung up and done something right then, but I was a bit of a deer in headlights at the impending disaster in front of me.

Goat-Grizzlies and Dragons: Fine.

BFFs, Boyfriends, Emotional Attachments: Not So Fine.

I'm not going to even bother trying to psychoanalyze that.

Nope.

Stacey placed both hands on her hips and physically barred the men to that side of the room. "So, you gonna to tell me what happened last night to leave my girl black and blue?"

"She'll have to tell you yourself." Phil didn't miss a beat as this kind of stuff was old hat. It was in that moment I realized how sad it was that lying on my behalf had become second nature to him. Well, lying in general seems to be a common wizardly trait, so what was one more?

"Uh huh." Stacey stared them down and while Phil may have been used to it, Harper looked like he might fold.

"Leave a message, or, you know, not." I heard Marcel's voice in my ear then a couple of annoyingly sharp beeps.

"Hey, it's Minni." I paused. I actually forgot why I was calling him. "I kinda broke my phone last night. I'll get it fixed or replaced tomorrow. I'll call. I… I see you. Bye."

Stacey now stood barely a hand width from the police detective who smiled awkwardly. He was totally going to break. I felt as if my world was about to implode and I had no one to blame but myself. I took a long deep breath and counted to three. I could get through this.

"Stacey." I stalked over to the group. "I was mugged in Central Park, fell into a pond, this man is the detective on the case." I *was* almost mugged in Central Park yesterday. The lie was not completely without factual merit.

"What?" She turned on me, eyes wide. "You okay?"

"I'm fine. I didn't want you to worry."

"Girl!" she scolded me even as she wrapped me up in a hug. "I never should have left you alone."

And I did not think this through, forgetting about the long-term effects of that stupid suggestion spell Drake cast on Stacey. It messes with the morality/guilt/reward complex and likely made Stacey feel ten times worse about the whole thing.

I pulled away and put my hands on her shoulders. "Hey, I'm fine. See? A few bruises. I've gotten worse dodging bike messengers."

"You should have called me." Her eyes flitted over at Phil.

Now I felt like an even bigger idiot. She's my best friend, but so is Phil. Stacey knows this, but she was acutely aware of the fact I only included him in my time of need, and not her. It's possible she thought I was mad at her, maybe even blamed her.

That's not even close to the truth, but my little ball of lies was blowing up in my face and Stacey was getting all the shrapnel.

I am the worse friend ever.

Is my secret worth all this? Not sure it even matters anymore. I'm going to end up losing her anyway, just like every other non-magical person in my life. I might as well let her keep her ignorance so she doesn't have to be afraid of the dark.

"Yes, I should have." I put as much regret into the words as I could muster, which was a hell of a lot. "I was on my way to Phil's anyway and he knew Detective Harper. Lots of stuff was happening so fast, it was crazy. I wasn't thinking straight."

I really wanted her to forgive me, not that I actually deserved it.

All she did was look sadly at me.

Harper cleared his throat. "Miss Masterson, there are a few things I need to go over with you. Sensitive police business."

For a moment I thought Stacey might argue. Policeman or no, there was no stopping that girl when she had the moral high ground. Instead, she grabbed Phil by the arm and dragged him towards the kitchen. "Come on, you can help me do the dishes."

I'm sure both men wanted to speak to me but this was the best I could hope for under the circumstances. As Phil was hauled away to be interrogated, erm, wash dishes, I gestured for Harper to join me on the sofa.

"Stacey doesn't know I'm a witch," I whispered as we sat down.

He raised an eyebrow. "How does that work?"

"Not very well," I admitted. "What did you guys need?"

"Well, for one, Gant wanted a welfare check done on you." The big man twisted a little uncomfortably on the retro cushions of my art deco inspired, cheap-ass sofa. "While he now thinks you're a victim, he knows you didn't tell him the whole story. Especially after we discovered you'd visited The Cloisters earlier that day."

"Would seem suspicious, yeah." It's good to know Detective Gant is at least half-way decent at his job.

"I told him I'd check up on you. It was everything I could do to keep him from putting a detail on you." His eyes darted over to Stacey and Phil as they stood at the sink, his voice lowered. "Canton was identified."

"And?" I prompted after he paused.

"His wife reported him missing a few days ago." He lowered his voice further. "She said he left for work like he always did but never came home. That was Monday. Seems he's been planning this for a while."

"Yeah." I rolled over the possibilities in my mind. "Mrs. Canton give any indication why her husband would want to destroy New York City?"

"It wasn't considered as a topic for discussion at the time," Harper answered wryly. There was a clatter and we both snapped our heads up to see Stacey stowing away the pans in the oven where I usually kept them. The dishes were done. They didn't mess around, pun intended. "We're going to interview her again, Phil and I. Thought you might want to join us. We can also discuss our friend, Drake."

I nodded, finally figuring out what was bothering me about the lighthouse. "He's been lying to us."

"Phil said the exact same thing."

"Alright." It wasn't hard to come to a decision. I stood and called over to Stacey and Phil. "I have to go back to the police station."

"Want me to come with you?" Stacey asked as she wiped down the countertop.

I really wanted to make her feel included but, "No, it's okay. It's tedious and boring paperwork. I'll come over tomorrow after work and tell you all about it. Cure your insomnia."

"Right." She held on to the vowel like she might bludgeon me with it.

Seems to be a reoccurring theme.

THIRTEEN[13]

Harper politely offered to drop Stacey off, but she opted to take the subway instead. I don't think she was too happy with any of us. But at least this meant we could talk freely in Harper's car, not that we knew where to start. There was Canton and his plan to destroy Manhattan, Drake and his lie about there being no other dragons in New York, the claws on the lighthouse, and the seemingly random Goat-Grizzlies.

"The astral projection you did last night to find Ignatius," Phil asked as Harper pulled into traffic, "that won't work again, will it?"

"Already crossed my mind," I told him as I buckled up. I was sitting in the back because I failed to call shotgun. "I don't think it will work again. Before I was looking for a dual energy signature. That's gone now, and you can't track an aura."

Phil gave a thoughtful nod of his head. "Searching via magic might not be worth the effort. We can't even be sure Ignatius is still in New York state, let alone Manhattan. But if Canton is on the island, he would have doubled his security precautions by now."

"If I were him," Harper added, "I'd be halfway across the world."

"Probably not that far, but he could be anywhere in New England." Phil turned back to me. "You remember those claw marks on the top of the lighthouse?"

"Three!" I practically shouted as I finally figured out what was bothering me. "Ignatius had three clawed feet, just like what damaged the lighthouse. But Drake said his father was in human form from the moment he was summoned. Could Canton have had him switch to a dragon form then back to human again?"

"It would fall under the use of the binding spell, but it wouldn't change the fact that it takes time for a dragon to change into human form." There goes Phil, being all logical. "I'm not sure exactly how long it takes to cast the transformation spell, but I know it's never been recorded to have been less than a year."

Duh, I knew that. In the legend of the Copper Knight, it took several years before the dragon in the story became human again. Of course, that was a fairy-tale based on fact. I was never sure how much of it was true and how much was romanticism added later.

"So it's probably not the other dragon either," I mused.

Phil's head popped up. "What other dragon?"

"Did I not tell you about the other dragon?" I thought I told him about that, honest. But by the look on his face, nope, I had not. "When I was projecting, I saw three total dual energy signatures. One was Drake, one was Ignatius. I didn't check the third one. I kinda forgot to."

"Wait, wait, wait," Phil trailed off as the wheels turned in his head. "Three signatures means three human form dragons. Unless… Can you be sure the third one was a dragon?"

"I'm sure it was a dual aura, very powerful."

He sat back in his seat and stared out into the traffic as he thought this through out loud. "Okay, assuming the damage to the lighthouse was done by a dragon and not some other three clawed creature, then there are two other dragons in New York that aren't Drake and Ignatius. One is in human form and the other in natural form. Drake said there were no other dragons in this part of the US, let alone New York."

"That he knew of?" I defended Drake, which made me only a tad bit nauseous.

"Possible," Phil conceded. "How much can we actually trust a dragon?"

"I'm going to say at least slightly more than a vampire." I mean, I'm willing to give Drake the benefit of the doubt. Okay, now I really am going to be nauseous.

"Not helpful," Phil replied dryly.

"You're welcome."

Phil was not amused. I was. But not Phil.

Before it got too quiet, I asked, "Have you contacted any of the councils?"

"Yes, but they don't think it's an immediate threat." Pretty sure I heard gnashing of teeth.

I frowned because, really. "What part of a rogue wizard wanting to destroy the fabric of reality isn't a threat?"

"*Immediate* threat." Yep, there was definite gnashing. "Clint's obviously been working on this plan for some time before we went and ruined it. They think it'll be a while before he could attempt anything again, and they have other, *more pressing*, matters in the meantime."

I rarely ever doubted Phil's assessments of situations, but the council does have a good point. "Do we think he's still an immediate threat?"

Phil scratched at the back of his neck. "Well, Clint can't hope to hold Ignatius for much longer. The binding will eventually wear down or the dragon will find a way out of it. If Clint wants to finish what he started he won't, he can't, wait too long."

Okay, point served to Phil. "You think he'll risk it and go back to The Cloisters?"

"Maybe..."

I studied Phil's silhouette, taking note of the fine worry lines etched around his eyes. I'd seen the man afraid before, terrified even, and this wasn't that. This was something I only saw on rare occasion: guilt.

"Phil, how do you know Canton?"

There was a small pause before Phil admitted, "He came into the shop a few years ago. He was a third generation Forsaken looking to reawaken his abilities. I set him up with Johannes and left it at that."

Johannes Ketz is this old, retired wizard that I've only met a few times. In 1938 he immigrated from Germany to New York and because he was also wicked good at chemistry, he set up a chemist's shop. He sold everything from medicines, to herbals, to potions. The latter only if you knew how to ask. When technology advanced to the point of forcing him to detach from the modern world, he retired from the shop and took up teaching.

He was pretty darn good at it from what I've been told. Phil studied under him for a while, as did many of Eli's brood. But even though Johannes was able to slow down the ravages of age through the use of magic, he still aged, and finally decided to completely retire last year. Got himself a nice cabin up in the Catskills and, as far as I know, he's still kicking around.

"Didn't Johannes find teachers for all his current students when he retired?" I asked.

"He did." Phil pulled his sender out of his carrier bag and started to flip through it. "I sent him a message, and it looks like he hasn't gotten back to me yet."

"Welcome to Jersey," Harper casually intoned as we passed over the George Washington Bridge. I'll be honest, I kind of forgot he was there even though he was driving the car. I know, situational awareness skills, I haz none.

Realizing where we were, my heart sank just a little bit. I craned my neck out the window to see if I could get a glance at Jeffery's Hook. "I can't believe we almost let the Little Red Lighthouse get destroyed."

"We don't know why the demon attacked us," Phil tried to console me. "It could have been because we're wizards or because we happened to get there first. Better us than some trust worker who wouldn't have been able to defend themselves."

"When has reason and logic ever made anyone feel better?" I quickly snapped my head up and caught his eyes. "Don't answer that."

He chuckled and put his sender away.

I remembered a question I meant to ask. "Hey, how did Canton get away?"

"He disappeared."

"Like, got away from you disappeared, or puff of smoke disappeared?"

"Puff of smoke. Well, more like shimmer." Phil scrunched his face all up as he thought about it. "Clint got stuck at a dead end and cast some kind of transport spell. I'm betting it's of the same school as the bigger spell he was trying to cast."

Harper asked, "So he slipped into the Shadow Realm?"

"Probably."

"But?" I asked, knowing that tone.

"I'm not sure how he cast it so quickly, while running down the hall…" his voice trailed off, not a good sign.

"Well, he did bind an ancient gold dragon." The guy must have some skills.

"Clint hasn't been awakened long enough to have that kind of skill level built up."

"You sure?" Harper asked. "Sometimes people are just naturals, or really knock out that learning curve."

"I… suppose," Phil admitted after a moment. "It's either that, or Clint isn't working alone. I'm not sure which I should be more worried about."

Harper groaned. "I hate it when you say things like that."

"Me too." I am not a big fan of Phil being worried about anything.

The rest of the trip was spent in silence, but thankfully it only lasted a few minutes. As we pulled up to the Canton residence, I couldn't help but think how normal the whole place looked. No white picket fence, but the lawn was deftly manicured with a small bird pond on one side, moderately sized tree on the other. A compact car sat in the driveway and a bicycle leaned against the garage door. The house was a smaller two story, mid-sized family kind of place. No front porch, only a small overhang with wind chimes singing in the breeze.

"We're sure Canton isn't here?" I asked as Harper parked out front.

"Gant and I came by earlier and spoke with the wife." The detective gestured with his head to a non-descript blue car down the road. "Since then we've had surveillance on it. Canton hasn't showed up. I kinda doubt he will."

"Surveillance, great," I mumbled, trying to avoid looking directly at the car. Harper could get himself into a lot of trouble letting civilians in on the investigation.

Harper killed the engine and slipped off his belt. "And since Canton is suspected of both kidnapping and The Cloisters break in, we're fighting the Feds on this case."

"The Feds are involved?" I squeaked.

"Came in after you left." Harper twisted in his seat to look at us both. "They have a video copy of your statement, but they'll probably want to speak to you themselves, FYI."

Oh, yay, now he tells me.

I glanced back at the cop car. "Um, aren't they going to take note of us visiting? I don't think as the 'victim' I should be here."

"I got that covered." Phil produced a necklace from the depths of his satchel. It was a pretty simple chain cord with an engraved pendant of sterling silver hanging from it.

"Ooo!" I love playing with these things.

It's probably no surprise that illusions are a mainstay of a wizard's arsenal. They came in real handy for hiding from witch hunters back in the day. They're also really fun at parties.

The spell is simple enough: it changes the way light refracts off your body. Your eyes are brown because that's the spectrum that's reflected and seen by the other person. Tweak the laws of physics a little and suddenly everyone sees blue instead. You can also use light to change the angles of your face and shape of your body, kind of like how photographers can work wonders with the right lighting and camera lens.

Of course, the more you get away from your body shape, the harder is it to hold the illusion. If you make yourself look like you're a good foot taller than you are, then someone could put their hand through your fake body if they meant to put it on your shoulder.

The pendant Phil handed me contained a basic illusion; it only changes some colors and simple shapes of the face. All I had to do was put the necklace on and pour some magic into it.

"How do I look?" I asked once I felt that the spell had completed. I glanced down to see that both my copper foci bracelet and the melted mess on my other hand now looked like a pair of matching silver bangles.

"Not bad," Phil said appreciatively of the spell's handy work.

"Like a raven-haired Emma Stone," Harper added with a slight nod of his head.

"Raven-haired Emma Stone? Oh, I could have so much fun with this." I resisted the urge to giggle, mostly.

"Yeah, no." Phil frowned at me but I could see he was hiding a grin. "You want to annoy the paparazzi, you learn how to make one of those yourself."

I pouted and let out a very long sigh. "Killjoy."

Harper popped the door of his car. "I'm the only one who should be here, so let me do most of the talking."

I slipped the pendant under my blouse which had I matched to a nice jacket and trousers. I always wear jeans unless I have to dress professionally for work. I guess this counted.

I hopped out of the car as gracefully as possible. Harper took the lead as we walked up the short drive to the front of the house. It still felt normal, almost too normal, like it didn't quite have a soul.

Harper pressed the doorbell. About a minute passed before a tall slender lady in her fifties wearing a pea green dress greeted us without so much as a feigned smile.

"Detective Harper," Mrs. Canton spoke and the average mean temperature for New Jersey dropped unseasonably.

"Mrs. Canton, sorry to be asking this so late in the day, but I've brought two profilers with me." He gestured to Phil and I. "I'd like them to have a look around, maybe ask a few questions. We won't be much of an intrusion."

"I suppose if I say no you'll just come back with a warrant based on nonsensical leaps of logic." The words were sharp and bitter. Before Harper could say anything, she stood to the side like a guardian statue: stiff, stoic and menacing. "Let's get this over with."

Harper gave the 'lady's first' wave, so I stepped up to cross the threshold. I causally put my hand on the door frame, sensing out for any magical barriers. I could feel the energy of a warding spell flowing through the wooden frame easily enough. It was impossible for me to tell without stopping and concentrating on it if the ward was your basic anti-monster fare or a more complex anti-magic spell. I'm pretty sure Mrs. Canton would have gotten suspicious if I just stood there staring at the door frame for five minutes.

Should have brought Ryan.

Mentally bracing myself, I stepped past the threshold into the home. A surge of magical energy lashed out at me. It wasn't much, but it would be enough to knock a magic user on their ass and make them think twice. I absorbed the attack, channeling the energy through my aura to disperse it to the ground. This didn't stop an arc of electrical energy from sparking between the frame and my fingers.

"Fu-udge." I stopped myself from cursing in front of Mrs. Canton. Needed to maintain that air of professionalism.

"You okay?" Phil asked.

"Yeah, I'm fine." I shook my hand. "Just a little static."

Mrs. Canton showed me no sympathy and nearly slammed the door behind us once we were inside. She rounded on Harper, her anger visibly boiling over. "You come in here and tell me my missing husband is involved in some kind of kidnapping and destruction of private property? Are these two going to prove he's a terrorist, too?"

Harper glanced over at Phil. "Have a look around." He turned back to Mrs. Canton. "Ma'am, why don't we have a seat and discuss the situation again."

"Discuss, discuss." Her whole body shook. "He's a good man and you go accusing him of such indecency."

"I know this must be very hard on you right now." Harper was gentle as he led her into the living room. "You should really consider our advice on staying with your sister."

The rest of the conversation faded in and out as Phil and I were left in the entry hall.

"Well, she's not a witch," I said as we started our search.

"Don't think she's a Forsaken, either," Phil added. "Let's find an office or work room."

"Doubt he has a craft room," I mumbled to myself.

The first floor of the home seemed pretty benign. There was the kitchen, dining room, living room, breakfast nook. A smaller eight-by-twelve area in the back was set up like an office. Overstuffed bookcases lined against one wall, dozens of arranged photo frames hung on another. A prefab desk sat in the middle of the room with a big comfy chair. Two filing cabinets were shoved in a corner, stacks of papers and files littered everywhere.

"What does Canton do for a living?" I asked Phil as I flipped through a few of the papers on the desk.

"Investment trader, stock broker," he said as he ran his hand down the spines of the books. "Something like that."

"Then I think this is the wife's office." I held up a folder with a pamphlet for a swanky looking event hall paper-clipped to it. A guest list with phone numbers and notations were inside. "She's some kind of event coordinator?"

"I'm not sensing anything magical in here at all." Phil moved from the bookcase to take a gander at the photos hanging on the wall.

I flipped another set of files and sure enough there was a business card stapled to the top of a folder. "Sheryl Canton, Platinum City Events, Indoor, Outdoor, Charity, Weddings."

"Look at this." Phil called me over.

There was a collection of seven photos on the wall arranged with one central, the rest flanking. The center image was of the Cantons at a party, their glasses held high with genuine smiles plastered on their faces, blurry figures of guests in the background. It looked like they were in a living room, buffet table peeking in at one corner. French doors in the back were open to show a small garden lit up with lanterns.

"They look really happy," was all I could say.

"Yeah." Phil went quiet for a moment before pointing to one of the photos hanging lower on the wall. "That's the New York City skyline."

"So they used to live in New York?" And here I thought Canton's general dislike of Manhattan was because he was from Jersey.

I took a closer look. Each photo showed the Canton's at different parties held in the same house. The change of clothing and Sheryl's hairstyles meant the images were likely mid-80s to late 2000s, nothing newer than that. It was definitely a different house than the one they currently lived in. Something in me felt a great nostalgia and sadness towards the events in the photographs. I figured it was just me feeling homesick. It's been a while since I've been able to return to Nebraska.

Phil glanced between the images and the office. "I wonder why they moved here?"

"Yeah, who would want to move to Jersey." I couldn't help myself.

"You know what I mean." He frowned at me, not appreciating my lame joke. "Look around this house, it's not a place where people entertain."

Now that he got me thinking about it, I realized the house wasn't really set up for parties. The living room was scarce on seating and the kitchen was very utilitarian. "Maybe money problems? Economy isn't what it used to be."

"Yeah, maybe." I don't think he was all that convinced. "Clint was obviously a very happy man, full of life. Now he wants to destroy Manhattan and willing to go through great lengths to do so. You don't wake up one day like that."

"I think," and I should have said this earlier in the car, "that you're taking this way too personally."

He scoffed and averted his eyes.

"Hey." I grabbed his arm so he couldn't turn away from me. "You didn't do anything wrong. You got him set up, got him a teacher, there was nothing else for you to do."

"I should have noticed something." He shook his head, not having it. "Instead, I just sent him along, didn't even think twice about him afterwards."

"Oh, dear lord." I sighed and ran my hand over my face in

annoyance. "Look, you're right. Canton didn't wake up one day and decide he was going to open a rift to the Shadow Realm in hopes of taking out the City for no other reason than it seemed like a good idea at the time. His moves have been calculated from the start. You couldn't have known."

I doubted Phil really heard the words but it made me feel better to say them. Eventually he would realize none of this was his fault. He's the least guilty party in this mess.

"Let's check upstairs." Phil moved past me and ended the discussion.

We found another office on the second floor that was definitely Canton's if all the stock reports were any indication. There was nothing else interesting in the room, nothing magical or supernatural. There was also no electronic equipment of any kind. I imagine being a stock broker must have become difficult when he started to use his magic and his aura attracted more wild particles and static.

A search of the bathroom resulted in plenty of DNA laced items that would have been handy in doing a tracking spell. But considering he went to all the trouble to block daddy Drake, I wasn't going to hold out any hope that he wouldn't have blocked himself, either. Not after the fiasco at The Cloisters.

We found a ladder up to the attic, so guess who got to check out the small cramped space? I saw spider webs but no spiders, thank goodness, but they really should get a pest controller up there regardless. At least the basement was clean of creepy crawlies. Also anything remotely magical. I checked the tool shed in the backyard while Phil went out to the garage.

We were rapidly running out of places to look.

"I guess he kept his business and personal life separate," I said when we met up in the kitchen. If Canton had left any kind of grimoire or magical artifact, then one of us would have found it. These items are imbued with their own magical energies and of course energy is my thing. Phil is simply more knowledgeable and knows what to look for. Between us, you can run but you can't hide.

Yeah, I know, Canton has already done both successfully.

It was rhetorical.

Phil gestured towards the living room. "Then we need to find his sanctuary."

Harper sat on the sofa, talking with Mrs. Canton who sat in a chair. The woman stood abruptly when we approached. "Well?"

"I'm sorry ma'am," Phil said politely. "We can't discuss an ongoing investigation."

"Of course you can't." The words dripped with disgust. "My husband has been missing for almost a week and no one cared. Now you think he's some kind of criminal?" She started to pace in frustration and couldn't say as I blamed her. If Canton didn't share any of his plans with her then this all probably came out of left field.

"Mrs. Canton," I said softly as my subconscious nudged me. I had touched Canton's spell, and while it was now gone, it still left a small residue in my aura, like charred pieces of a burned photograph. "I need to ask you a few questions."

"Questions," she huffed. "More questions."

"Can I ask when and why you two moved from New York to New Jersey?" I had no real reason to know that this was important, but I felt like it was. I realized the sadness I had felt earlier wasn't my own feelings being projected. It was a subtle reaction to the little bit of Canton's magic I still carried.

Sheryl cleared her throat and looked away. The room became layered with an uncomfortable silence until she said, "We had a lovely little place. Smaller, yes, but with so much character and grace. I loved that home." The woman shook her head and slumped her shoulders. "Two years ago, Clint said we had to move. No rhyme, no reason, no argument. We had to leave."

Things started to make a little more sense. He moved to Jersey to get her out of the blast zone. Or at least that's what I made of the situation. Of course, that meant Canton thought he'd only be affecting Manhattan, and not the world. Maybe he knows something about the spell we don't. Or vice versa.

"He gave no reason at all?" Phil asked for clarification.

"No." She gave a soft, resigned chuckle. "But it was a long time coming. You see, Clint had worked for a brokerage in the

Walker-Tidwell Building."

"He was there, when it happened?" Harper asked and I was glad at least he knew what she was talking about. He later filled me in that the building experienced a rather horrendous gas explosion which nearly leveled the building. This was about ten years ago, before my time, but it must have been right before Canton came to Phil.

"It was only by luck that he was late that day," Mrs. Canton continued to explain. "The rest of his coworkers didn't make it. He was never quite the same after that."

"Did he seek help?" Harper asked, glancing over at us.

"He saw a therapist for a while." She threw her hands up in defeat, her voice coming out faster and ragged. "He kept saying he should have been dead. No matter what I told him, what anyone told him, he considered himself a walking corpse and slowly became one."

Quiet settled between us, no one sure how to respond to the candid revelations of a woman who long ago resigned herself to these events even if she wasn't sure on the specifics. Canton had… was suffering from what, in my non-professional opinion, was some mix of Survivor's Guilt and PTSD. That's hard enough for regular people to deal with. Throw in magic, and literally nothing makes sense anymore.

Harper was the first to find his voice, "Why didn't you tell us this before?"

Mrs. Canton sighed, a slight quiver to her voice. "When you came to my door, I thought it was to tell me he was dead. I was expecting that. I could handle that. But everything you told me, about The Cloisters and kidnapping that woman, I still don't know what to think."

"We'll do everything we can to find your husband," Harper promised her. "We'll get this figured out."

"Empty words," she muttered back. "Always empty."

Harper looked to us to see if we had anything else to add. I had nothing because my brain had done a literal reboot after this revelation.

"We'll show ourselves out," Phil said politely.

We got to the hallway and I couldn't hold it in anymore. I whispered to Phil, "He's not a crazy wizard. He's hurt, he needs serious help."

"He's still trying to destroy New York," Harper reminded me.

"But why?" Phil asked. "How did he make that leap?"

"Detective," Mrs. Canton called out as I opened the front door. "There's something else I didn't tell you."

"Yes?" Harper said as we all turned back to see her standing at the end of the hall.

"The old house…" She didn't seem a hundred percent confident she should be telling us this. "We moved, but we still have it."

"We did a background and financial check." Harper sounded like he was trying too hard not to be contrary. "It didn't come up under your holdings."

"We sold ownership to Porter-Lynn Real Estate, it's my brother-in-law's business," she explained. "He's doing us, me, a favor and holding it off market. I'm still paying the property taxes… I had hoped we'd move back."

"It's sitting empty?" Harper asked. "No one lives there?"

"Yes."

Harper kept his expression neutral and police-like. "Why are you only now volunteering this information?

"I was mad before," she admitted. "Clint had his troubles, but this… he couldn't be doing this. It has to be all wrong."

Sorry, lady. Something is very wrong, just not what you think.

"I'll keep an open mind," Harper promised her. "What's the address?"

"I'll write it down for you," she said and moved towards the kitchen. "It's off Saint Nicholas Avenue, in Washington Heights."

Okay, I admit, it wasn't until after Mrs. Canton gave us an address and the key that I put two and two together.

"This can't be a coincidence," I mumbled as we piled into Harper's car. I took the front this time so Phil would have room to go through his bag of magical goodies.

"No, it still could be," Harper said as he turned over the engine and threw the car into reverse. As he went to look over his shoulder, he must have caught my questionable glare. "The Cloisters and lighthouse aren't exactly secretive locations are they?"

"Fair," I conceded and buckled up.

"You know," Harper continued as the car rolled backwards, "some people don't believe in coincidences, others believe in them too much. I wish it were only as simple as one or the other."

"Okay." Phil wasn't listening to us. "How long until you have to report this new information?"

"A couple of hours?" Harper shrugged as he pulled out into the street. "Hopefully Gant hasn't stumbled onto it himself."

"Could he?" I mean, I've been arrested more times than I could count but my only real experience with detective work comes from watching reruns of *Elementary* and *Law and Order*.

"Gant's a smart man," Harper admitted. "He'll have it on a list of known addresses. He might have already checked it out."

"He wouldn't know what to look for," Phil pointed out.

"If anything is even there?" I said because if Harper was right about coincidences, then the house could be a red herring.

"Still, best lead we've had all day." Phil was cautiously optimistic.

I realized I was still wearing the illusion necklace. Slipping it off, I was back to looking like my old self. Phil was distracted so I pocketed it.

Oh shit, it's still sitting in my laundry. I should not put that through the washer.

Traffic back to Manhattan wasn't as bad as we feared, which was good because finding a new clue gave us a sense of urgency even though there wasn't any need for one. Let's be real, Canton couldn't hope to hold Ignatius spellbound for much longer, and once the dragon broke free he would roast the wizard at a nice four-hundred… thousand-ish degrees… Celsius? I don't know. Hot, really freaking hot.

We also threw a big wrench into his plan, so what could he hope to do now? Use his own Plan B? I hoped he didn't have one.

What? I can be optimistic, too.

"Okay, remember, you're not cops," Harper said as we filed out of the car about two doors down from the Canton's former address. The sun had dropped behind the skyline leaving a haze over the city that sent shadows across the street. "I still have to be able to explain anything actionable to Gant and the Captain, so try not to do something that will get me fired."

Harper grabbed a couple of flashlights and latex gloves from the trunk of his car. I slipped on the gloves but put my hands in my pockets. I didn't want to look conspicuous or anything. We walked down the sidewalk as if it was any other day, any other street, any other group of people. Across the way, a lady sat on the stoop of her house smoking a cigarette, glued to her phone. Otherwise the area was relatively quiet.

Casually we strolled up the steps, Harper on point. When he made a grunting sound that could easily be translated into 'that's not good', we all tensed.

"What is it," Phil asked over the man's shoulder.

"Door's ajar." Harper slowly unholstered his gun.

"Gant?" he questioned.

Harper did another scan of the street. "I don't see any police cars, marked or unmarked."

"Okay then." Phil slipped his blasting rod from his bag. "Left."

"Right," I quickly called dibs, sending energy to my foci.

"Guess I get center." Silently, Harper edged the door open, the hinge creaking too loudly for comfort. The detective raised his gun, sighting down the barrel.

A stairwell to the second floor dominated the entry hall, meaning there was no left, only up. Phil slowly took each step, blasting rod extended. Harper headed down the hallway to what I presumed would be the kitchen area at the back of the home. There was a large arched opening leading into an empty sitting area. I crept through it with one hand up, the electrical symbol glowing lightly on my bracelet.

The room was clear, but it opened into another. It was darker for the lack of windows, nearly pitch black. As I passed what little light was cast through the curtains from the street lamps, I swear I could hear each board creaking under my feet regardless if they made any sound. I took a deep breath and soldiered on, after all, I was a witch, a sorceress, I can control electrical current and I'm a lot tougher than I look.

Yeah, we'll go with that.

A tall shadow detached itself from the wall inside the room and approached me at a leisurely pace. I nearly panicked, but instead drew myself up to full height, reached out, and slapped the damned man square across the face.

"Ow!" Drake whimpered, very unbecoming of a dragon of his stature. "What the bloody hell was that for?"

"Oh, come on, seriously?" I snapped.

All he did was smirk at me, so I slapped him again.

FOURTEEN[14]

"Right." Drake squared his shoulders and seemed to grow half a foot taller. His golden eyes flickered like flames in the low light. "Strike me again, I dare you."

I brought my left hand up but he caught me at the wrist. His fingers wrapped tightly around my copper foci, warping it out of shape so it dug into the bone. I sent a charge through the bracelet, nothing too big, just enough of a buzz to let him know what I could do. Staring up at him, I did my damnedest to stare him down.

Irrational anger tore through me, a screaming wraith of my emotions. I wanted to believe this was Drakes fault, all of it. But truth is more insidious than fury. I'm the one who didn't tell Stacey about magic, and further screwed up the suggestion spell. I got myself arrested because I stayed behind to try to wake up the guard, which I failed to do. I even caused the blackout that likely led to my almost mugging at the beginning of all this.

It was my fault Marcel stormed out the way he did.

A line from the story of the Copper Knight echoed through me: *A good man is simply an evil one who's decided everyone else is as important as they are.*

Momma tried to tell me the Copper Knight was wrong, of course, but I'm not sure she believes that. Why would she keep the line in the story if a part of her didn't think it was true?

Harper came around the corner, gun drawn and trained on Drake.

"No, wait!" I nearly yelled at Harper who stopped but kept his gun up. "This is the dragon. This is Aiden Drake."

Drake released my wrist, saying, "I may have frightened the poor girl."

I gave Drake a very annoyed look, poor girl my left foot up

his ass. But the anger was starting to wash itself out of my system and I felt just a tad bit sick to my stomach. I worked on fixing my bracelet, letting the cold copper soothe my irritation.

"You're Drake, huh?" Harper asked, lowering his weapon only a little bit. "Thought you'd be taller and more intimidating."

"Hiding a false sense of bravado in humor is very tacky." Drake straightened the cuffs on his suit jacket. "And you are?"

Harper used his free hand to show his badge. "Detective Harper, 34th Precinct."

"Drake?" Phil said as he came into the room. "What are you doing here?"

"I imagine the same as you," Drake replied near casually.

"How'd you find this place?" Phil asked as Harper finally holstered his gun.

"I have my own resources," Drake answered as if we should have already known. We probably should have. I mean, if you have enough money and influence you can do anything you want, right? Isn't that the dream?

"Care to share?" Harper asked.

"No." Drake almost smiled as he said it, but then got down to business. "This house is a dead end. There are no signs of someone squatting here. Well, recently anyway."

"We'll be the judge of that." The bitterness in Phil's voice was likely a direct result of his anger over what happened at The Cloisters. Because of Drake's impatience, everything had gone from pretty darn bad to possibly apocalyptic on a good day.

While Drake's actions had pissed off Phil something royal, Drake didn't seem too fussed. Perhaps he also believed it was only a matter of time before Canton lost control and Ignatius broke free. It was certainly a valid expectation.

"Just wait here," Phil grumbled at the unflappable Drake. I figured Phil would want to confront him about the possibility of there being more dragons in New York. I guess he wanted to cool down first. It wasn't often I saw the man so frazzled, not that I fared much better. Man, there was just something about that house... It just got to you, you know?

"Waste of time but so be it." Drake sat down on the window seat with only a slightly undignified sigh. I wondered where his bodyguard was. Perhaps outside in one of the vehicles?

"Heading back upstairs," Phil called out as he disappeared around the corner.

Leaving Drake alone, I walked with Harper into the library, although books no longer lined the shelves. The room opened up to another larger dining area which I recognized from the photographs in their Jersey home. A small but adequate kitchen was off to the left and the downstairs toilet was under the stairs. Dark, finely finished woods and moldings lined every possible corner and edge.

"What a beautiful place." It took me a second to realize I'd said that out loud.

"Yeah." Harper opened every cabinet he could find, flashing his mag-lite into them. I wish I had thought to bring one but I usually use the flashlight app on my phone, which was still in pieces at Phil's.

I'm not sure I want to think about how many messages I'm going to have once I get that thing fixed. Though, you know, I'll probably just get a new one. Been meaning to upgrade it anyway. This seems like the perfect time for a change.

After opening up the refrigerator, which was turned off and empty except for a box of baking soda, I admitted, "I think Drake might be right. I'm not sensing any magical objects in this building at all."

Harper squatted down, checking under the sink. His dark features made him difficult to read in what little light there was. "It's as easy as that?"

"Sometimes." Well, really, "Most of the time, yeah. You have to actively hide magic otherwise it can be a beacon, or a buzzing, or a nudge."

"And if he's *actively* trying to hide it?"

"Then you *actively* try to find it." I tapped a finger against my temple. I'd been sensing out, looking, feeling, for any changes in the normal order of things. Sometimes even the absence of something can be an indicator of the presence of other magical items.

"Wait." Harper cocked his head to the side. "You've not been looking with your eyes all this time?"

"I, well…" Okay, he had me there. "I've been looking, you know, you can't not look." Yes, I am a genius.

"What if what you're looking for isn't magical?" Another very good question, you'd think this guy was paid to do this?

"Then I guess your eyes are as good as mine," I told him while trying not to shrug. "But I think anything he'd leave behind would have a magical signature."

"Everything?" he asked as he moved to check the cabinets above the sink, his flashlight reflecting shadows across the kitchen.

I leaned back against the counter and tried to think of an item that wouldn't show up against the backdrop of base energies. "Well, I mean, there's amulets, foci, wands, grimoires—"

"Grimoires," he interrupted me. "I've been meaning to ask someone. If they are basically just wizard journals, then why are they called grimoires?"

"It's a leftover word from another language?" I shrugged and went to check the pantry. "I honestly have no idea."

"Alright then." Harper chuckled, shaking his head. We had a few more nooks to examine, but everything was empty. Harper gestured to the last door and said, "You want to check out the basement with me?"

"Nah." I glanced around the dimly lit rooms, the home feeling small, hollow. "Phil will try there next when he's done upstairs. I think I'd rather check outside instead. Get some air."

"Alright." Harper moved past me without question and opened the basement door. He made his way slowly down and I could hear the creaking steps of the stairwell. The eerie sound did nothing to ease the tension of an empty home without a threshold. The building had been vacant for so long, I bet even vampires could stroll into it without so much as a stumble.

Through the open rooms I could see Drake sitting on the window seat. The light from his phone sharpened his features, making him appear more like the monster he was. I wondered idly again where his guard had gone off to, though Drake could obviously take care of himself. He's hella strong and can shoot dragon flames from his hand—that's pretty sweet. But it wasn't the napalm of the elder dragon, so did that mean Drake couldn't create napalm as a human? Or does he get to decide how to produce the flame? Curiosity bounded through my mind and I can see why Great-ish Uncle Gaerwen spent so much time learning about them.

Dragons are still jerks though.

Drake glanced up and it startled me.

Mom was right. It's rude to stare.

I nodded and turned towards the double doors leading outside, trying to play it off. The doors swung outwards, a light breeze gently pushing past as I made my way onto the patio. Making sure I wasn't going to lock myself out, I let the door close behind me.

The sun was already down but the temperature wasn't uncomfortable. Out there, the air was a little bit cleaner, a little crisper. The breeze continued and I could smell nature's distinct perfume from the rows of ivy climbing over the fence. The small stone patio jutted out then dropped three steps into a grassy area which was past due a trim. The small size of the yard worked to its advantage, making it all cozy and peaceful.

There was a toolshed in the far-right corner, but it proved to be empty save for some actual spiders and a possible nest of squirrels. Closing it up, I strolled around the fence line. I made note of the shorter discolored areas in the grass where a table, chairs, and a barbeque once adorned the lawn. I thought of the photos at the Canton's. There was so much happiness in this home. Joy, hopes, dreams.

I know Canton went through a traumatic event, but it just didn't make any sense to me. Why would he want to wipe Manhattan right off the map? Harper said in the car that typically these kind of negative emotions target inward, that they tend be more self-destructive.

But there is no one-size-fits-all for grief.

I plopped down on the patio steps gingerly as grogginess started to settle in. The stone was cool and gritty under my palms, even through the gloves. I leaned back on my elbows to stare up at the stars, or at least the voids where the stars should be. That's one of the few things I really miss about my parent's place. Back home you'd always find a nice clear, never-ending sky.

My jaw became unhinged as I let out a mighty yawn. The power nap I took earlier was wearing off. It also didn't help that I was now permeated with sadness over the whole situation. Canton wasn't the crazy lunatic I thought he was; he was ill. Crazy I could deal with, but this, this was totally outside my wheelhouse.

There was noise coming from inside. I looked over my shoulder to see Phil meeting Harper at the basement door. The two walked down the steps and disappeared into the darkness. Drake continued to sit at the window, phone in hand. I don't know if was texting or on the internet. Hell, he could have been on Tinder, which, you know, seems fitting for a fire dragon.

Another involuntary yawn caught me off guard, almost dislocating the bone. I sat straight up and stretched, trying to keep the sleepiness at bay. I took in deep breaths and that seemed to make it worse. The garden was so serene. It didn't matter that it was tucked between several other homes, or that the air was filled with the typical sounds of the City. There was this sense of peace, of finality.

My latex gloves felt sweaty so I tugged them off. I hunched over with a sigh, my temperament having gone from angered to melancholy in the space of half an hour. I thought of Stacey and what the dragon had done to her. It was a subtle spell, but it could have lasting effects. Marcel, ugh, I'd have to sort that one out later when I wasn't chasing a man intent on killing me. Well, not me personally, but it's implied since I live in Manhattan.

Of course, all my problems would be solved if New York City ended up being ripped to shreds as it merged with the Shadow Realm. That would make things a lot easier, wouldn't it?

Perhaps it's not such a bad idea.

A leaf flew past, catching on my shirt. I grabbed it and

tossed it back into the wind. It didn't even occur to me that I was starting to hear voices.

Empty, that's what I am right now. I should be dead.

I almost agreed with him and that snapped me out of my daze. I looked all around, twisting my body and whipping my head about. I was alone, except I could feel another presence, just as I could feel myself breathe.

People weren't meant to hold such power in their hands.

It's a curse.

The words were heavy, pushing down on my shoulders until I found myself laying back against the cold patio stone. I closed my eyes and listened to the unfamiliar voice. I was far too interested in what it had to say.

Maybe I'm dead and this is some kind of hell? No, not hell, purgatory. Stuck between worlds, stuck in apathy, unable to move from one to the other.

Wouldn't hell be better than this windowless world?

A second voice joined the conversation, this one like acid etched lead. Invisible forces pressed my head against the stone, slowly placing me in a vice. My pulse quickened. I had trouble catching my breath.

Paralyzed by fear, I was thrown to the floor. But it wasn't me, it was Canton. I felt his memory smother me. The floor cracked beneath us as shock waves propelled debris upwards. We didn't know what to do. Crawling across the floor, we could hear others, familiar voices calling out.

Exit, that's what we needed to find. We could see the exit lights through the haze. A glint of metal catches our eye, the wedding band glows softly against our skin. We're drawn to it… our grandfather's wedding ban.

Petrified. Frightened.

They did this to you.

Horrified. Scared.

We don't want to be here, we want to be with our wife. We twist the ring, not knowing why we do it. The world glows brightly and we fall into a shadow, my shadow. That's when we hear it:

Shadows are where it's safe.

Concrete, dirty and cracked, is where we land. Impossible. The street is full of people screaming, sirens blaring.

What are they looking at?

"*Oh, no*… no no no…"

"DOMINIQUE!"

"No, no…" Tears stream uncontrollably past my temples to gather in my hair. I want to sit up. I want to run, run away from the smoking remains of an office building.

There is no smoke.

My body was paralyzed with fear.

Not my fear.

"Snap out of it woman." Strong hands roughly pull me into a sitting position.

Reactively I lashed out, arms swinging wildly, trying to destroy something that isn't there. But it was there, *I saw the building burn. I was there.*

I wasn't sure of anything anymore, not even of who I was.

Clutching at the man's clothing, I doubled over and heaved, choking on my own nausea.

"What's going on here?" a panicked, angry voice joined the conversation.

"I believe she had an empathic episode," the first man answered.

"No." I shook my head, which made me even sicker. This wasn't right. My brother was the empath of the family, but I couldn't remember his name. I nearly screamed.

"Minni." The second voice was closer, squatting down next to me. "Remember who you are. Remember your name."

"I am *Clinton Christopher Canton*. No, *yes*, who are you?"

"Minni, look at me." He placed his hands on my neck to hold my head steady. The crying had stopped but there was still a glaze over my eyes. I could barely make out his features, but his voice sounded so familiar and I think that terrified me more. "What is your name? Tell me your name."

My mouth felt raw and dry as if I breathed in the smoke

from my hallucination.

"Dominique..." he prompted, and was that a touch of doubt in his eyes?

"Dominique." The word felt familiar to me, an old t-shirt worn a thousand times, always pronounced with a strong *o*.

"Dominique," Phil repeated the name again, following it with the soft *sh* sound I always used rather than the hard *ch*.

"Dominique... Channery..." I spoke the names, letting them wrap around me like a soft blanket on a cold night. "Katrina..." The nightmare started to fade away with every remembered syllable. "Mahala Gwendolyn Rhiamon Masterson."

My father named me. He won best two out of three in a game of rock, paper, scissors.

"God, Minni," Phil said as he let go of my neck. "That was a little close."

"Did that seriously just happen?" I asked as I started to get my motor functions back under control. I realized Drake was still holding me up, but my limbs felt like jelly so I was stuck in that position. Joy.

"You had an empathic episode," Phil stated the obvious as he pulled a bottle of water from his bag. "A dangerously uncontrolled one at that."

"Empathic episode?" Harper asked.

"Empathy is the ability to share another's feelings and emotions," Phil explained as he handed me the water. "Feelings can imprint on places if they're really strong or repeated enough."

"Yes," Drake agreed. I was finally able to extricate myself from him and sit up by myself. "Miss Masterson seems to have picked up on some emotions that Mr. Canton left behind."

"You said there was no magic here?" Harper asked, or at least it sounded like a question.

"It's not magic, it's physics," Phil explained as he checked my pulse and temperature. "Strong emotions, repetitive emotions, they're just another form of energy, and energy can neither be created nor destroyed. It has to go somewhere."

Drake stood, straightening out his suit. "Sometimes magic

can amplify emotions or make a wizard more susceptible to them. I'd say both Miss Masterson and Mr. McCree were being affected by whatever strong emotions Mr. Canton left behind."

Phil nearly glared at Drake, then blinked and shook his head. "You might be right. We were feeling out for magic, that could have opened the door for an empathic backlash."

"Could have?" Drake was very condescending, which was not appreciated, even if he was right.

"I touched Canton's spell at The Cloisters," I said between gulps of water. "He probably developed it here and left a trace of it."

"And as we know, you're a little siphon of wild energy." Drake gave me a smug grin and I had the strangest feeling he was hiding something beneath it. Man, I am paranoid.

I gave him a sour look, then noticed the red and white smudges down his pants legs. "Sorry for upchucking on you." I wasn't actually sorry for him, but he may have been wearing Armani and that's a real tragedy right there if it doesn't come out.

Drake didn't bother looking at the mess. "Did you at least gain us anything useful?"

I took another swig of water and gave myself time to sort out the haze of jumbled images that were disappearing into the white noise of my mental landscape. "He wasn't late."

"He wasn't what?" Harper asked.

"Work." I involuntary coughed at the memory of the smoke. "He made it to work on time; he wasn't late. He was there when the gas pipe exploded."

"Damn," Harper muttered and everyone got quiet for a moment. "How did he escape if none of his coworkers did?"

"Teleport." The word fell from my lips and I could feel the weight of the ring on my finger. "He triggered a teleportation spell that was on his grandfather's ring."

"That's right." Phil looked towards the house as he remembered. "When I met Clint, we figured out it was his grandfather who was the one who forsook, but late in life. He didn't mention a ring though."

"The ring could have been one of his grandfather's focus items," Drake suggested conversationally and I, unfortunately, was inclined to agree with the man again, ugh.

I replayed the memory in my mind, or at least what was left of it as it started to fade away. "Extreme emotional distress, that's how he triggered it. He wanted to be out of there. So he just fell through the shadows."

"Impressive."

"Extraordinary."

"Did what now?"

"Teleportation spell." Phil used his teaching voice. "It can be done several different ways, but all are tricky. The trickiest is also the most effective. Basically, you create a wormhole that bends the universe using the Shadow Realm as a conductive medium."

"Right." Harper stared at us blankly. "Of course."

"You fall through one shadow and come out of another," Drake interjected impatiently. "His grandfather must have developed a workable spell and inscribed it onto the ring."

"And because Clint is a blood relation, he was able to trigger it," Phil agreed with only slight annoyance. "And that also let him bypass any possible wards or traps."

"But he was still untrained." I shook my head, hoping that would speed up the process of the memories dissolving. "Canton had no direction, no control. He got out, that was it. He's lucky he got far enough out of the, um, blast zone?"

Drake made a 'tch' sound. "Well, this explains how he got away."

By the evil eye Phil gave Drake, he had some choice words for him since Drake was the one who messed up everything at The Cloisters. But instead, Phil stayed on point. "It also explains Clint's obsession with the Shadow Realm."

"There was something else." It was the only piece I tried to keep a hold of, but as typical it was the first to go. "There was another voice... I don't know if it was a person, or a demon, or magical, or what."

"What did it say?" Phil asked.

"It was supportive of Canton's plan to destroy the world, or Manhattan. I didn't really get any details though."

"This makes sense." Harper looked like he finally had a grasp on something. "If Canton is being coached or manipulated by an outside source, then that would explain his M.O. and why it doesn't track. Someone is using his grief as a rudder to push him in a direction they want him to go."

"Or some *thing*..." Drake added.

"Man, not helpful," Harper replied candidly.

"Canton needs psychiatric help," I said, knowing full well Canton would have been limited in his options. He couldn't rightly tell his therapist what really happened that day, that he magically fell through a shadow. They'd think he snapped and lost hold of reality, which he kind of did. But you can't fix something that's broke when you're only taking apart the undamaged gears. "Like *real* psychiatric help. Phil, isn't there someplace we could send him, people who know the truth?"

"Bellevue used to have a ward for magic-related cases, but they closed it down after the vampires were run out." I remember Phil telling me about all the people who had been attacked, saw something they shouldn't, or were otherwise affected by the vampires. They needed someplace to go where the doctors didn't think they were completely crazy. "I'll have to check around. It's been a long time since I dealt with someone who probably needs to be committed."

"This is all well and good." Drake seemed to be only a patient man when it suited him. "But at the moment, we're all missing the bigger picture here."

I was about to say something really snappy and clever but was stopped by the expression on the dragon's face. I'd seen that look before. "Goat-Grizzly?"

"Yes."

"Oh, for the love of..."

FIFTEEN[15]

"Goat what?" Harper was bemused; he didn't know to be scared.

I turned towards Drake as I stood. "Where's your bodyguard? And by bodyguard, I mean that iron sword of his."

"Running an errand." Drake gritted his teeth, his eyes darting around and hand twitching at his side.

"Someone want to fill me in?" Harper's voice suddenly took on an edge. He wasn't stupid. If two wizards and a dragon were taking a situation seriously, probably best you do, too.

"Know the damage to the Little Red Lighthouse?" I asked.

"I saw photos." Harper unholstered his gun. "The Feds have the place on lockdown."

"It was attacked by a shadow demon," Phil explained, rummaging through his bag. Wizards have a lot of tricks up their sleeves, but the problem is always being prepared and having your spells in place. "The creature wasn't fazed by my plasma bolts or Minni's electrical blasts."

A howl filled the air, our heads spinning around to locate the beast. The first two had hidden up high so I looked towards the roof. I also took the chance to get another dig at Drake. "We could really use that iron sword about now."

"Inside," Harper barked the order and we all complied. "Do you think if we made a run for the car that whatever this is would avoid being scene on the main street?"

"I'm honestly not sure," Phil admitted as he shut and locked the doors.

Drake messed with his phone. "The creature will either attack us now in public or hunt us down and attack us in seclusion, just as the second one did to Miss Masterson."

Harper turned sharply towards me. "Second one?"

"The first one showed up at the Little Red Lighthouse," I explained quickly. "A second one attacked me and Drake outside Paradiso a few hours later. So yeah, this weekend… Not been one of my best."

"Okay." Phil kneeled on the floor, tearing through his bag. "What we need to do-"

A blistering howl screeched through the building, causing windows to shudder and wood to creak. There was an undeniable thump as Goat-Grizzly the Third landed in the middle of the lawn.

"Drake." I turned to the dragon in a fit of déjà vu. "It may be too risky to use inside, but how does your magic stand up against shadow creatures?"

"It's a shadow creature?" Harper asked, though he didn't really wait for an answer before fiddling around with something on his belt.

"I don't know," Drake admitted… Wait, he actually admitted that. "In my dragon form I could easily tear it apart, but even dragonkin have issue with Shadow creatures. They are not from the same plane of existence. It makes things complicated."

Goat-Grizzly slowly approached his prey. The house would have bits of steel throughout its structure, but unlike the lighthouse, it wouldn't be enough to repel Grizzly completely. We could try running to the basement; that might work. Except the creature would probably bring the whole block down on our heads trying to get to us. Depends how dedicated it was to the job.

"I got this." Harper stepped forward, gun drawn and sighted on the monster. "Cover your ears."

I was about to say something about lead being useless, but I did not want to argue with the look on his face. Instead, I brought my palms up to try and block the noise of six consecutive shots ringing through the room. The first round broke the glass of the door. The second didn't look like it did anything more than annoy Goat-Grizzly, its mouth opening in a growl to show off his rows of shark-like teeth.

I know there's a reason I keep forgetting about the teeth.

As the third and fourth bullet struck the monster's torso it began to falter, the wounds not closing up as one would expect from a shadow demon. The last two shots sent Goat-Grizzly to the ground, heaving and shuddering like a wounded animal. For a moment I felt sorry for it. Then I remembered it wanted to eat me, or at least kill me, maybe in that order.

Another pitiful howl and Goat-Grizzly began to sizzle and melt into goo, staining the grass and stone where it laid and died.

"How in the world?" I muttered, the smell of spent ammo hanging heavy in the air.

Harper smiled and slid the magazine out for me to see. Three rounds left. They were regular copper jacketed bullets but with a flat tip where it looked as if someone had barreled into it, bits of grey peeling over the edges.

"Hollow points, they break apart on impact," Harper explained as he swapped the magazines and holstered his gun. "Instead of a lead core, these have iron."

"Ouch." I smiled approvingly.

Harper walked towards the broken door, getting a better look at the damage outside. "Best you all leave. Someone's called 911 by now for sure. I can explain myself being here but not you guys."

Most normal people don't believe in magic, so when they hear a mystical howl the first thing they're going to think is not 'wow, some magical shadow demon is on the prowl'. Instead, they write it off in their mind as something that makes more sense like an animal, a television, or the wind. Sometimes you consciously make this leap, other times your brain does it for you and you don't even realize you've heard the sound at all.

Gun shots, on the other hand, may go ignored but not unnoticed.

"There might be people watching outside." Phil pulled out a little jar that once held women's powdered makeup. It now contained a gritty green substance. "Invisibility dust, doesn't last more than five minutes though."

"Plenty of time." At least, I assumed so.

"How quaint." Drake's jaw tightened as if he was suppressing a smile.

"You got a better idea?" Phil asked, flicking a pinch of dust at me. The dragon slightly nodded in acquiescence and Phil threw some of the dust at him before dousing himself. "I saw an alley down the road as we came up. It's on our right going out. We head there and wait for the spell to wear off. All of us."

Drake gave another meaningful tilt of his head. I think he was trying to keep himself from laughing. If Phil noticed, he wisely ignored it and moved on. A few mumbled words later and both men disappeared.

The invisibility spell is related to the illusion spell I casted earlier in that it's all about refraction. During the casting phase, the dust activates and builds a reflective barrier around you where light bends, reflects, and refracts. Most of what is behind the invisible person is shown and any gaps are filled in by the human eye. And as anyone who wears glasses will attest to, there are more gaps in your vision than you will ever realize.

The spell powder is cheap and easy to make, but the effect doesn't last long. What it lacks in durability it makes up with quality. The worse that could happen is someone sees some kind of movement out of the corner of their eye. On the double-take, they'll see nothing and chalk it up to a natural phenomenon such as wind or ghosts. Depends on the person, really.

"Let's go," Phil's disembodied voice called out through the darkened room.

Thankfully, whoever developed the spell had the sense to make sure the invisible person could see themselves. I'm not quite sure if you're seeing through the spell or you're filling in the gaps with what you know should be there. After all, your body didn't just disappear leaving only a floating head. Subconsciously you have you realize this.

I didn't want to end up running into anyone, so I didn't rush and kept a few steps behind. The front door opened a little as if someone was checking outside for any complications. Seconds later, the door swung lazily open and I counted to five before attempting to go through. I figured it was Phil at the door and Drake wouldn't be very thoughtful about trying not to run me over.

Holding onto the rail, I slowly made my way down the steps. I noticed a couple of people across the street looking carefully through the blinds of their house. Had they thought anyone was on the street, they probably would have quickly disappeared. There are thin lines between being curious, being helpful, and not wanting to get involved.

I then allowed myself to hurry, one hand extended as a guide to keep myself from running into the others. The alley was farther than I thought it would be and a cop car came sailing down the road, siren blaring. I wasn't sure how Harper was going to play this off, but if the police decided to do a grid search before we could get away, well, we'd have a hell of a time explaining this one to the cops.

I'm already in the hole for being a kidnap victim and I know when to fold them. Ah, man, I'm sorry. Now I got that song stuck in my head, too.

I entered the alley and walked far enough in not to be seen casually from the road. Tempting as it was to call out, I found myself strangely timid. I've talked to myself on more than one occasion, but I seem to have a natural aversion to talking to empty space.

A little flash caught my eye and Phil became visible again as thousands of grains of reflective sand were seemingly being dumped over his head and spilling down. I lifted my hand to see the same dust fall from my fingertips. I gave an involuntary shake to rid myself of the spent spell components.

"Minni." There was a note of relief in Phil's voice as he caught sight of me, then his head whipped around both ways. "Drake?"

"Here," came the amused voice of the dragon as he stepped from behind a dumpster. Drake finally broke into a chuckle. "Invisibility dust."

"It's cheap, it stores well," Phil defended his use of the powder, which was truthfully more of a parlor trick than anything else. "It worked."

"Indeed it did." Drake was downright jovial now. I think Phil and I were missing an inside joke. "I suppose we should now walk to the road before we are deemed suspicious?"

I hate it when Drake has a point. Wordlessly, we went to the other end of the alley and casually stepped out onto the sidewalk. There were some sirens in the distance, but nothing that warranted our attention for the moment. There was a Dunkin' Donuts down the road. I almost suggested we all go there but Drake started talking.

"I'll call my car around." Drake pulled out his phone. "I suppose I can offer you a lift seeing as yours is currently occupied."

"How generous of you." I stressed the words and rolled my eyes.

"Why didn't you tell us there was another dragon in New York?" The question came so rapidly from Phil that it startled me. I snapped my head to look at him but he was watching Drake's reaction closely.

Drake went unnaturally still, holding his phone mid-air. He had already dialed a number. "Yes, sir. ... Mr. Drake?" I barely heard the voice on the other end as Drake continued to stare at Phil, every effort being made not to show any emotion.

Only moving his arm at the elbow, Drake lifted the phone to his ear. "I'm on the east side of the block. Bring the car around."

"Yes, sir," the driver was able to say before Drake cut the connection and slipped the phone into his jacket's breast pocket.

"Now." Drake fixed his lapels and buttoned his suit jacket. "What's this nonsense about another dragon?"

"We have evidence that at least one other dragon is operating in New York City right now." Phil bluffed. We only had suspicions at best. "You lied to us."

"Lying would require me to omit facts I was previously aware of." Drake spoke with all the smugness we've come to expect from him.

"There's so much here not adding up," Phil continued on, getting into Drake's face. "It should have taken Clint decades to progress to the level he's at; he had to have had help. Someone or some*thing* is keeping an eye on him, helping him by sending shadow creatures to cover his tracks."

"So you jump to the conclusion that this other dragon is involved?" Drake mused with a tilt of his brow. "Could be here on holiday."

Damnit, another point to Drake.

"Was it really random chance your dad was the one taken?" Phil asked sharply.

"I admit there is a possibility that my father was targeted specifically." By the tone of Drake's voice, I got the feeling he was understating things. I also wondered if Drake was once again imagining what our insides might look like on the outside.

"A possibility." Phil crossed his arms and gave the man his best disapproving glare. I think it's more effective against wayward wizards than annoying dragons. "Do you know of any other creatures that have dual auras or something similar?"

Drake glanced between us. When his eyes fell on me, I didn't get the feeling he was considering just how much fun eviscerating me would be. Instead he watched me, nothing quizzical, nothing comical, nothing patronizing. I think I preferred it better when he considered me a possible lunch snack.

"None that I know of," Drake said slowly, deliberately, the way you speak when you're pretty damn sure about something but that grain of doubt has wormed its way in.

I took him at his word. I'm not entirely sure why. It's not as if I suddenly got some mystical insight on the matter. It's... you know those times when you just know something in your gut, despite everything else? That's pretty much how I felt, and trust me, I checked. Drake didn't hit me with a suggestion spell. "Okay, I believe you."

"How reassuring." His disdain dripped back onto his face and I felt strangely comforted.

I tilted my head and stared blankly at him. "You know, I'm pretty sure I'm going to slap you again before all this is over."

Drake smiled. "I believe you."

"Going back to before," Phil interjected before we had a chance to do or say something stupid. "Why would your father be targeted? Other than the obvious."

Drake worked his jaw before answering. "You would think our kind would be above such pettiness."

"I suppose every race has to have at least one weakness." I meant it sarcastically, but it went right over Drake's head and I got a thoughtful nod from him.

"Dragonkin have their own hierarchy, one similar to that found in nature," Drake said the words as if his kind were outside the realm of the animal kingdom. "As I told you, gold is the ruling class, which presents its own issues. My father is one of the triumvirate. I'm sure you can figure it out from there."

"Okay, someone wants daddy Drake out of the picture cause he's the boss," I said as Drake's car pulled up to the curb. "But why go to all this trouble? Their plan could result in the destruction of the Shadow Realm or, hell, magic itself. The word 'overkill' comes to mind."

"A question worth asking," Drake acknowledged as a man hopped out of the car to open the passenger door. "Though the better line of inquiry you should be focusing on is what will Mr. Canton do with my father now that his first plan has failed?"

Drake slid into the back seat, the driver dutifully holding the door. As the man went to shut it, I grabbed the frame to stop him. "And while we're doing that? What about you?"

"I'll be figuring out if this is a coincidence." There was deadly mischief in his smile, as if he'd been wanting to do something for a long time and was simply waiting for a reason. "I'll be in touch."

Stepping back so the driver wouldn't hit me with the door, I grimaced. I'm sure Drake would contact us again, but that didn't make me feel any better about the whole situation.

"Well, crap," Phil muttered as the car sped away.

"That about sums up the situation," I agreed.

"Well, that." He adjusted his bag on his shoulder. "And we just lost our ride."

I looked down the street, Drake's car disappearing around a corner.

"Nuts."

SIXTEEN[16]

We decided to head to my apartment first because it was closer and, to be perfectly honest, neither of us really knew what to do next. There were a few options for trying to track down Canton but none with more than a snowballs chance.

While Phil borrowed my desk computer, I searched for something to cut off the melted bracelets. I was having no luck when there was a knock at the door.

"Kinda late for a visitor," Phil said, not so subtly reaching for his bag.

"Could be Harper, or maybe Drake?" I headed over to the door, forever the optimist. I mean, the only person it couldn't have been was Stacey. She would have just let herself in.

For a moment I thought it might be Marcel, and the thought terrified me as much as I wanted it to be true.

The peephole revealed my visitor to be a woman, middle aged, dark hair pulled back, a very serious expression on her face.

"Who is it?" I said loudly enough to be heard.

"Agent Ross, FBI." She flashed a badge. "I need a few words with you, Miss Masterson."

Well, Harper did warn me this might happen. But… "Isn't it kind of late, Agent Ross?"

"I tried calling," she replied flatly. "I spoke to Detective Harper, he assured me you'd be home."

I was paranoid, but that's hardly new. Nothing felt off to me so I undid the dead bolt, keeping the chain latched so I could open the door a crack. "Badge, please," I said semi-nicely. The woman, probably early forties now that I had a better look, slid her ID into my hand. It seemed legit to me and I do have some experience in the matter.

"Come on in," I said after slipping off the chain and swinging the door open wide.

"Thank you." Ross nodded politely, striding in swiftly, posture straight, eyes taking in everything. I noticed she carried a gun but made no movements towards it, nor tried to hide it. All part of the uniform.

"It really is late." I used my best tired voice as I handed her back the badge. "I don't know anything more than I told the police."

The woman smiled and sighed as if I was a child who had yet to figure out the square peg goes in the square hole. "Perhaps getting straight to the point is best for everyone, Miss Masterson."

"Okay," I said cautiously.

"You're a witch," she stated matter-of-fact. "And you were decidedly not kidnapped."

"I beg your pardon?" I managed to keep a straight face, though I'm not sure how.

"I'm a second generation Forsaken," she continued impatiently with a smattering of annoyance. "My mother decided to forsake when she was a teenager. Been tempted to reclaim my heritage, but being an FBI agent has its perks."

A quick check of Ross's aura confirmed that she was indeed, a Forsaken.

"What do you want?" Phil asked only moderately politely.

She turned halfway to him and smiled. "What we both want, Mr. McCree."

"I want a billion dollars and Anthony Mackie." I really do, Marcel knows this and he's okay with it. "Somehow I don't think that's what you meant."

That garnered a chuckle from the agent. "Yes, well, what I want is a bit less… fanciful."

"Got my attention, shoot." Perhaps not the best turn of phrase when the other person is packing heat.

"I have two magical crime scenes on my hands." She either didn't get the joke or was ignoring it. Happens a lot around me. "Your fingerprints all over both scenes. I do mean that literally."

"We are not responsible for the vandalism." Phil was quick to assure.

"Oh, I know." Ross waved him off and started to walk around a bit. "I've checked you two out. You're janitors. You and your little coven, if you can even call it that, clean up messes, though I think this time the floor got mopped with you."

I guess when you put it that way, we are janitors. We're always cleaning up what the high-and-mighty wizard councils can't be bothered with. Normally we do a pretty good job of it, too. We've had a couple of really off days.

"How do you know about us?" Phil asked.

"I work for the FBI," she answered wryly. "Most of my colleagues are in the dark about magic. I've been tasked with the job of keeping it that way."

"So, are you Mulder or Scully?" I really need to stop antagonizing people I've just met. It's not healthy.

"Is that why you're here?" Phil asked the more pertinent question.

"Yes." Ross paused for a moment before continuing. "I can make both of your involvements in the lighthouse completely disappear. But you," she looked straight at me, "are far too involved in The Cloisters case. All I can do is make sure Mr. McCree here doesn't come up as a person of interest in the FBI's investigation."

"What do you want in return?" I asked.

Ross sat down on my sofa, making herself comfortable without even asking. "First, tell me everything you know about the two incidents."

I'm not really a fan of open ended requests. They rarely end well. "How do we know that you'll do what's best for the victims in all this?"

"What victims?" She tilted her head slightly. "There's you, Jeffery's Hook Lighthouse, and the Cloisters. Oh, there's the guard in the coma but there's nothing I can do about him."

I was about to point out the actual kidnap victim, Ignatius, but stopped myself. The dragon could take care of itself once we freed him. He wasn't who I was more worried about. "The wizard that caused all this, he's a victim here, too."

"Is he now?" That got a lifted eyebrow and smattering of emotion from the Fed.

"Yes," Phil supported me. "Clint is performing magic he shouldn't be able to. There's a possibility he's being coached."

"By whom?" Ross didn't question the other parts. That had to be a good sign, or a really *really* bad one.

"Not sure yet." I was honest with her. "But we have good reason to believe someone is helping him."

"That doesn't mean he isn't a full and willing party to his actions." Ross pointed out.

"It is if they went to Canton when he was vulnerable and manipulated him."

Ross was having none of it. "One way or another, Mr. Canton needs to be stopped from causing further damage. I need something to take to my bosses."

"We thought about putting him in an institution." Okay, so I thought about it. The others kind of nodded before getting distracted by Goat-Grizzly the Third.

Ross frowned. "An institution?"

"Yes," Phil spoke up. It was good to know he was in my camp after all. "We believe he's suffering from a type of PTSD coupled with the usual stress and perception crisis that comes with learning you're a magic user."

"PTSD?" Ross questioned, glancing between us.

"He almost died in a building fire a few years ago," Phil explained.

"Right, that was in his file." Ross crinkled her brow in thought. "That doesn't explain why he's going around destroying local landmarks."

"Which is why he needs help." I almost added a 'duh' onto that statement.

Ross regarded me for a moment. "Well, if you think he's a puppet, then there has to be a puppet master. I admit I'd rather bring that person in instead, if it's a person."

"We don't have all the facts yet," Phil told her, begrudgingly. "But we do know Clint is being manipulated. We'll find out who's doing it."

"I see," was all she said.

"Please." I didn't want to plead, but the last thing we needed was for this to be taken out of our control. "Give us time to clean up the mess like the janitors we are."

She crossed her arms, unmoved. "And what do I tell my bosses?"

"Whatever you need to." I mean really, I'm not going to do your entire job for you. "Let us deal with Canton and we'll make sure you're able to close the case."

Ross studied both of us for a moment, her eyes sliding back and forth. Eventually she put her hands on her knees and stood. "Fine. I can only give you a day or so. After that, well, someone is going to get the short end of the stick."

"Understood." Barely veiled threats never seem to go out of style.

"Good." She held out her business card. "When you have something, give me a call."

I took it with a slightly sarcastic smile, then showed the woman out.

"You got a plan?" Phil asked.

"Of course not." I tossed the card onto the coffee table. "Was hoping you did."

Phil started to rub his forehead.

"Johannes ever reply to your send?"

"Ah, good question." Phil pulled his satchel from the floor next to the computer desk where he had dropped it.

That's when a thought struck me. If Agent Ross had been looking into my background, her search could have gotten back to my folks. Magicians are too paranoid not to keep track of such things, governmental enquiry and rumor spreads quickly among us. I grabbed my sender from where I left it on the island. Skipping through the pages, I came to the last received entry.

Minni, we've been hearing the FBI has been looking into you today and the NYC blackout was magic related. Are you okay? –Dad

Yep, thought so. I grabbed a pen to send a reply.

Dad, the blackout was the result of magic, some funky stuff has been going on. Don't worry, me and Phil are looking into it. Tell everyone Hi for me. – Minni

No point in worrying him about events outside his control. I held my hand flat to the paper and sent the message across the ether towards the intended recipient. A slight glow hummed against the words then died away slowly.

"Everything okay?" Phil walked over, keeping a distance that equated to 'I'm being nosy but respectful at the same time.'

"Yeah." I shrugged and left the book open in case I got an immediate reply.

"Johannes sent word." His tone was neither hopeful nor anxious. "He said Clint left his schooling before he retired." Phil lifted his own sending journal to quote it. "*'Clint came to me and said he found a teacher who was more specialized in the type of magic he wanted to learn. I advised him best I could, warned him about possible scams and charlatans, but he thanked me for teaching him the basics and went on his way.'* So the question is, did this other teacher approach Clint or did Clint approach them?"

"From what I gathered through that empathy episode, the voice approached him." Not exactly evidence that could be used in court or anything. "It would help if we had an idea who, or what, this teacher was. Or if these two people are even the same."

"Johannes doesn't know." Phil snapped his sender shut and held it in both hands, subconsciously strangling it.

"Okay." I took a deep breath, trying to rev myself up. "Where do we start looking for the next clues?"

"You don't." Phil started shoving stuff back into his bag. "It's late and we're both exhausted. You have work tomorrow—"

"Ah, rogue wizard on the loose," I interrupted him. "I think I'll take a sick day. And come on, you're just going to go home and start flipping through books."

"Yeah, but I haven't thrice battled a shadow demon, absorbed draconic magic, astral projected, been arrested, sucked into an empathy mergence, and… I'm forgetting a few things here." Phil put his hand on my shoulder. "I know you have more energy reserves than the average wizard, but even you need to rest."

I really hate it when he's right. "Call me if you find anything?" And that's when I remembered my phone was still in pieces on his bathroom sink. "Damn."

Phil chuckled and grabbed his stuff from the table. "If I find anything, I'll send."

"You better," I said as he slugged his bag over his shoulder.

I drained Phil's static then he bid his farewell, heading out into the night, leaving me to attempt to get some sleep. I wasn't sure I was ready for that yet. I'd let too many things fall to the wayside, like laundry. I started a new load, then headed back into the kitchen to check on my sender. I found a message waiting for me.

Minni, We're getting reports out of New York of some strange stuff happening. Ritual scenes, shadow demons running loose, it all sounds very worrisome. You stay safe and let us know if you need anything. Love you, Mom

I suppose I could have asked my family for advice, but it seemed fruitless. We couldn't even be sure Canton was still in New York. If I was him, and I didn't have a Plan B, I would want to put as much distance between Ignatius and myself before the dragon broke free of the binding.

Mom, Don't worry, the worse is over, a lot of clean up now, damage control. I'll give you a call next week and tell you all about it. Love you too, Minni

I sent the message to my mom knowing she'd still worry anyway. Nothing I could do about that, either.

I put on the news and there was another update about the lighthouse. A community action project had already been put together to get it fixed up. Canton's name and driver's license photo was shown again in conjunction with the vandalism at The Cloisters. They were calling it some kind of civil disobedience thing—that was the story my new friend Ross was going with. I suppose Canton was a bit too old and white to be a gangbanger or terrorist.

I sighed and sunk farther into the sofa. Canton, Drake, Stacey, Ross, Marcel… the whole situation was a mess. There had to be some way I could fix things. Put it all back the way it's supposed to be.

The news rolled into sports and I was done for the night. I couldn't find anything to remove the melted bracelets that were *still* stuck on my wrist, so I changed for bed and put my sender on the night stand. If I got a message it would glow and hopefully wake me up. Failing that, Phil has a key to my apartment; he's just more judicious with it than Stacey.

It wasn't long before sleep overtook me, a bit gentler this time. I was sure I snored as I slept, tossing and turning when it became too painful to sleep on my bruised backside. My new fashion accessory didn't help matters much either.

What is one of the most pitiful looking things in nature?

A crushed sunflower.

It just doesn't look *right*, you know?

But that's what happens when there's a struggle between two people. They tend to lose any regard for the world around them. They are much too involved with killing, or trying not to be killed, to be respectful of their surroundings.

The newly opened area in the sunflower field wasn't terribly big, but it was enough to allow the light of the harvest moon to glower down on them through the thinning rain clouds. David lay on his back, his body wet and matted with blood. In the low light it resembled some kind of black alien goo trying to invade his body.

Lording over him was the guy from the diner, blood stained and angry. My brother was lying near-dead on the ground and that man had put him there.

His eyes darted to his weapon of choice, an aluminum baseball bat, once blue and green, now streaked with blood. It lay between us where the man had dropped it to go check on David's life expectancy. By the scowl on his face, it seemed he'd have no quarrel with adding me to the list of Masterson's dead at his hand.

Now, I'm a wizard—no, I'm a *witch*.

I was born with *magic* in my *blood*.

The *laws of physics* might as well be *guidelines*.

I could bend the elements of this world and reign down the *righteous fury* of *hell and brimstone* onto the pitiful creature who dared laid a finger on my kin.

So what did I do?

I dropped into a dead run, snatching up the baseball bat before he could reach it, and swung it with all the might of a country-grown Nebraskan.

Suck it, bitch.

SEVENTEEN[17]

At some ungodly hour I stumbled into the bathroom. No fireworks this time. Making a round trip, I grabbed a bottle of water from the fridge before heading back. I downed at least half of it before setting it next to the sender. No messages. I guess Phil was still at a loss, or passed out at his desk drooling on some seventeenth century codex.

Wouldn't be the first time.

As I sat down on the bed, I wanted to grab the covers and curl into another ball. But sleep wasn't going to make my problems go away. I supposed I could have messaged Marcel on the desktop computer, asked him to come over or something. Maybe we could work things out?

I could fix things with him, put it all back the way it's supposed to be.

The way it should be…

"Ho, damn," I said out loud once I realized my thoughts weren't entirely my own.

Okay, legitimate question here: Why are all my best ideas extremely dangerous and stupid?

I picked up the sender but I didn't bring a pen with me. By the time I snagged one from the living room, I realized there was no way Phil would let me do what I was planning. He'd say the risk didn't outweigh the reward, perhaps in a more stylish and less cliché way. He'd also be right, of course, but he couldn't try to stop me if he didn't know what I was doing.

Forgoing sending a message, I decided to just do it.

Needing supplies for my spell, I snagged a photo album from the coffee table. The first several pages were taken at different family gatherings, reunions, and ceremonies. The next images were from my time spent at Purdue. Eventually it showed me in New York City, going on all the various adventures Stacey dragged me into. She never quite understood why I find hard copy photos so interesting. I just like things I can touch, that I can feel, you know?

My New York driver's license sat on the island, it only reads Dominique Channery Masterson. I picked it up, then went to the bookcase to grab a wooden box which held a few personal items and trinkets of sentimental value. If my plan was to succeed, I needed a baseline for reality. I'd recently renewed my renter's insurance, so I grabbed the envelope with the paperwork.

All this tucked under an arm, I went back to the bedroom. I straightened the crumpled blanket to sit down dead-center of the bed. I checked the sender to see if maybe Phil had come up with something in the ten minutes since last I checked, but no, nothing.

Systematically, I laid everything out around me. I selected specific photos from the album and grouped them so I could see all the familiar faces. The renewal notice and driver license were towards my feet. I took the trinkets out of the box and laid them randomly about: a ticket stub, a string of beads, a postcard.

It would have been better to have someone there with me, just in case, but I didn't want anyone to talk some sense into me. I laid back against the pillows, closed my eyes, and took slow, even breaths, relaxing my muscles and letting the stress of the day melt away. I began to pull myself out of my body to astral project, not quite letting go of the tether. I needed one last component. In the shadows of my mind still lay the trace of memories and emotions of Clinton Canton.

I scratched at them, dug what I could from the crevices, and held them close. Then fully cut the connection to my body. I was left to stare down at myself with nothing but Canton's thoughts to keep me company.

I was trying to use the remnants of the empathy mergence to either locate Canton, or find some clue as to where he might be. Of course, this meant attempting a controlled empathy mergence. Slightly less dangerous than an uncontrolled one...

Slightly.

Words echoed in my head, voiced deep in the emotions of a broken man. He just wanted to fix everything, put it all back the way it was supposed to be. But he was looking at a twisted and warped image, distorted in his grief and anger, washed in lies and manipulations.

I listened to him, the linger shadow of this thoughts, as I drifted throughout the astral plane. I let them be a dowsing rod, pulling me along through the world. I passed through the walls of my bedroom into the night air. I hung in the darkness of the alley for a moment, listening.

The voice got louder, morphing from a whisper to a static voice on the end of an AM radio. It was the same mantra:

I can fix this.

He repeated it over and over again. I wasn't sure if he was trying to make himself believe it, or if it had simply been the last thread of hope he could hold on to. Somewhere in the white noise was another voice I could barely make out. It's only familiarity being that I'd heard it before, at Canton's old house.

If you destroy magic, then everything will go back to the way it was. The way it's supposed to be, it told Canton, and you almost wanted to believe it. It felt so… confident, and sure.

Won't that destroy the world, or at least Manhattan? I asked the voice but it wasn't talking to me. It wasn't listening to me. I knew that, but for a moment I forgot.

I know what I have to do. I could hear Canton so clearly now, as if he was speaking in my head. *It's risky, but it will work.*

What's risky? I asked and his thoughts answered me.

I became overrun with a sense of knowing. Canton was at his cousin's design studio on 37th and 8th. I knew what spells he was preparing to cast. The few remnants of Canton's memories had latched on to their rightful owner. They created a linked chain that dragged me into the depths of his subconscious.

I was drowning, caught in the current of an emptying spillway of emotions.

My eyes flitted open.

I sat up as if I'd been held against a crushing wave that

vanished but had left me under water. My head spun left and right, taking in the scene around me.

I didn't recognize where I was.

The crinkling of paper drew my attention to the items once dotted around my body, now tossed sideways or stuck against my sweaty skin. A license clung to a leg.

"Dominique," I whispered the word but it didn't feel right.

I picked up a photograph taken at Coney Island. Two women were laughing into a phone raised above their heads to capture them both. I tossed the picture aside, feeling that it should mean something to me but I couldn't understand why.

Papers, cards, and trinkets slid around, trapping me on the bed. I kicked and swept, knocking much of it to the floor. I felt a pang of remorse as a postcard folded under the weight of my body. I grabbed it, desperately trying to ease the crease out of the thick card, unsure why that was important. The front image was a collage of landmarks, but it was the single word written on the back in felt-tip pen that caught my attention: *Peek-a-boo.*

"I see you," I whispered. The words made me feel warm and happy and frightened, and I didn't know why.

A glimmer caught my attention and I turned to the headboard, panels of copper shining dimly. I had bought it at an auction. I felt awful about outbidding an old lady, but I wanted it so badly. There was a crazy moment of bouncing back and forth between bids. I hadn't even noticed how high the price had gotten. Stacey took one look at it and told me I was insane.

I remembered.

I placed the flat of my hand against the cold metal, catching my warped image in the reflection. Memories of my mother's voice spoke softly to me, telling me the history of the Copper Knight, loyal and true. He made a mistake, but he ended up doing what was right.

How did mom always end the story?

"He waited for her."

My pulse and breathing quickened, and from all outward appearances I was having a panic attack. I suppose I was.

"Dominique Channery Katrina Mahala Gwendolyn Rhiamon Masterson," I shouted the words, pressing my forehead against the copper.

Not Clinton Canton.

This time I took Canton's emotions and lit them on fire. Burned them to the ground and salted the ashes so they could never take root again. Then I washed it all away in a flood of my own self-loathing. I laid crying on the bed for too many reasons to count.

I blew a breaker, but this time the blackout was contained to my apartment.

The spell wasn't the smartest thing I'd ever done, but not the stupidest. It did garner me the address of where Canton was hiding, so I think I did all right. But he was in the Garment District, and magic doesn't exactly run in leaps and bounds in that area, well literally speaking anyway. This meant Canton was going to need a powerful source of energy if he wanted to complete his spell.

He needed more than a dragon performing magic... He needed a dragon's magic.

When I regained most of my function, I grabbed the sender. *Phil, yell at me later but I used empathy to locate Canton. He's at 37th and 8th. Gather Vivian, Ryan, & Harper if you can, and pick me up, we don't have much time. He's going to perform a Rasputin. - Minni*

First I fixed the breaker, then I began straightening up all the loose papers and items I had knocked about. I put them away as I waited for Phil's response and for my own self to completely calm the hell the down. I noticed a few mementos had gotten damaged. I hope this will all be worth it in the long run.

Phil's return note appeared in haphazard script.

Minni, on phone to Harper, he'll pick you up. Good work, crazy and stupid, but good work. – Phil

Phil, Meet you there. We have until dawn. – Minni

I checked the clock. Four in the morning. It was plenty of time to stop Canton from making a huge mistake. Of course, that does nothing to stop me from making my own bad decisions.

Aiden Drake, CEO of Pennington-Kettering Enterprises. Your father is in the Garment District, but I won't tell you which building until

I get there. You could go barging through all of them, but you'd probably tip Canton off and it would be The Cloisters all over again. Wait for me. That isn't a request. – Dominique Masterson

I placed my hand over the message, pausing as I reconsidered letting the dragon in on this. He was arrogant and impulsive, but not completely stupid. If he learned his lesson from last time, or uncovered anything useful in the interim, then maybe he'd actually turn out to be an asset rather than a hindrance.

And I didn't fancy the notion of having to deal with an enraged ancient gold dragon who might be having difficulty understanding that we're friend, not food.

Sending a message to someone who you either don't know, or don't know well enough to have had access to their particular symbols, can be a little challenging. I brought up Drake's image in my mind, both his human and dragon forms. I focused on these images as I cast the spell, willing the words to him and him alone. Hopefully he would have a sending journal nearby and that would catch it; if not, it would appear on any writable surface.

I then got dressed in jeans, a faded Purdue t-shirt—I have a zillion of them—and a sensible pair of sneakers. I still had that mangled mess of melted bracelet on my other wrist but I'd just have to deal with it. I grabbed a bottle of water and a protein bar, and I was good to go.

Waiting outside my building for Harper, it wasn't long before the detective pulled up and I quickly slipped inside.

"37th and 8th?" he asked for confirmation as I buckled up. I gave him a mumbled yes and he pulled out into the road. "Phil didn't tell me everything, but he said you did something incredibly stupid in order to get this information."

"It was… a calculated risk." Yeah, that sounds respectable.

"Sure it was." He didn't believe me. Can't say I blame him.

As he drove, I filled him in on how you use empathy and astral projection in order to locate the person attached to the emotions. It's not an easy spell, being as you need the actual emotions first, which usually aren't left lying around like Canton's were. Also, it invites the foreign thoughts and personality to take over the wizard performing the spell.

I had everything under control.

I did!

It wasn't long before we got to the intersection. Harper pulled over in front of a tourist gift shop. Turning off the lights and engine, the world went silent around us.

"What's a Rasputin?" he asked.

"Excuse me?" I was watching a random person hurrying down the sidewalk.

"Phil mentioned something about Rasputin." Harper leaned back in his seat, one hand on the steering wheel, relaxed despite everything. "Rasputin, as in crazy Russian cult leader or coincidence?"

"Not a coincidence." The story of Rasputin and his rise to power was something I had actually paid attention too in my magic classes. "Rasputin was a wizard and a master at a Black List spell called *auric transfer and redirection* which is a long ass name so everyone calls it a Rasputin."

"And this auric transfer spell?" He pushed for more answers. Not that I could blame him for that, but I really wished we could just sit there in awkward silence instead.

"Basically, you steal a person's aura and therefore their magic." Which is as bad as it sounds. "Once you take it, you have the option of transferring the energy to your own aura, but you lose a lot of potency doing that. It still increases your magical ability, though."

"Other option?"

"You can redirect it." I paused to settle on my words. "You take the pure, raw, magical energy and use it as fuel. Make the spell bigger, or more powerful, or both."

"Oh, like the overpowerment spell Canton used?" He caught the connection before I did.

"Yes and no." I gazed into the side mirror, looking down the street into the semi-darkness. "The idea is the same, but an auric redirect is much more powerful. The increase in the strength of your spell is directly proportional to the strength of the magical being it came from. Magic users can study all their lives and never be able to unlock the full potential of their magic. There is almost nothing stronger than the pure auric energy of even the weakest of wizards. If the overpowerment spell is a bottle rocket then an auric redirect would be a heat-seeking bunker-busting missile. A thousand of them if it comes from someone as powerful as a gold dragon."

"But I thought the aura couldn't be broken?"

"It can't." I chewed on my lip, turning back to look at him. "It's an all or nothing kind of spell. You can't break the aura or the willpower attached to it, so it just becomes a supplement to your own. Less of an extension of your power and more like a sack of potatoes you can carry around and lob at people. You really have to know what you're doing with the spell or else *whoosh*." I made a mushroom cloud with my hands. "You burn yourself up."

"Sounds dangerous." Master of understatement there.

"As far as I can remember, Rasputin only ever used the spell to increase his power. That's how he was pretty impossible to kill."

"Canton's going to transfer the dragon's magic to himself," Harper realized. "That way he'd be strong enough to perform the original spell?"

If only.

"No." I shook my head and wished what I knew wasn't true. "Even Ignatius on his own wouldn't be able to perform the spell Canton wants. That's why they were at The Cloisters, they had all that extra magic at their disposal."

"Oh, but if Canton has the dragon's aura as the fuel, in place of The Cloisters…"

"He'll be able to use it to power his spell," I finished the thought. "It's even trickier than the overpowerment spell, much too dangerous, but that's his Plan B."

Harper had to think about that for a moment. "How does one take another creature's aura anyway? That can't be healthy."

"You're right." I thought back to everything I had learned about Rasputin and the spell. "He's going to sacrifice Ignatius at dawn."

"Damn," Harper muttered. "I know Canton has mental issues, but that just sounds downright evil."

"'There is no such thing as a good man,'" I quoted the Copper Knight. "'Only an evil one who's decided everyone else is as important as they are.'"

EIGHTEEN[18]

"You know, I think I've been here before." I mumbled into the silence.

"You have?" Harper asked.

"Well, not this building, but down the street." I gestured in that general direction. "There's a store that specializes in binders. Ryan has me take him there since the store isn't magic compliant."

"Why does Ryan need specialized book binders?"

"Huh?" I stared blankly at him for a moment. "No, chest binders."

"Oh, right. I forgot about that. But, well, this *is* the Garment District," Harper mused. "I think that one is probably just a coincidence."

"Yeah…"

Phil, Viv, and Ryan walked up the street. We hopped out of Harper's car and joined them on the sidewalk. Phil's greeting was simple. "That was reckless."

"It worked." I can get a little Nietzche sometimes.

Phil looked at me with only minor disappointment, then said, "Alright, where is he?"

"Top floor, it's a double penthouse." I pointed to a twenty-something-story concrete building dressed in whites, browns, and nothing but squares. It was functional, lacking the decorative moldings or fancy set windows adorning some of the other buildings. The bottom two floors housed a home improvement store, the business dark except for a few security lights. There was a glass door offset to the side. "That's the way up."

Harper had his cop face on. "How we gonna do this?"

"Give me a second." Phil was still formulating his plan. The rest of us continued to stare at the face of the building, trying not to look suspicious.

It was Ryan who eventually posed the all-important question. "Why couldn't he be hiding in the Dunkin'?"

I followed his gaze down the street, the smell of baked goods sitting lightly on the air as the staff got ready for their early morning customers. I think I noticed the shop earlier, but my brain didn't really register it because this was, what, the fourth Dunkin' Donuts I'd seen in the past forty-eight hours?

Am I paranoid enough to believe there is a global pastry conspiracy against me?

Maybe.

"Want to get a latte before the end of the world?" Vivian asked casually.

"Yes, please?" A plan with no drawbacks.

"We get through this and I'll buy everyone breakfast," Phil promised, knowing we'd hold him to it. "Ryan, wards?"

The kid was still staring at the orange and purple sign. "Nothing down here. Too public." His head swung around to glance up at the building. "I'm betting there are trip sensors. Anything magical gets close and he'll get a warning."

"But you can handle it, right?" Viv asked.

Ryan grinned. "Why does anyone even bother asking me that anymore?"

Phil opened his bag to retrieve his blasting rod. "Okay, here's the plan. Ryan will go first, checking for trips and wards, I'll be right behind. Vivian and Minni, you're in the middle, be prepared to cover us. Harper, follow last, keep an eye out for any surprises. Be careful of normal people, too. We don't want anyone getting hurt who didn't sign up for it."

You know, we should bring Harper on these things more often. With him around we could use the 'on police business' excuse and have a real cop there to flash his badge.

Not that, you know, we've ever tried to pass ourselves off as cops before.

Okay, like maybe a dozen times, tops.

Ryan made quick work of the locked glass door. He tricked

the building alarm into not tripping. There wasn't much to the foyer, a few mailboxes on the wall and a door labeled OFFICE. Beside it was one of those big black boards with the stick on lettering noting each floor's business. I recognized the name Kirchhoff Fashions as being the design house of Canton's cousin.

We headed to the stairwell out of habit, elevators are too dangerous a weapon if you knew what you were doing. Ryan held us up at the door, pulling a pair of rune covered wire cutters from his pack. He mumbled a few words then tapped the frame three times. "All good now."

The stairwell was about as you expect: dull, grey, and vertigo inducing if you looked up. Dutifully we started the trek to the penthouse, Ryan leading the way. We stopped at every third floor, Ryan disabling trip sensors. I had faith in him, but at the same time I hoped he hadn't missed any. One run in with a dragon trying to roast me alive was enough thank you.

Speaking of, there had been no sign of Drake yet. I didn't think he could have beaten us there without anyone noticing or anything blowing up. Though, I'll admit, I wouldn't have been too upset if we walked into the penthouse to see Drake sitting with a cup of tea, waiting to gloat on how he had done all the work for us. I'd give him a sarcastic remark for good measure but be secretly pleased. Well, as long as Canton was still alive.

The number of the floors kept getting bigger and we all got a tad winded. We finally got to the penthouse. End of the line.

"Ryan?" Phil asked.

Ryan tilted his head, examining the frame. "Major wards, bit nastier than last time, but cake."

"Once it's down, we're going to have to throw up a barrier to keep him from phasing out."

"I can do that." Ryan sat down on the floor, off to the side. "After I knock his ward down, I'll put up a shield. He won't be able to skip out this time."

"And if he sics the dragon on us again?" Viv asked.

"I dunno, run?"

"Good plan." Harper deadpanned.

"I'll take care of the dragon." I should probably think before I speak, it would help. "I can dodge or block any fire or kinetic energy he throws my way."

Phil didn't even question it and turned to Viv. "That leaves me and you to take out Clint. Let's try to disable him first, I don't want to resort to extreme measures. But however Canton goes down, the binding spell he has on Ignatius breaks."

"He may not give you an option," Harper interjected. "He believes what he's doing is the right course of action. You tried swaying him once. That didn't work."

"Thanks to Drake, we don't know if it would have. But we do what needs to be done." Phil didn't even stutter.

There was an awkward silence before Harper said, "Where do you want me?"

"Cover Ryan." Phil glanced down at him. "He's going to have to hold that barrier and we're going to make a ruckus. Keep the norms from getting curious."

"Will do." He nodded and stepped back where he had an unobstructed view of the descent.

"The door is locked," Ryan said as he finished making his ritual circle on the ground, complete with a piece of rune covered duct tape. "You'll have to pick it. Like before, his ward comes down and he'll know we're here."

"No time to be subtle then." Phil pointed his blasting rod at the door handle. "When you're ready, kid."

Ryan took a second to look mildly indignant then went to work bringing down the ward. We waited for the code to be spoken three times. "*Decido, Decido, Decido.*"

Phil mumbled something and shot a bolt of plasma at the lock, which promptly turned to slag. A quick and rough kick by Vivian sent it flying open barely a breath later. Phil ducked into the room with both of us on his heels.

A curved receptionist desk sat in front of a false wall, basically a slab of lumber put up to hold the Kirchhoff Fashions logo. Behind it was an open expanse filled with tables, racks, and mannequins. To the left and right were offices, dark and empty through the picture windows. The only illumination was from different security lights and random table lamps left on.

"This way." Phil wasted no time cautiously moving through the opening between the false wall and the edge of the offices.

Light reflected eerily off the mannequins. Naked, bald, and creepy, they stood around haphazardly as if someone had been too lazy to put them away properly and would take care of it later. They looked like they could come alive at any moment. To be honest, I'd rather fight an emotionally unstable wizard trying to destroy magic.

If we could even find him.

Glass exploded into the room from the far windows, howls echoing through the hollow space. I threw my arm up and reflexively built a kinetic shield to stop the shards. A mannequin's head bounced off the barrier, another landed at my feet.

"Shadow demon!" Viv shouted.

Okay Goat-Grizzly. I'm getting really tired of your shit.

The ceiling was too low for Goat-Grizzly so it ended up all hunched over, caught on the roof beams. It was actually pretty hilarious. Of course, I only think that now as I'm no longer running for my life. At the time, it was pretty terrifying as it ripped its way through the naked mannequins.

A table came sailing by but we managed to dive through an open office door. Possibly not the best of tactical retreats. Something heavy banged against the outside wall and a gaudy piece of art made from mangled bits of metal fell and attempted to impale me.

Viv grabbed at my arm, getting little more than a fistful of shirt, but she managed to pull me out of the way. We moved to the corner of the office behind an ornate desk I was sure wasn't going to last the night. Hell, I wasn't even sure *I* was going to last the night at this rate.

"Thanks," I said as got my breath back.

"*Zikher*." Viv gave me a nod and trained her blasting rod at the door, waiting for Goat-Grizzly to bust through.

I had an idea. "We should call for Harper. He can shoot it."

Phil rummaged through his bag. "We're risking enough as it. Gunshots ring out and the police *will* come."

"We don't stop the wizard, it will hardly matter," Viv pointed out.

His retort was cut off as half the wall ripped away. Crunching particle board and screeching metal layered on top of the howling from the beast. Goat-Grizzlington the Fourth was met by a plasma bolt, a fireball, and a surge of electricity. That only stalled the monster as it reared back and once again got tangled in the ceiling tiles.

"Think, think," I mumbled to myself as I twisted my bracelet around my wrist. The smell of burnt, wet dog filled the air as Goat-Grizzly came in contact with bits of steel and the elements within it. "Anyone think to bring iron?"

Phil pulled a crowbar from his bag. "Best I could do on short notice. I should invest in an iron sword."

"Yes, you should." I grabbed the weapon as I had another idea. "It'll have to work."

He didn't want to let go. "What are you doing?"

"I distract Goat-Grizzly, you stop Canton from casting the spell." I basically wrenched the crowbar out of his hand. "If he succeeds, then you know what we have to do."

"Minni." Phil stopped himself, like he couldn't decide if he should argue or not. There was that slight movement of his jaw where he was going to say something, but instead nodded and left it at that. I know I was the one who was supposed to take care of the dragon, but we had more immediate threats.

Goat-Grizzly howled as it ripped through the ceiling, pulling down wires and metal. The air sizzled as the stench of burnt hair intensified. The steel content of the building wasn't going to be enough to take out the monster just by touching its skin, but it would slow him down. If I could just jam the crowbar down its throat, then I'd have it made.

"Hey, ugly!" Brandishing the weapon in both hands, I waved it in tall arcs back and forth to get the demon's attention through the holes in the wall.

It growled, showing me his shark teeth—again with the teeth—but it made no attempt to come closer.

Keeping as much eye contact with the demon as I could without tripping over debris, I started to walk out of the room as Goat-Grizzly watched me intently. I could hear Phil and Viv moving around but I dared not take my eyes off the creature. Veering off to the left once I cleared the door, I created a space behind me where the others could get away.

"We're clear," Phil yelled and there was the patter of running feet.

That left me with one important question. "Okay, now what?"

You know, asking that to a goat-headed Shadow Demon who wants to eat you is probably not the brightest idea. They're only ever going to have the one answer.

Goat-Grizzly lunged forward and I skidded back, swinging the crowbar wildly. I was doing fine until my feet got tangled up in excess plastic limbs and I went down hard. Previously bruised and sore areas screamed in pain as I tried to scramble backwards. One of Goat-Grizzly's large paws swiped down at me, grabbing at my ankle.

The crowbar still in hand, I used the hook end as a handle and I sliced at the demon. Sizzling, howling, and a stink I hope you never have to experience accompanied the hit as Goat-Grizzly reared back. I kicked at his paw and received little resistance as I pulled myself free from his grasp to scramble to my feet.

I headed towards the open end of room, dodging display tables and hopping over arms and legs and the occasional head. It wasn't long before I realized I'd led Goat-Grizzly around in a circle. It had taken maybe a minute, and I was at a loss as what to do next as I panted and tried to control my breathing.

A mass of plastic body parts came zipping past, a few making contact and I stumbled. Afraid Goat-Grizzly would grab me again, I flung myself to the right. When I connected with the floor, I slid a few feet before using a pillar to hop back up again.

Not looking back, I dived into the office I'd previously taken shelter in.

"Stupid, stupid," I berated myself for getting stuck in a corner, again.

I spun to face the torn entrance, crowbar still in hand thanks to the death grip I held on it. But a lot good it would do me if I couldn't get close enough without getting mauled.

I had another idea, and did I mention all my best plans are insanely stupid and/or dangerous? I did? Oh, good.

The metal artwork that fell earlier sat sideways on the ground with a ceiling tile split atop it. The piece was designed as if someone had picked through the aftermath of a tornado-redecorated house, then welded all the little bits of scrap metal together to form a vaguely flower shaped bouquet. There were a few copper and possibly titanium bits, but mostly it was strips of steel with a few bars of good old-fashioned iron.

Knocking the tile off, I grabbed the artwork by the underside to pull it off the floor. It was heavier than I thought, and as I came to discover later, worth about fifty thousand dollars.

Pretty sure it was insured. Pretty sure.

Howling accompanied the creature as it ripped away more of the drywall to widen the gap it had created. I held the mangled artwork as a shield and waited for Goat-Grizzly to work its way into the office. As it ducked to get through, I knew this would be my only opportunity. Taking a deep breath into my burning lungs, I started a dead run, rushing at the demon with all of my hundred and sixty pounds behind me.

There may have been screaming and the possible use of a catch phrase.

Slamming into the creature, I drove the spiked ends of the metal bouquet into Goat-Grizzly's stomach, the rancid stench threatening to make me hurl. A loud, angry howl rained down on me and I instinctively backed away in time to dodge a rather pitiful attempt to swipe at my head. The artwork fell to the ground but the damage was done. The monster was dying, slowly, as it could not heal itself of its internal wounds. It was unfortunately not enough to kill it outright.

There was a dull thud as the demon dropped to its knees then sagged into a doubled-over position. A sickly spat, spat, hack filled the air. I think it was a cough, but I could be wrong. It was like watching a wounded animal die and I couldn't bring myself to do that.

I picked up the crowbar from where I had left it in favor of the more artsy weapon. Goat-Grizzly, too weak, too defeated, or sensing what I was going to do, didn't bother trying to attack me as I got as close as I dared. Using the hook end of the crowbar as leverage, I drove the metal down into where the monster's heart would be, if it were a mammal.

"Maybe they'll leave you alone this time, big guy," I offered as I watched the creature dissolve into ectoplasm. I still don't know if that was the same demon each time, or four different ones. I guess it doesn't really matter. None of them asked to be treated like this.

They were only weapons.

NINETEEN[19]

Taking a moment to get my breathing back under control, I looked around at the total wreck of the place. I'd hate to be the insurance adjustor on this one.

I wasn't sure which way Phil and Viv had gone, but I could hear shouting coming from the other end of the room behind a faux runway. My keen powers of observation led me to believe they were probably over in that general direction.

Crowbar in hand, I jogged across the room and ducked behind the dividers at the front end of the catwalk. Mobile curtains and clothes racks turned the area into a maze. I stumbled into an open space which had a large window facing out onto the terrace.

Things did not look good.

Despite it being two-on-one, Canton held his own, deflecting and shielding against Phil and Viv who weren't trying to go for kill shots. Canton, on the other hand, seemed to have no such qualms, but found it difficult to land a hit on the two moving targets.

I needed to get out there and help.

I considered breaking the window, but I thought I'd sneak up on Canton and take him by surprise. I made my way through what I guess was a hair-and-makeup area as I looked for the door outside. What I found was a metal circular stairwell leading up to the second floor of the penthouse which sat atop the first like a tiered cake. Getting the high ground on Canton sounded like a good idea at the time.

Bounding up the stairs, I was greeted by a few more false walls, storage boxes, and several work stations. I saw a set of double doors that led onto the smaller upper-terrace.

Oh, and a dragon.

Ignatius' massive form took up the whole terrace, his front legs hanging out over the ledge, his tail trailing across the floor, and his wings tucked in. There was no way I was going to be able to get out there without alerting him to my presence.

I did find it strange though that he wasn't doing anything, wasn't attacking. He looked as if he was just chilling, catching a breeze. Seeing as he wouldn't attack unless ordered to, or wanted to, I figured I was safe. After all, he would have seen that I was there with his son earlier. He'd have no reason to attack me, right?

Pressing my luck, I opened one of the doors. It swung outward and I hit his tail after a couple of inches. I wasn't going to get through without a little nudge.

Ignatius turned slightly to look over his shoulder and I froze, ready to bring up my thermal shield. I didn't know dragons could frown because I'm pretty sure that's all he did before turning his attention back to the battle, scooting his tail so the door would swing broader. This all made me slightly confused but it didn't stop me noticing the sigil painted on his scaly forehead.

So not good.

Taking a deep breath, I opened my Third Eye so I could see the flow of magical energy. At first I was almost blinded by the glow of everything around me. From the battle below to Ryan's shield, the magic was getting pretty thick up there. I closed my eyes and mentally filtered out what I could before opening them again. Better, but I still had to squint as I moved farther out onto the terrace to get a closer look at the dragon.

It was exactly as I feared.

Canton had started the auric transfer early, probably when we busted in. I could see the flow of energy from Ignatius to the terrace below. Canton would be using some kind of collector to store the aura-turned-magic energy before redirecting it. It was the safest option, but even that's relative. Once the aura was completely transferred into pure magic, then you might as well stamp a sell-by date on the container because it would eventually break down and go boom.

Like, goodbye Manhattan, boom.

I couldn't stop the magic transfer. Well, I could, but the magic already in the collector would snap from Ignatius' aura. It would complete its transformation into pure magic and he'd never be able to get it back. Ignatius would be left with a severally damaged aura that would probably never recover, never contain the levels of magic that it used to. Sure, it would save him right here, right now, but could I really do that do another magic user?

Even if they, and their son, are arrogant pricks?

If I slowed the transfer, then as long as the connection stayed intact, we'd have time to think about a possible reversal. To slow it, I was going to have to get to the focal point of the spell to touch the flow of energy. The focal point being the sigil which, as previously mentioned, was on the dragon's forehead. A head that was currently leaning several feet over a terrace.

"Um, Ignatius?" I nervously tried to get his attention.

He swung is head around to look at me and I could see the sigil more clearly. The problem was that with his massive shoulders, his wings tucked at his sides, and the rest of his bulk being, well, bulky, there was no way I was getting close to the sigil without climbing. How did Canton put the darn thing there in the first place?

"You got to trust me, okay," I spoke softly as one would to a child. Kind of ridiculous since I was talking to a mystical creature probably twenty times older than me. "I need to get to that sigil."

There was a nearly imperceptible nod from the dragon and I took that as a go ahead. Putting down the crowbar, I stepped on a potted plant to climb up onto the balustrade, and the wind chose that moment to pick up. My hair whipped around in the air, trying to whack me across the face. I remembered I had a hair tie in my back pocket. I quickly tucked my hair halfway through a loop just to get it out of my face. It would be a painful knot to remove later.

Oh well.

Ignatius tilted his head down, but his elongated spiked nostril made it difficult to reach his forehead unless I got closer. Carefully I stepped over his hand—claw? I could feel his hot breath against my body and memories of my fire-breathing reminded me of how dangerous my position was. I could step back but that would mean standing on his hand. I'm pretty sure he'd take issue with that.

Did I ever say how big this dragon was, and how many horns and knobs it had? Imagine trying to climb across a full grown elephant-rhinoceros-chameleon hybrid. Though from this distance, I could see small vines of silver in his golden hide. Man, he must be really old to have that kind of gray.

The sigil on his forehead was written in the charcoal paste Canton seemed to favor. Ignatius' aura presented as a gold sparkly twine covered in a haze of pixie dust as it was pulled from his body. It was tethered to a sphere sitting on the terrace below. The auric container itself looked more like a garden gazing ball on a concrete pedestal than a magical artifact.

From my precarious perch I could see the three wizards continuing to battle it out, Canton having driven my friends farther down the terrace. I was actually glad for this. I didn't want to draw attention to myself because I was a sitting duck up there.

Taking a deep breath, I laid my hand on the sigil, careful not to smudge it as that could inadvertently break the spell. I shut my eyes to work inside my mind's eye to get a better view. Ignatius' aura sparked golden, but it wasn't as active as I had seen it before. Fizzling out, the bright gold was now worn down to a dull sheen. It poured off his form like a steadily flowing river which had a metric ton of gold glitter dumped into it. I could see the container it was connected to and it glowed white hot.

My jeans began to stick to my legs from the heat of the dragon's breath. I might have gotten in a little over my head.

Well, the only way to slow a raging river is to build a dam, right? It made sense to me, although, I got a degree in electrical engineering, not structural engineering. For the lack of a better idea, a dam would have to do.

Willpower is a natural insulator to auric energy. This is partly why it's so hard for wizards to break through another's spell. If I was going to do this, I was literally going to hold back the tide of flowing energies through the strength of my willpower alone.

I can do stubborn.

Reaching into my magical essence, I gathered up as much pure willpower as I could. Instead of applying it to my aura, I molded and shaped it into a form which shone pitch black against the world. I folded the mass, metaphysically speaking, around the stream of Ignatius' aura, closing it so the energy slipped through it like a needle and thread. Slowly, I turned the edges of the donut into a more conical shape, narrowing the far end as I did so. The flow of the aura began to slow, backing up in the funnel, trickling out the front.

I was absolutely stunned that it worked.

Shutting down my mind's eye, I became acutely aware that I was panting, either from the exertion of forming my willpower or the intense heat of the dragon. I was also soaking wet with sweat, my head beginning to pound in the frontal area, a possible sign of dehydration.

If the end of magic as we know it doesn't kill me, heat stroke probably will.

"Alright, Ignatius," I said calmly. I'm pretty sure I was calm, yeah, I was totally cool and collected. "That should buy us some time."

There was a small shifting of the dragon's head and a grunt that I interpreted as a sarcastic 'that will do for now, peasant.'

Hey, he's a dragon, what else would he say?

So, what do you think are the odds that as I tried to climb off Ignatius, a stray fireball would come hurtling towards us? Man, this weekend was the worst, I just could not get ahead.

I didn't even see the flaming mass until it impacted on the terrace, the ledge rocking violently as it cracked. I was going to jump to the bottom terrace. Ignatius, however, took that moment to rear away from the flying debris, seemingly forgetting I was there. His wing clipped my chest and since there was nothing holding me to the ground, I went sailing backwards into the air.

Annnnnnnnnnnnnnnnnnnnnnd, I'm dead.

Okay, obviously I didn't die because I'm sitting here talking to you, but at the time, I was pretty sure I was street pizza.

See, at first I thought I was going to fall onto the terrace below which, while painful, was very much survivable. Then as my body rotated in the air, I realized Ignatius hit me so hard I flew far enough to clear the edge of the building. I could see 37th street, cars the size of toys, and my stomach lurched as gravity started to claim me as its victim.

My mind raced to think, do something, anything that would stop my descent: wind, thermal energy, featherfall. The names of spells rushed through my head but as I tried to slow down my thoughts to make any sense of them, the faster I seemed to fall.

I suppose my life should have passed before my eyes, but I literally blanked out. It was just me and my impending doom, the cold wind rushing past and my body feeling strangely heavy, weighed down by nothingness. Happiness and regret canceled each other out in the void.

Two sharp pains in my side sent shocks through my system, my head whipping back and forth as massive clawed feet grabbed me in midair.

Dragons are essentially an unholy gene splice of cats and birds of prey. Their claws are designed to grab food which they then hold tight so as not to let them wiggle away. Ignatius grabbing me resulted in two small puncture wounds to my leg and side. The sudden stop meant a nasty case of whiplash that left me dazed for a good fifteen seconds.

As Ignatius flapped his wings, his body bounced in the air which didn't help me at all as I tried to hold myself steady against his scaly leg. It took a moment to process the fact that I was, indeed, not going to fall to my death.

Night wasn't over yet.

TWENTY[20]

Getting my wits about me, I looked down to see Phil and Vivian battling it out with Canton. My friends had gained the advantage and had Canton on the defensive. He stood behind the auric sphere, using it as something of a shield. They'd have to be more cautious in their spell casting because they wouldn't want to hit it and set it off uncontrolled.

"Okay, Ignatius, thank you for the save," I said as pain shot through me. I could still feel my legs, so I was pretty sure there were no serious neck or spinal injuries. Felt like I was going to hurl, though. "Can you set me down now, please?"

Flapping his wings sharply, Ignatius flopped me around like a dead fish as he got closer to the fight. I thought he was going to drop me behind Canton so I could flank him, which would have been a really good tactical move.

Well, that's kind of what happened.

Ignatius' clawed feet tilted backwards like he was going to gently toss me to the ground. Not my first choice in getting down but I could handle it. He pulled back farther and got into position as he sighted his target.

"No," I shouted as it dawned on me. "NO! Bad dragon!"

Smooth and swift, Ignatius threw his claws forward and for the second time in only a few minutes I went sailing through the air, not of my own free will. I'm pretty sure I was screaming at the top of my lungs, but Canton never looked back before I plowed into him.

I wouldn't have called it a controlled landing, more like a physics experiment gone wrong.

When I hit Canton, I latched onto his suit jacket for no apparent reason I can fathom. He was completely unprepared and lurched forward under the sudden weight. We both went down, straight into the aura collector.

When Canton touched the sphere, there was a release of energy neither of us were ready for. Imagine touching an exposed wire—magic exploded around us. We didn't get the full force of the energy in the container, but the little bit of Ignatius' aura that was released had turned into pure, concentrated magical essence. We were repelled by it, sprawling against the stone terrace. Just like an electrical current can wreak havoc on a heart, the energy overloaded my aura.

If I were anyone else, I'd been in serious trouble.

I captured the wild energy and did the only thing I could do. I fought. I riled against its turbulent ebb and flow as it tried to consume my own magic. It buried down deep in hopes of taking my aura for itself. But as I've said, energy is what I do.

"Minni." I heard my named called as I finished tucking the magic away where it couldn't do me any more harm. "Minni, you okay?"

"M' kay," I mumbled, opening my eyes to see Phil leaning over me. He shined a light in my eyes and my head pounded, the Philadelphia Orchestra playing an all drum and brass symphony in my head.

"You might be concussed." He sounded worried but relieved at the same time. "Can you count backwards from ten?"

I rattled off the numbers while glancing over at Canton. Viv leaned over his prone body, her hands splayed out as she tried to get a read on him. My head lolled back and the sky above seemed a little bit brighter than last I remembered, but I was being thrown around by a dragon at the time. "How long was I out?"

"Not long, a minute, maybe two." That was good, meant less chance of real brain damage. "Can you sit up?"

"I like it here." I closed my eyes and seriously considered sleep. "It's comfy."

"Minni!" Phil shouted and tapped my face gently.

"Fine," I grumbled, my eyes flitting open.

"Can you move your foot for me?" Phil asked and I gave

him a funny look as I moved my right foot clockwise. "That's good. I think you managed no broken bones but you're gonna need to get checked out, just in case."

He rambled on about a couple more things but I'd stopped listening. Ignatius had perched again on the upper terrace and was staring down at me. I raised my hand weakly and pointed at the beast. "That… was totally not cool!"

Phil looked confused. "You didn't plan that?"

"You think I wanted to be a human bowling ball?" I kept looking up at my raised arm. "There's blood on my hand."

Whatever Phil was going to say was cut short.

"Seems I missed all the excitement," Drake said idly as he sauntered in through the broken remains of a glass door, body guard in tow.

"Managed quite well without you," Viv commented as she placed her jacket under Canton's head. I guess he was alive, but the man seemed absolutely catatonic.

"What's wrong with him?" Drake asked clinically, perhaps annoyed that he wasn't going to get to beat Canton senseless.

"He got pushed against the aura collector," Phil spoke harshly. "He received a charge of pure magical energy without preparing himself. His aura basically shorted out."

Ignatius said something, or at least I assume he did because he made some guttural noises. Drake cocked his head as if he was listening.

"Ah," Drake said when Ignatius stopped. "It seems father was commanded to not take any action against the wizard." He chuckled and looked down at me. "He was also supposed to let the spell do its work and not get into a fight. Mr. Canton said nothing of helping a wizard find their way back to Earth. Seems he misjudged the distance."

Seriously? "Misjudged my a—"

"Guys." Harper came running out onto the terrace with Ryan. We're having a regular ol' party. "The police are on their way. If we're done we need to go, now."

"Not sure we should move her yet." Phil was referring to

me. I gave him an indignant look but made no effort to get up.

"Of course she can be moved," Drake spoke dismissively. "We need Miss Masterson to reverse the transfer."

Yeah, there was still the issue of the auric transfer and the garden gazing ball of doom. Man, it was a wonder we didn't knock it over and destroy Manhattan ourselves.

Phil got to his feet to confront Drake. "You can't expect her to attempt to reverse an auric redirect even if she wasn't injured. The spell's too dangerous."

"You forget that if the energy has no place to go it will explode," Drake pointed out a bit too cheerfully. "It will take several square blocks with it. If not the whole island."

"We can put a shield around it, contain the blast." Phil countered, fidgeting slightly.

Drake gestured to Harper who was now looking over Canton. "Your police are coming. Do you want to risk moving the sphere?"

Phil tensed, getting into the dragon's personal space and gritting his teeth. "You can't ask her to do this."

"I wasn't asking." Drake spoke so lightly no one but the three of us could hear him. "Miss Masterson survived a blast of pure magical energy, among so many other things these past few days. We both know what she's capable of."

"You can't make her," Phil nearly growled.

"I can," Drake assured him, "and I will."

In a matter of seconds, Phil and Viv had their blasting rods drawn against the dragon who held his hand aloft, flames flickering between his fingertips. Harper and Drake's bodyguard followed suit, pointing handguns at each other.

Really?

Really?

These guys were going to get into this *right now*?

"RYAN!" I shouted. "Get over here."

The kid was hiding behind the frame of the broken door. He tentatively started to walk forward but he would have to pass through the line of fire.

"Don't worry," I told Ryan as I sat up, slowly. "Drake ain't gonna do nothing."

Ryan slinked through and no one lowered their weapons despite my assurances. I gestured for him to give me a hand, a small wave of nausea hitting me as I got to my feet.

Clearing my head, I went face to face Drake. "You aren't stupid. A standoff, up here, norms coming, and your father dying by the second? You need to cut the transfer, and your loses, or work with us to fix this."

The man's gaze darted over to Ignatius who had taken a new perch on the lower terrace behind the magic time-bomb. The elder dragon now showed signs of his aura being drained, his scales washed out and his breathing labored.

"There is no time to reverse the spell," Phil admitted, lowering his blasting rod. "By the time we figured out all the variables to do it safety, Ignatius will be gone. He should be dead already but Minni slowed it down."

"Miss Masterson can reverse the spell," Drake reiterated.

Phil spread his hands wide. "You're grasping at straws."

"I can *cut* the transfer," I said neutrally, watching Drake. "Ignatius lives."

"He's lost most of his power." Drake met my eyes, his arm still outstretched but the flames dying off. "If that happens, he might as well be dead."

"So let him die now," I offered coolly with a slight shrug of my shoulders. "Have him go out a hero, saving Manhattan."

"He's my father." And there it was, some honest to goodness emotion from Drake. An unadulterated fear that he wore in his eyes like a man who had never worried a moment in his life because there was nothing beyond his reach.

I continued to stand there, unmoved. I had plenty reasons not to care about him, or his father.

Drake's lip trembled slightly. "Please."

I tried not to smile at my victory, that would be crass.

"See, that wasn't so hard." Okay, so I smiled a little.

"Minni," Phil said warningly.

Ignoring him, I turned to Ryan and pointed to some iron benches lining the ledge. "Pull one of those in front of the sphere, would you, I need to sit down."

Sirens sounded in the distance, the police and fire department were starting to arrive. Everyone glanced between themselves, confused, but at least they all lowered their weapons.

"Minni," Phil yelled after me as I went to the bench. He even grabbed my arm to stop me.

I jerked out of his grasp. "Reversing the spell is the best solution. The magic bomb gets defused and Ignatius is restored."

"You know what could happen if you do this."

"It was always going to be this way, Phil. I never had a choice." Magic is non-linear and doesn't always obey the arrow of time. "The memories of David, the sunflower field. I was told this was going to happen from the very beginning. I see that now."

Phil said nothing, what could he? So I sat down, my body screaming at me as a reminder that I wasn't exactly in the best of shape at the moment. I chose to ignore its needy blabbering.

Concussion-smucussion.

Drake finally caught up to the conversation. "You're going to do it?"

I pointed at him while shooting the dirtiest look I could muster. "I'm saving your dad, but not for you. That little act was payback for Stacey, you limey English wet crumpet."

I hope that was a pretty bad insult. It made sense at the time, but it could have been the minor brain damage talking. And, well, maybe it was a bit petty of me to hold his father's impending death over his head, but I'm pretty sure I can live with it on my conscience. Someone needed to put that dragon in his place and stick up for the non-magically inclined.

Drake's mouth opened as he took in a breath, but his retort died on his lips. Instead, he nodded. I wanted to gain some respect for the man for that, but in the end he was getting what he wanted — his father saved — and he knew that. I couldn't be sure just what he was thinking.

The sirens reached a crescendo and Harper started herding

everyone. "We need to go, now."

"You go," I said as I closed my eyes and went into my mind's eye. "I have to stay."

The gazing ball of doom shone brighter than the sun in the metaphysical world. I had to build a mental filter so as not to fry a few brain cells while looking at it. I could also see the thin line of Ignatius' tether flowing into it.

Phil was still right next to me. "Minni, what if the council finds out—"

"Go," I told him sternly. "I know what I'm doing."

My choice, my actions, my consequences.

I heard the push and shuffle of people moving and Phil's general lack of not wanting to go. Harper said something about holding off the police as long as he could.

Now, I know what you're thinking. That I'm insane.

I should be going to the hospital, not performing risky magic likely to get me killed. You're thinking the concussion is affecting my judgment. You might point to my recent relationship troubles as a reason for my lunacy.

The simple answer is that I know exactly what I'm doing and have total confidence in being able redirect Ignatius' aura back into his body without blowing myself up. I was only hoping I wouldn't have to because this could lead to questions I'm not supposed to answer.

One question being: have I ever performed a Rasputin?

To which the answer is an unequivocal: yes.

TWENTY-ONE[21]

At some point, I passed out. I gained consciousness in a hospital, if the plethora of tubes, needles, and beeping machines were any indication. Upon thorough consideration of all the facts on hand, I decided to go back to sleep, where the dreams are.

I was sitting on a bed of broken sunflowers, my brother's bloody head in my lap. His breathing shallow, his eyes fully dilated and his pulse near non-existent, he was completely non-responsive.

Forming a ball of light in my hands, I tossed it up into the sky. Once it got high enough, it sparked like a firework, a wizard's emergency flare. Hopefully one of my family members would see it and get there quick. Then we could get my brother to a healer.

But David was long past help.

We're talking about my little brother here, the youngest of the seven Masterson siblings, the really annoying one who always cheats at board games. I wasn't going to let him die. He was born with necromancy abilities, but that doesn't make him evil, that doesn't make him a threat.

I glanced over at the fallen attacker, beat into submission by his own baseball bat.

There was blood on my hands.

"And she's awake," I heard a voice say as I found my way back to consciousness. A tall, red-haired nurse started raising the hospital bed for me. Her name tag read Natalie. "Looks like I lose the betting pool again."

"How long I been out?" I asked when I could finally form words, my throat dry and voice coming out as frog-speak.

"About two days," Natalie cheerily informed me as she passed over a plastic cup of water. "It's Wednesday morning. I'm going to fetch your doctor, you sit and rest."

Two days, that wasn't awful.

I mean, it was plenty of time to heal both body and mind. I was covered in bruises that were already turning yellow. The cuts and puncture marks were bandaged and scabbed over nicely. My aura and energy reserves where at a comfortable base level after having exhausted myself performing the auric transfer.

Then I noticed my focus bracelet was missing… and that's when I panicked. My heart started racing, which caused a monitor to screech in alarm.

"Woah." An older gentleman in a white coat and sporting a handlebar mustache walked in, Natalie in tow. "You're okay, you're safe now."

He looked me in the eyes and told me to breath, take deep calming breaths. I was too tired to argue. I told myself the foci could show up in my personal belongings. The melted bracelets on my other wrist were gone. They could only have been removed by cutting them off. Did my copper bracelet suffer a similar fate?

I could always create another foci, but it's not the same. It takes years to fully break in a good focus item. It becomes more than an item. It's an extension of yourself.

I'm not really sure saving the world was worth losing it.

"I'm Doctor Morgan. You can call me Gerald, or doctor, or doc," he finally introduced himself. "Let's take a look at you, shall we?"

I didn't fight the doctor as he examined me, checking my eyes, blood pressure, breathing, sensitivity, and reflexes. I think by that point he could have wanted to stab me with the world's biggest needle and I would have been meh about it.

"That's good," he said once he was done asking me to move various limbs, fingers and toes. "Scans didn't indicate spinal damage, but we weren't positive you didn't suffer any motor damage from your fall."

"My fall?" Memories of flying over the terrace with nothing but ground far below me came flooding back. My stomach gave an involuntary lurch.

"You might not remember everything that happened and

that's okay," he said softly. "The mind does that sometimes, to help you heal."

"Right," I replied and dropped the subject until I knew what my cover story was.

The doctor wrote something in my chart and put it away. "Well, you're healing up just dandy. You'll be out of here in no time."

I smiled as best I could. "Great, thank you."

Natalie stopped the doctor as he turned to leave. "There's a policeman outside who's been waiting to speak with her. Is it okay if he comes in?"

"I don't see why not," he said. "If you think you're up for it, Miss Masterson?"

"Yeah, sure." I shrugged, hoping it was Harper and not Gant.

"I'll send him in."

They left and I realized I was in a private room. No way was my health insurance covering this. Something was definitely up, but I couldn't fathom what.

Various bouquets of get-well-soon-flowers dotted around. All of the arrangements contained lilies, my favorite. Two were from work: one a gift from the company and the other from those in my department. Stacey and Phil were represented along with members of the coven. Sitting right next to me on the table was one from Marcel.

I hoped the cop would have come in already to distract me, but no luck. I had to open the card attached to the expensive looking flowers Marcel sent. It only said one word: *Peek-a-boo*.

"I see you," I spoke softly in return.

I tried to put the card back in the crappy paper envelope but all it did was tear. Then after what seemed like an hour of being unable to put it on the plastic spoke thingy, I shoved the whole thing down into the flowers and pushed the vase as far away as I could.

There was a knock and Harper came in wearing his usual detective uniform of a blazer and badge. "Hey, Minni, how you doing?"

"Good." I was visibly relieved it wasn't Gant. "I'm good. What happened to me?"

"What really happened?" He pulled up a chair next to the bed. "You did it. You returned Ignatius' aura and he flew off into the night before anyone was the wiser."

"Pity, I would have liked to have seen you explain a dragon in the middle of New York City." I reached for the pitcher of water as I was still thirsty.

Harper laughed, taking the pitcher and pouring me a glass because I was still feeling weak. "I told everyone I was following a lead. I got there just before they did and found you and Canton passed out. It's a big mess, everyone is happy to take my word as gospel."

"Well, that's something." I took the offered water cup. "Is Canton still catatonic?"

"Yeah." Harper frowned as he pulled a notebook and a pen from his jacket's breast pocket. "Phil found a doctor, a Forsaken, who's going to take care of him."

As much as I was pleased to hear that, I suddenly had to wonder. "Drake didn't argue?"

"Didn't say a word, and I didn't ask."

Why does a dragon's lack of bloodthirstiness worry me?

Harper flipped through his notebook, settling on a page. "Okay, we need to go over your cover story."

"Shoot." Again with saying that to people with guns.

"Alright, you were found lying on the bench, passed out, lots of debris and damage to the area," he mumbled a bit, furrowing his brow. "What we decided on is Canton wanted to finish what he started and that meant kidnapping you, again, when you went out for a morning coffee."

"Right, makes sense."

"We're chalking up the damage to grenades."

"Grenades?" I rose an eyebrow questionably, which sent pain streaking back across my scalp. I reflectively reached up and touched the sensitive bruise above my temple.

"It's what the FBI is using as their cover for The Cloisters: either grenades or improvised home explosives." He flipped to the next page. "Now, you were attacked by Canton and fell from the upper terrace onto the debris. It sorta matches your wounds."

"So I dragged myself to the bench and collapsed?"

"Or Canton dragged you." Harper noncommittally shrugged. "You can claim shock and trauma, play off the whole thing like you can't remember and no one will question it. We only need confirmation you left your apartment in the morning."

"Well, I did leave my apartment that morning." I settled back into the pillows. "Simple is always better."

Harper wrote a few more notes then closed the book. "The D.A. could charge Canton and try him in absentia, but I think with enough push from the FBI they'll be happy to let it all go away for now."

"The FBI is okay with that?"

"I had a visit from Agent Ross," he explained. "She's pretty satisfied with the results. If there is no trial, it's easier to cover up the magic angle. I don't think we'll have any problems on their end."

No trial meant the less likelihood someone would ask questions about what really happened. Somehow though, this didn't make me feel all that better. "How bad is Canton?"

"I asked Phil the same question." The detective frowned. "He told me Canton has a chance. His mind is still there but it's scattered from his aura shorting out. Eventually it will right itself, but not any time soon."

"Damn," I said and my tummy grumbled loudly.

"Sounds like you need some solid food." Harper chuckled.

"I need something." Like my head examined?

"You eat and get some rest." He stood and pocketed his notepad. "You're going to have a ton of visitors when the hours open."

"Nice to feel loved," I replied, but really, the last thing I wanted right now was attention.

"Oh." Harper stopped himself when he got halfway to the

door. "I hope you don't mind, but after you passed out I took your focus bracelet so it wouldn't get entered into evidence. Gave it to Phil for safe keeping."

At that most wonderful news, I swear my eyes widened to the size of saucers and I made strangled pterodactyl noises.

TWENTY-TWO[22]

When visiting hours started, the first person through the door was, of course, Stacey. After giving me a monster hug, she grabbed me by the shoulders and said, "If you weren't in a hospital bed right now I'd slap you right across the face!"

"Um, thanks?" I think?

"Why didn't you tell me you were kidnapped?" She sat on the edge of the bed and loomed over me in all her Amazonian glory. "Why did you lie to me?"

Yeah, I knew that question was coming, and I'd had an hour to think about it. "I didn't want to make you worry or feel bad." And that was the best I could come up. I'm beginning to think I'm not very good at this friendship thing.

"Really." It was not phrased as a question.

"I went home, I made the choice to go back out again." I needed to stick with the facts as I told them to the police. "That's on me, not you. Well, it's on the guy who decided to kidnap me in the first place, but I know you and how you think." Especially since you were mind-whammed by a dragon. "I thought the whole thing was over with. I wanted to forget about it. If I'd known it'd only get worse, I would have said something."

"I'm your best friend." I knew she'd say that and I didn't have a counter-argument for her. "You should have told me."

"I'm sorry," I offered meekly. "I screwed up."

It's what I do.

"You're sorry?" She paused, frowning. "You're the one in the hospital and I'm making this about me. This is so messed up."

"It's not your fault," I told her, speaking only the truth. "I'm not a very good friend."

"Come here." Stacey hugged me, possibly to keep herself

from crying, I couldn't be totally sure. When she pulled away she looked me in the eyes. "You are not a bad friend. Just next time, don't leave me out of the loop, okay?"

I still don't think I agree with her, but I wasn't willing to let her go. It was selfish of me, but I needed her. I needed that foundation of normalcy she gave me. "I promise, next time I'm kidnapped by a crazy man who thinks he's a wizard, I will totally call you first."

"Oh, don't make me hurt you," she laughed.

"I'm already hurt!" I pointed to the various tubes that shackled me to the bed.

"Technicality." Stacey shrugged it off and smiled, almost back to normal. "If you need to talk, you know where I am."

"I know." I squeezed her hand. "Thank you."

"Am I interrupting something?" A voice called from the doorway, one I didn't recognize, so it was a bit of a shock when I looked up to see Drake standing at the threshold.

"And you are?" Stacey answered for me as I sat there with a spectacularly dumbfounded look on my face.

"Detective Drago," Drake said as he walked in sporting a light New Jersey accent. "I won't be long. Just need to clear up a few points on Miss Masterson's statement and I'll be off."

"Oh, okay." Stacey smiled and stood from the bed. "I bet you could use a cheeseburger right now. I'm gonna see if I can sneak one in for you."

"Yes! Ketchup, honey mustard, and mayo, please."

"All three?" Stacey turned to Drake, jutting her thumb at me. "She has the weirdest taste buds of anyone I've ever met."

"You don't say," he replied politely.

"Seeya in a bit." She headed out the door.

I waited till I was sure she'd be out of ear-shot. "That's a nice accent there, *Drago*."

"I think so." He was back to his English-ish accent.

"What are you doing here?" I asked him directly.

He gave me one of the most pathetically sad looks. "We never did get off on the right foot, did we?"

"Nope," I replied without hesitation. "Please don't tell me you wanna be BFFs or something."

"Hardly," he retorted. I was slightly offended, *slightly*. "But you're a formable sorceress Miss Masterson, with a rare gift. I'd rather prefer you as an ally than a foe."

Was it just me, or did that sound way too ominous?

"What do you want?"

"Dragon's never owe a debt to anyone, ever," he answered gravely. "Not to humans, not to other dragons, and especially not to wizards."

"Smart." What? It is.

"My father saved you from falling to your death, but he was the one who put you in the position in the first place," he began, his voice methodical in his statements. "You saved his life at risk to your own, so he will give you Mr. Canton's life in return. He will make no move for revenge against him or his family."

Yeah, and your dad also decided to use me to work on his bowling game but, you know what? I'm just going to let you have that one cause I'm nice like that.

"Sounds fair." I've never been much of a stickler about favors. I would have saved Ignatius regardless. But it was good to know daddy Drake wasn't going to go all medieval on Canton. We still don't know who was manipulating the poor guy.

"As for myself, I owe you much." Drake had a little trouble saying the words. "You found my father, twice. You risked your life to save him. You even thought to include me in the raid at the studio."

"About that," I interrupted him. "What took you so long?"

"Your message scribed onto a hallway mirror." He splayed his hands apologetically. "No one saw it for some time."

"Huh." It made some sense, and I was inclined to believe him. It was better than thinking he purposely held back in hopes we'd clean up the mess for him. If that was true, then I suppose he really did owe me, big time.

"Even I will admit it is difficult to put a price on acts of bravery and thoughtfulness," he said casually.

"You know, it's fine." I was starting to feel uncomfortable. I wanted to go back to when he was more likely to eviscerate me. That I could deal with. "I went after Canton for my own reasons. We happened to share a common goal."

"Regardless." His nostrils flared, eyes sparked, and there may have been smoke coming out of his mouth. "You helped me and mine. That is a debt I will not allow to hang over our heads."

"O-okay," I said numbly.

Mental note: if a dragon wants to pay you back for a good deed done, don't argue.

Drake took a breath and straightened his suit. "I have arranged to pay for your personal healthcare in regards to the injuries you sustained." That explained the private room. "I've also taken care of Mr. Canton's healthcare as well. Mr. McCree is to have the medical expenses forwarded to myself, or, well, a shell company. His wife will receive a fair pension she was previously unaware of."

I stared blankly at him. "You're doing all that, for Canton. The man who kidnapped and almost killed your dad?"

"Would you rather I do what I truly want to do to him?" There was a boiling undercurrent of rage there, like a crusted over lava flow.

"Probably not."

"Heya." Stacey stuck her head through the door while waving a pudding cup. "Nurse Ratched wouldn't let me get you anything decent to eat. Is it okay to come in?"

Drake slipped back into his Jersey accent. "It's alright ma'am, I believe we're all finished here. Unless you have anything to add, Miss Masterson?"

"No, we're cool." We were even.

"Very well then." Drake bid his farewell and left without looking back.

"I wonder where he gets his hair done," Stacey asked once he was gone. "And those contacts. Kind of wild for a cop."

"Yeah." It's amazing what magical beings can get away with these days.

"I found Tapioca." Stacey handed me the pudding cup and a spoon.

"Yum, thanks." I do like me some Tapioca.

"Huh." Stacey started to get this dazed and confused look on her face. "I don't know why I even bothered trying to get you a burger. They're so unhealthy and you're in a hospital, not to mention your diet is already atrocious. I must be losing my mind."

Yeah, so, *that* happened.

Drake whammied my friend, *again.*

Next time I see him, I'm going to punch him in the face.

Repeatedly.

Anyway, Stacey went on to explain what I missed while I was out. Marcel had been by, a lot. She had to threaten him with severe bodily injury to get him to go home, shower, and sleep. I asked her not to let him know I was awake yet. That would give me a few hours to get my head on straight about our relationship status.

Who am I kidding, I'm going procrastinate the hell out of it. I'm here, aren't I?

Stacey also told me Phil had talked to my parents and explained to them what happened. They were looking to 'book the next flight out that they could' which was a story for her sake, of course. A cut through the Shadow Realm would have them here in a few minutes, but I probably wouldn't see them until the weekend. It's not that they don't care, but for several reasons it's best for them to wait, not draw attention to the situation.

Towards lunchtime, a few of my work friends came by. They'd been worried when they found out why I hadn't shown up on Monday. Getting kidnapped by a deranged cultist is going to make future office water-cooler talk awkward. Wish someone would have thought my cover story through a bit more.

Nurse Natalie said a reporter wanted to speak to me. I said hell no, and don't release my name either. I swear, if I find myself on the news, I will black out this city again, on purpose this time. Hopefully it won't be too long before this was all old news anyway, replaced by the next sound bite. I can bide my time.

Phil finally made his appearance after lunch. He'd spent the whole morning putting together a special charm. It would cover him on his walk up to my room and back again without sending patients into critical care because everything shorted out. It took nine hours for him to make the charm, but it was probably only good for four hours of use.

The first thing Phil did was hand over my focus bracelet. I slipped it on and closed my eyes, feeling the cool metal warm against my skin. Taking deep breaths, I poured energy into the copper and felt it rebuild my protective barriers.

"You two want to be alone?" Phil chuckled.

"Shuddup." I tried not to grin, no longer feeling naked without my foci.

Holding in a laugh, Phil passed over my sending journal which was filled with new notes from my family. I quickly scanned them, and they all basically read the same. They knew I'd be okay, I was strong, they were proud of me, and I should visit more.

That last one was from my mother.

"Drake been by to see you?" Phil asked.

"Yeah," I answered as I quickly wrote off a note to my mom. I needed to get something to her or else she'd just worry, and worry some more, and that's no good for the hydrangeas.

"He's having my bathroom remodeled." There was a note of incredibility and awkwardness in Phil's voice. "He said some stuff about debt and how now I can't claim any."

I put my pen down and sent on the message. "Dragons are apparently more paranoid than wizards. They are also known for hoarding gold. I guess it makes sense that they'd want to put a price tag on everything, or attempt to, in order to avoid even the semblance of debt."

"But is he even in my debt?" Phil scratched at his neck. "You did all the heavy lifting."

"Maybe he wants to make sure there was no question?"

"I suppose." Phil was still boggled. I could tell by the confused wrinkles scrunching up his face.

"Maybe he likes you?" I said, only half teasing.

Phil's confusion turned into a thoughtful frown to cover a blush. "He is pretty handsome, shame about that oppressive cloud of arrogance that hangs around him."

"I know, right?" I couldn't help but laugh. "But hey, I don't have to worry about meeting my deductible, so I'm happy."

Phil changed the subject. "I have Clint isolated. There's so much loose magic in him right now, he can't be around patients on electrical equipment."

"You didn't send him to a healer?" I asked as I scanned more notes in the sender.

"Wanted to," he admitted. "But his wife is still clueless, as are some of the Feds and cops poking around. If Aiden is going to foot the bill, might as well use it. Oh, the security guard from The Cloisters, he got transferred to this hospital, too."

I looked up at Phil. "Still in the coma?"

"Clint didn't leave any notes as to how he performed the Siren Calling spell and we can't find his grimoire. Without knowing who taught him these high level spells..." he trailed off, trying not to sigh as that's a sign of giving up.

"We'll figure it out," I tried to reassure him. "Maybe he'll come out of it on his own?"

"It's possible." Phil wasn't convinced. He glanced down at his charm, which had been blue when he came in and was now almost purple. "I better go before this wears off."

"The hospital might appreciate it," I teased, trying to lighten his dour mood. "Oh, thanks again for bringing my focus and the sender."

"You're welcome." He gathered up his stuff and stood, giving me a quick hug. "I might not see you again until you're out. These charms are a pain to make."

"Nah, it's cool."

"Alright, you get better." He headed for the door.

"Hey." I stopped him when I realized I'd forgotten to ask him something. "Did Drake say anything to you about the other dragon in New York?"

"I asked him about it," Phil admitted, stopping and turning

only a few feet from the door. "He said it was 'an internal matter that was being dealt with.' I let the wizard councils know about the situation. They might be able to find out what that means, but the upper echelons of dragon hierarchy do like to keep their private matters… private."

"You think Drake will let us know if he finds the guy who pulled Canton's strings?"

"Probably not." He shrugged, adjusting his bag. "I have a feeling it's going to be one of those moments where we'll just have to be satisfied we were able to stop a lot of people from getting hurt and accept everything else as the way it is."

"I hate those kind of moments." And there's a lot of them in magic. "Well, not the saving of people part, that's pretty cool."

"Same." Phil gave an appreciative sigh, then pressed his lips together, trying not to frown at me. "I just hope no one thinks too hard about how a wounded and possibly concussed witch with a high school level of magical knowledge managed to reverse a Black Listed, high level spell without any prep and pretty much everything else against her?"

I only had one answer to that. "It had to be done."

"You did the right thing," he agreed, but there was so much sadness there. "You've been doing real good lately, that counts for something."

"Somehow I doubt it." What can I say, I tell it like it is. "If one of the councils comes after me, don't try to stop them, no one else gets hurt."

"Minni—"

"Just how it's gotta be, Phil." I sighed and nearly collapsed into the bed. "You didn't sign up for this; hell, I didn't sign up for this, but it is what it is."

He was angry at me now—that was easy enough to see in the sudden tense lines between his brows—but he wasn't going to argue. "It's your choice, Minni," he finally said. "I don't have to like it though."

"Didn't ask you to."

Natalie chose that moment to come check something or

other. Phil made his retreat with only a nod of his head. Yeah, Phil's my magic bestie, but it's a lot more complicated than I might have previously mentioned. All good relationships are, I suppose. Or maybe just the ones I get myself into.

Once the nurse was done, I toyed with the idea of watching some TV, but even that didn't sound appealing. Stacey had left and she wouldn't be back until way late. She promised not to text Marcel, though he still could show up at any moment of his own volition. I did not want to think about what I was going to say to him, or how much I missed him.

I turned my thoughts towards the Canton situation. Too much was left unanswered and most of the facts didn't exactly fit together. It got to a point where my mind was filled with nothing but a series of random interconnected questions, a maze built of probability and conjecture.

"Bah," I said as I hit the call button.

Natalie returned a few minutes later. "Everything okay?"

"I'm fine." I gestured to the half dozen cables hooked up to me. "I'd like to go for a walk though, can I do that?"

"Yes, I think so. It will do you good to stretch out those kinks." She smiled and started to work on detaching me from my monitors. I didn't have any needles or anything in me anymore, so at least there was that. "You're not going to run away on me, are you?"

"Nah, too lazy."

"That's the spirit." She turned off the machines. "Don't go too far or stay out very long. I *will* hunt you down."

"Si, *mi capitán*," I replied as I slipped off the bed.

"Get going." She shooed me out the door with a disapproving click of her tongue.

I was actually doing pretty good, all things considered. I could have gone home but the doctor's wanted to keep me under observation. I wasn't sure if that was because of my physical injuries or my mental health. Earlier, the doctor not too subtly hinted that I might want to see a therapist for the trauma that I went through. I suppose that was fair of him to suggest. After all, the version of the story he was told was pretty sketchy.

My version of the story really isn't much better, is it?

Goat-Grizzlies, dragons, empathic merges, cops, gazing ball of doom, falling off a building... I survived it all.

This time.

I seriously tried not to think about it as I wandered the halls. Eventually I ended up in front of an open door two floors down from where I was staying. If anyone noticed me, they didn't seem bothered by my presence. I slipped inside to find two occupied hospital beds, both with sleeping patients.

Well, they weren't actually sleeping.

A man lay in the far bed, his breathing even and shallow as machines beeped and booped away. Pushing a chair next to him, I eased myself down and got comfortable. Taking his right hand, I closed my eyes and relaxed. I slipped my mind into his as before, walking through the fog towards the faded beacon. The taxi was still there, and I crawled through the back seat into a spring day at Central Park.

The hospital pajamas I wore in the real world translated into how I visually perceived myself in his mind. I wasn't in nearly as big a rush this time, so I took a moment to change my clothes. I envisioned myself in this nice light blue summer dress with strappy sandals, just 'cause I could.

I went back to the clearing from before but it was empty. Walking around, I got a little lost. The park wasn't laid out properly thanks to his incorrect memories. Eventually I stumbled upon the familiar entrance to Cleopatra's Needle, on the wrong side of the park.

Seriously, it's all screwed up.

But it was pretty, the trees lush and full, their leaves casting moving shadows as a breeze blew through. The guard sat on a wooden bench in front of the Needle while his son drew on the pavement with chalk. Rembrandt the kid wasn't, but the crude rendition of his home and family, while cliché, was kind of sweet.

Well, it was cute until I remembered this wasn't actually his son, only a memory of him.

"Wait, do I know you?" The guard asked from his seat.

"I thought you might not remember." I gestured to where the boy was busy scribbling away at a bright yellow sun. "I came to ask you to leave, but it looks like you have everything you could ever want here."

"Yes." His eyes followed the child who scooted across the ground to grab another chalk stick.

I glanced up to see the sun peeking through the rustling branches. I will say, you picked a gorgeous day to recreate in your dreamscape. "Aren't you the least bit curious about what was happening out there?"

"Should I be?"

"I think so. It's a pretty interesting story and, I have to say, I was pretty awesome."

"Really now?" You were not exactly impressed with me.

I sighed. "Okay, the wanton destruction of public property—that's on me—but momentarily displacing Delaware? Yeah, that… that was totally the dragon's fault."

"Huh?"

"Right, so, on Friday, I may have cut the power to New York City. It was an accident. I'd drawn enough electrical energy from the local power grid to crash it. Some kind of cascade failure occurred and, *boom*, there went Times Square. And I completely slept through the whole thing."

TWENTY-THREE[23]

The sun didn't move in the guard's mindscape, it was a perpetually lovely midday afternoon. This might have had something to do with why Minni told her story with perhaps more flare and detail than was really necessary. The concept of time had gotten away from her.

But they say it's always good to talk things out when you go through a traumatic event, and the comatose guard was the definition of a captive audience.

"That's some story," he said when it was all over. "I appreciate that you got arrested trying to help me, but I'm staying right here."

"You realize that's not your son, right?" Minni asked in all seriousness. "That's just a memory. It's static, it can't grow, or learn, or evolve."

"I don't care. You can understand that, can't you?"

Perhaps she could. "Just because I can understand it doesn't mean I'm going to let you get away with what you did."

"I didn't do anything." He crossed his arms and sat a little straighter.

"Exactly, you did nothing." She almost laughed as she spoke, then her face blanked. "I'm sorry, what's your name again?"

"Frank Dubins," he answered sourly. "And you never asked."

Minni didn't bother to apologize. "The way I see it, Frank, you allowed Canton to put this spell on you so he could have run of The Cloisters. That's the only way to explain how Canton got inside without breaking in or getting caught."

Dubins went back to watching his son play. A breeze blew past, trees rustled. "I was a dead man no matter what."

"Only if he succeeded in casting the spell. You could have told someone, but you didn't." She threw her hands in the air and gave a chuckle of incredulity. "You figured, what the hell? You'd just go along with the scheme and that way you could get something out of it."

"I had no choice," he defended himself, nearly shouting.

Minni had a cold blankness in her eyes. "Well, you have a choice now."

"W—what?"

"Option one," Minni started, her tone even, clinical. "You wake up, you tell your story to Phil and whatever council he wants to put you in front of, keeping out certain details about myself, of course."

Dubins nearly snorted. "And risk the wrath of wizards who have a distinct desire to make everything go away quietly. I don't think so."

"Okay, well, there's also option two," Minni said sweetly. "I make you wake up, and I won't be very nice doing it."

"You'll make me?" The man laughed at the absurdity of it. "Unless I got it wrong, this spell is finished. It did its job. I'm here in this, whatever this is, and you can't make me leave it or do anything I don't want to."

Minni stared at Dubins until he became uncomfortable in the silence. That's when a long, broad smile crept across her lips. "Do you really think I came to New York City because I wanted to live in a cramped cage of anti-magic, so far away from my family where I can't even see the stars?"

"You said—"

"That wizards are very paranoid," she spoke bitterly with a tinge of acid on her tongue. "That we're constantly being hunted, driven out of our homes, and forced to Forsake our magic." Her smile turned derisive. "And we tend to muck up our relationships because we have issues telling the truth."

"You… you lied to me?"

"I barely know you, of course I lied to you."

Dubins frowned. "So, this whole story…"

"Oh, it's all true," she assured him, leaning back against the bench. "I did all those things, saved the world—or at least Manhattan—set a bathroom on fire, and developed a distaste for dragons, among other things..."

"Then what did you lie about?"

"Leave here peacefully and you won't find out."

Minni's voice unsettled Dubins, but in the end, he believed he had the upper hand. "No, out of the question." He pointed at his son still drawing on the cold pavement. "I did this for him."

"You did it for yourself." Minni's accent came out strong and thick. "And that's not your son."

"STOP SAYING THAT!" Dubins jumped up out of his seat, hands clenched at his sides.

"I am sorry you lost him." Minni tried to calm down, but her words were still laced with anger. "I really am, but you willingly went along with some would-be mass murderers just so you could end your days in a memory."

"You forgave Clint for his part in it."

"Canton was being manipulated in his grief," she retorted harshly. "You knew exactly what you signed up for and did it anyway."

"You can't prove that." Dubins bore down on her, anger in every crease and fold of his face. "And even if it's true, who gives you the right to judge me?"

"I do," she answered as if there was no question.

"Feeling a bit full of yourself there?" Dubins nearly laughed. "It doesn't matter, I'm staying right here."

"You really aren't getting it, are you?" She frowned, letting out a slow breath. "You don't have a choice."

Dubins narrowed his eyes at her. "You just said I had a choice. Make up your mind, woman."

Minni gave him the same look her mother would give her when she tried to sweet talk her into an extra slice of pie for dessert. "I said you had a choice as to how you're leaving this place, either of your own free will, or not. Do keep up."

"I'm not leaving."

"Yeah, you are."

"Make me."

Minni tilted her head slightly. "Okay."

His retort died on his lips as the wind picked up, barreling down through the tree-lined walkway at breakneck speeds. The once lush trees died instantly, their leaves turning copper and gold. They fell from the branches and were caught up in the heavy torrent. The sun went away, replaced by a Blood Moon which left an eerie glow across the shadow of the stone Needle behind Minni.

There was no hiding the trembling in Dubins' voice. "How are you doing this?"

"I told you, the mind is nothing but energy," she answered simply. "And energy is what I do."

Dubins took an involuntary step back and his face went pale. "You couldn't… you wouldn't…"

"Why wouldn't I?"

"I listened to your story." He had to shout as the wind kicked up fiercely around him. "You're not that kind of person."

"Were you not listening?" Minni swallowed a painful laugh. "I'm a murderer."

"Wh… what?" He looked at Minni as if her being a killer was so hard to believe.

"What do you think happened to the man in the sunflower field?" she bit back. "He killed my brother. David never would have made it to a healer. So I took that man's life, *ripped it out of his body*, to keep David alive."

Dubins stared in horror at Minni as leaves pelted against him. The ground rumbled and he took a few steps back. Then upon realizing he was truly no longer in control of this world of his own creation, he ran.

Rolling her eyes, Minni stood as Dubins bolted down the walkway as if he could actually hide. With a snap of her fingers, the wind stopped causing Dubins to fall over flat. He got to his hands and knees, only to find himself hoisted up and thrown over a shoulder. Dubins noticed the red, gold, and blue costume of the woman holding him. "What the hell?"

Minni's willpower had taken on the form of Wonder Woman, mostly because the very scientific reasoning of 'why the hell not,' and was currently holding him steadfast. The avatar turned around so Minni could get a good look at Dubins' face, although she had to bend down and tilt her head to meet his eyes.

"I came to New York for one simple reason," she told him coldly. "To hide."

He let out a gurgled response, flailing slightly.

"That's the deal I made," Minni continued, grabbing his head to hold him still. "Phil isn't just my friend, he's my warden. They only reason they didn't put me to death is because they took pity on me, for why I did it. But mostly because they might yet find me useful."

All Dubins could do was shake, his eyes wide in terror.

Sighing, Minni let go of him and started walking down the path. The Wonder Woman avatar followed closely behind, Dubins over her shoulder. They veered off into the grass which had turned brown under the Blood Moon. The stroll was punctuated by the eerie rustling of leaves that echoed across the vastness.

Reaching the taxi, Minni opened the door and stood to the side as Wonder Woman literally tossed Dubins into the back seat. Not needed anymore, the image faded away, taking with it Central Park. All that was left was a blank void and the yellow taxi sitting quietly, eternally patient.

Minni slid into the seat next to Dubins, shutting the door. "Here's what you're going to do, you're going to exit this taxi, then when you wake up, you're going to talk to Phil, tell him everything you know."

His lips trembled, holding on to that last bit of pride. "You can force me awake, but you can't make me talk… can you?"

"What I can do," she replied thoughtful, narrowing her eyes, "is march right back in here and wreck you up so bad you'd wish I had let you die."

Dubins had a choice, and it was no choice at all. "You're sadistic, you know that?"

"No," she assured him with a soft smile. "I'm just evil, but I understand that everyone else, *most* everyone else, are just as important as I am."

Minni reached across Dubins and grabbed the door handle. When the door popped open, she pushed him out into the fog. His form shuddered, dissolving into wisps of glitter-tinged smoke that drifted through the air.

Minni followed, finding her way back to the beacon she had set for herself, slipping from his mind to in her own. She saw that only twenty-nine minutes had passed in real time, though that didn't really surprise her. Dubins started to stir, his breathing reaching a more normal pace. It would take some time before he recovered enough to actually become conscious. She wouldn't be there for that.

Her work done, Minni strolled back to her hospital room, exhausted. Just because she could do something didn't mean it was easy, especially since she didn't have a lot of practice at it. It wasn't like she enjoyed manipulating someone's very consciousness. And if one of the councils discovered what she did to Dubins, they'd either conveniently ignore it or cite parole violations and put her death. Minni was pretty much banking on the fact that she was still very useful to them.

The door to her room was open. That wasn't surprising, but she could see the shadow of someone moving around. Edging closer, she quietly peered in to catch a glance at who it might be. The council surely would have known by now that she was awake, and had they come for her, she would face her fate. She wouldn't fight, but she'd argue that she did it to save Manhattan. That had to count for something, right?

Instead of black-cloaked figures, standing in the room was a man nearly a head taller than her, lean but muscular. He always dressed as if it was forty degrees outside, his rust-colored leather coat well worn, distinguishable in any crowd. He was turned slightly away from the door, his thumbs working the keypad of his phone, a pensive look on his face.

Minni stepped into the room. "Peek-a-boo."

Marcel glanced up sharply, relieved. "I see you."

They stood like that, Marcel taking in her appearance, his smile turning into a frown at her exhausted and bruised state. There was no writing off what happened that weekend, her alibi was set in stone.

"Minni—" he started, but she held up her hand and saw it was trembling.

"It doesn't matter," she whispered as she balled her fingers into a fist.

The man lightly tugged on his lower lip as he kept himself from saying something, anything. Minni didn't need words right now, so when Marcel wrapped his arms around her, she closed her eyes and collapsed against him. He held her tight, rocking softly as she began to cry, tears soaking his burnt orange scarf.

Maybe she'd tell him one day that she's a witch.

Today would not be that day.

Tomorrow didn't look good, either.

But until she was ready, he'd wait for her.

ABOUT THE AUTHOR

Jessica D. Coplen is a born and raised Oklahoman who loves to travel and learn new things. She received a Bachelor's in History from Northeastern State University in Tahlequah, Oklahoma. She lived in Warwickshire County, England (Tolkien's shire) for several years after college before returning to Oklahoma. Besides writing, she enjoys reading, carpentry, going to movies, travel, and painting her nails. She's been caffeine free since 2010 and it was one of the best decisions she's ever made.

Jessica likes to think of herself as living proof that life changing events don't have to be all that life changing.

Special Sneak Peak
Book Two

Copper and Cobalt

Copper and Cobalt

I drummed my fingers on the countertop. "So, I'm thinking you can buy me lunch at that little bistro two blocks over. I know you love that monstrosity they make."

He pressed his lips together, crinkling his nose. "You think anything with sprouts is a monstrosity."

"Yeah." I gave him my best duh expression in return.

Phil chuckled and tapped at the keys. "Sounds good. Ryan can watch the store, I'll bring something back for him."

"Where is Ryan?" I asked, grabbing my phone from my pocket so I could text Stacey, my non-magical BFF, about plans for later that weekend.

"Upstairs, cataloguing some stuff," Phil answered, then looked towards the door as the little bell dinged announcing a new customer. "Welcome."

I was in the middle of my text, totally ignoring my surroundings—which is why I would make a horrible spy—when Phil rushed around the counter. At that same moment I heard the clatter of one of the display tables getting knocked over. Glancing up, I saw the powder blue clad figure of a man slump to the floor. Phil rushed to his side.

"Should I call 911?" I said as I hurried over, wondering if maybe the person only tripped and knocked down the display.

Phil leaned over the collapsed man who looked to be in his late forties, maybe early fifties. The clamminess of his skin and generally sunken appearance made it hard to tell. He looked sick, like plague-carrier sick.

"I'm gonna call 911." I clicked out of texting to get to the dialing keypad.

"Wait." Phil had one hand on the man's forehead while the other hovered over the general region where the heart should be. I'd only gotten the 9 dialed so I paused, trusting my coven leader, because I tell you, this guy looked like he was about to die at any moment.

"Ryan!" Phil shouted at the top of his lungs as he started to clear away the fallen boxes of soap the man had taken down with him.

Loud thuds preceded Ryan running out of the back room, skidding to a stop a little wide-eyed at the scene.

"I need all the Prussian Blue we have in the store," Phil ordered and Ryan only paused for a second before disappearing into the back again. "Help me move him."

Realizing he was talking to me, I pocketed my phone and grabbed the man's legs as Phil reached under his arms. Together we carried the stranger into the back where Phil had a makeshift breakroom complete with battered leather sofa.

We laid the customer down, then Phil immediately moved to the shelf where he keeps his office supplies. You know, the usual: pens, sticky-notes, highlighters, exorcism kit...

"Get his tie off," he told me as he rummaged through one of the boxes. "Help him breath."

"Uh, okay." I still had no clue what was going on but hey, sounded reasonable to me. I watch a lot of movies.

Trying not to be too rough, I tugged at the tie, getting it loose enough to just slip out of its knot and from around his neck. I also undid the first two buttons on his dress shirt. I grabbed a random hoodie that was laying on the back of a nearby chair and folded it up to make a pillow. I didn't want to really tilt his head up, just make it lay more even with his body.

I made the stranger about as comfortable as I could. Then as I started to turn back to Phil, I felt a cold grip on my wrist.

"Seren cobalt." The man stared at me with vacant, glassed over eyes.

"Seh-ren cobalt?" I muttered, wondering if I had heard right.

His eyes rolled into the back of his head as he passed out again, his grip loosening and his arm falling from the sofa to brush the floor.

Great, see, this is how horror films start.